CAPTURED

The Duel, Book 2

Mary Lancaster

ARE YOU SIGNED UP FOR DRAGONBLADE'S BLOG?

You'll get the latest news and information on exclusive giveaways, exclusive excerpts, coming releases, sales, free books, cover reveals and more.

Check out our complete list of authors, too!

No spam, no junk. That's a promise!

Sign Up Here

www.dragonbladepublishing.com

Dearest Reader;

Thank you for your support of a small press. At Dragonblade Publishing, we strive to bring you the highest quality Historical Romance from some of the best authors in the business. Without your support, there is no 'us', so we sincerely hope you adore these stories and find some new favorite authors along the way.

Happy Reading!

CEO, Dragonblade Publishing

Additional Dragonblade books by Author Mary Lancaster

The Duel Series
Entangled (Book 1)
Captured (Book 2)

Last Flame of Alba Series
Rebellion's Fire (Book 1)
A Constant Blaze (Book 2)
Burning Embers (Book 3)

Gentlemen of Pleasure Series
The Devil and the Viscount (Book 1)
Temptation and the Artist (Book 2)
Sin and the Soldier (Book 3)
Debauchery and the Earl (Book 4)
Blue Skies (Novella)

Pleasure Garden Series
Unmasking the Hero (Book 1)
Unmasking Deception (Book 2)
Unmasking Sin (Book 3)
Unmasking the Duke (Book 4)
Unmasking the Thief (Book 5)

Crime & Passion Series
Mysterious Lover (Book 1)
Letters to a Lover (Book 2)
Dangerous Lover (Book 3)
Merry Lover (Novella)

The Weary Heart
The Secret Heart
Christmas Heart

The Lyon's Den Series
Fed to the Lyon

De Wolfe Pack: The Series
The Wicked Wolfe
Vienna Wolfe

Also from Mary Lancaster
Madeleine
The Others of Ochil

CHAPTER ONE

"YOU MUST BE very brave, Hera. I am afraid your father is dead."
Lady Hera Severne, who had just swept into the salon for tea, to discover her aunt and uncle looking solemn, came to an abrupt halt and frowned at such a huge pronouncement. For some reason, she felt she must have misheard.

"His Grace is dead?" Hera said cautiously.

Her aunt, Lady Hadleigh, dabbed at her eyes with a tiny square of lace. "A tragedy for all of us. Struck down in the prime of his life."

Hera sank slowly into the nearest chair. Curiously detached, she wondered if the world expected her to show grief like her aunt's, but she didn't seem to feel any. His Grace had been a distant figure whom she barely knew and, if she was honest, didn't much like. But he had always been a massive presence in her life—like God, she thought irreverently. One never saw him, but one knew he was there with power over every aspect of one's life.

"How did he die?" she blurted. His Grace was not yet fifty and had always seemed in vigorous health.

Her aunt and uncle exchanged glances, and Hera felt a surge of irritation. Even in this, was her information to be censored and filtered, as though she were a child or an imbecile?

"It was a duel," her aunt said.

Hera blinked. "*A duel?* His Grace fought a duel?"

Aunt Hadleigh waved her tiny handkerchief in apparent distress. "With some upstart young army officer. I daresay he forced a quarrel on His Grace to impress his foolish friends. Perhaps they are all Jacobins!"

"Army officers?" Hera asked, frowning. "Have they not been fighting revolutionary France for years? In fact, they are about to do so again."

"That is not the point," Lord Hadleigh growled. "The point is, this fellow, whoever he was, killed your father and orphaned you and Victor."

And quite suddenly, what Hera felt was not grief or sadness, but hope. Her brother was now Duke of Cuttyngham. She could stop this charade of husband hunting through the endless balls and routs, concerts and plays, Venetian breakfasts and morning calls. There was an escape.

She sprang to her feet. "Forgive me, Aunt, Uncle. I believe I would like to be alone. Will you excuse me?"

Hera didn't wait for permission. She hurried from the room and up the stairs and along the passage to her own bedchamber. Here, she closed the door firmly and walked straight to the desk. Taking the three-day-old copy of the *Morning Post* from the middle drawer, she spread it out and turned the pages until she found the advertisement that had interested her.

A Companion is sought for varied duties. Must be educated, sensible and discreet. Remuneration and leisure time generous. Apply with details of family background and experience.

The advertisement intrigued her because it didn't sound like the usual position of a paid companion. And generous leisure time was unheard of! From this house, where she could do nothing without a train of chaperones and servants, it sounded like bliss. She could *choose* what to do with this time, not feel it eaten away by pointless trivia in search of a husband she did not want and would never suit.

His Grace was dead. Victor, her brother, was the duke, and he would understand. Poor Victor, trapped now more than ever. But at least he could free Hera. And the poor duchess, their stepmother.

Hera was no fool. But she understood she was in the fortunate position of being able to walk away from any post she did not care for. She sat down and wrote a letter expressing her interest and asking for more details. Without mentioning names or titles, she gave a brief description of her upbringing and education. To avoid any future difficulties, she emphasized that she was an orphan and had no family dependents or guardians.

She hesitated over the signature. Hera was an unusual enough name that it might well be recognized. Should she just sign H. Severne? That seemed rather cold and impersonal, and perhaps even secretive. After a moment's thought, she wrote Harriet Severne, deciding that name was close enough to her real one that it should not trouble her too much—should her letter ever come to anything. Which she doubted, since the advertisement was already four days old. The position was no doubt filled already. But at least she had tried, and there would be others.

THE JOURNEY BACK to Cuttyngs, where His Grace would be buried, was accomplished with a strange sense of unreality on Hera's part, as if her brain could not quite comprehend that the godlike figure of her father no longer towered over them all, whether in his absence or presence.

She wondered if her aunt, his sister, actually felt any of the grief she kept expressing. She seemed more agitated, excited, even, than grief-stricken. So did Uncle Hadleigh, in a more subdued kind of way. The unkind might have suggested the pair were hopeful of a good legacy. After all, Hera had lived in their house for almost two years. They deserved a little more than formal thanks.

Once, Hera had been desperate to escape the constrictions of Cuttyngs, the angry unhappiness of her brother, and the misery she sensed beneath the relentless cheerfulness of her stepmother. The prospect of weeks of gaiety, of theatre and dancing and devoted young men, had called to Hera, so that she couldn't wait to exchange the unhappiness of her home for the wonder of her aunt's.

Hera sighed. It had been a childish view. Her first Season had palled after the first week or so, when it had finally come to her that her purpose here was not to have fun but to attract a husband. And when she did, she would find herself in a different trap, like her poor stepmother trying so bravely to put a happy face on neglect, humiliation, and unreasonable restriction. Mistress of her home in name only.

Her Grace was free now. They were all free of him—except Victor, who had finally decided to go to Oxford in the teeth of their father's opposition and was now trapped even more securely by his new responsibilities. It might be the making of him. After all, no one could live completely through books. But it was crushingly bad timing for him.

Nevertheless, she looked forward to seeing Victor, to long walks and riding at more than the sedate trot that was as fast as one could go in London. At Cuttyngs, without the heavy hand of her father, she might find a little peace to draw breath and think of another future.

But it was inevitable, she thought, that everything would be different with the huge presence of her father snuffed out.

Except everything looked the same, from the huge iron gates guarded by deaf old Dan, up the long, curving drive to the great house. And as usual, only the servants came out to welcome them, footmen scurrying with luggage, while Betts the butler and Mrs. Irwin the housekeeper waited on the steps to usher them inside.

"Welcome home, my ladies, my lord," Betts said lugubriously. "On behalf of all the staff, may I offer you our deepest condolences?"

"Thank you, Betts," Aunt Hadleigh said, sailing into the house before Hera could speak.

"Are we in time for supper?" Hera asked practically.

"It has just been served, my lady. Mr. Severne is in the dining room."

Of course Cousin Anthony would be here. "With Her Grace?"

"No, my lady," Betts replied.

Perhaps widows had to dine alone. There was a lot of foolish custom to follow. Poor duchess. "And I suppose Victor is in the library as usual?"

"His Grace is dining there alone."

"Of course he is." She cast a quick smile at Mrs. Irwin. "Am I in my old bedchamber as usual?"

"Yes, my lady. It is all just the same," Mrs. Irwin replied.

"Then I shall run up and wash my hands."

Cousin Anthony had already dealt with the soup and the fish by the time Hera entered the dining room. But he was now enjoying a glass of wine to wait for the others to catch up. He rose at once, coming to meet her with both hands held out. "My poor child, I am so sorry."

Steeling herself, she allowed him to kiss her cheek, then pulled away, hurrying toward the table. "My aunt and uncle will be down directly, so you had better tell me quickly what happened. How did my austere parent come to be dueling with ramshackle army officers?"

Anthony wrinkled his nose. "He received an insult he could not overlook, and the officer *was* a gentleman. Horsewhipping, sadly, was not an option, and the man refused to apologize. As you know, His Grace was a stubborn man, and neither Frostbrook nor I could persuade him out of it. I do know he meant to miss, but…" He trailed off and smiled apologetically. "I should not be talking to you of this. Rest assured the officer will be arrested and tried, hopefully, for murder. At least for manslaughter."

If his comments were meant to comfort her, they missed their mark. Instead, she felt uneasy. But she could ask nothing more, for her aunt and uncle joined them, and while dinner was served, Lady Hadleigh bemoaned the tragic loss of her brother, the even more tragic orphaning of his children, however adult they were, and the manners of young men who no longer knew their place in Society.

"How is Her Grace?" Hera demanded, determined to change the subject.

"Ah," Anthony said, laying down his fork. "That is what we would all like to know. Her Grace is not here."

Hera blinked. "Not here? But Her Grace is always here!"

"As is only right and proper," Aunt Hadleigh insisted. "Especially on the death of her husband! Where on earth has she gone?"

"That is the other thing we would all like to know. She left without a word to anyone, but I have people looking for her. At least we know what direction she took."

"You mean she left before my father died?" Hera asked, frowning. Part of her rejoiced for her stepmother's escape, although, like Victor, she was about to be sucked back into supposed duty.

"Certainly before anyone knew of it here."

As soon as the meal was finished, Hera excused herself and went straight to the library in search of her brother.

As always, the sound of someone entering the room took a few moments to register with his brain. It gave her a moment to glance around the lovely room and reassure herself it looked as it always did, lined with shelves full of books, to a double height, with a balcony running around the upper level and a narrow wrought-iron spiral staircase running between.

The curtains had been closed over the long, shapely windows. Books were piled up on two of the bigger desks, including the one where Victor sat, gazing at the pages of a large tome, though, for once, Hera had the impression he was not reading it.

Victor's dark beauty almost took her by surprise. As though nature had made up for her brother's physical infirmities by giving him the face of an angel—a fallen angel for the most part, for it was often scowling with impatience or bad temper.

The frown was only faint just now, drawing down his dramatic black brows not so much in anger as in concentration. Something bothered him. She was glad to be here to help, glad *he* was still here, still the same, still her ally. No words were necessary to tell her that. Victor was the only person in the world she trusted or cared for.

His dark eyes shifted and came to rest on her. He didn't betray surprise, but his eyes lightened, and his lips curved into one of his rare smiles. "Hera. I heard you arrive."

"You had better greet my aunt and uncle before they retire. It will make my life more bearable, and it is the ducal thing to do—*Your Grace.*" She curtseyed mockingly and dropped into the chair at the next desk, which was turned toward him.

Victor wrinkled his nose. "I never expected it to happen this early. I thought I had years."

"Does it put a stop to Oxford?"

"So far as I am concerned, I think it probably does."

"Perhaps it is a good thing. Freeing us. After all, you can still read, and you can visit scholars and other libraries whenever you please, now. Who needs a degree? You're already better read that anyone else I've ever met."

"Well, considering the well-bred cloth heads you must meet in London, I shan't let it go to my head."

"Better not," she agreed. "Where is Her Grace?"

Victor's face changed. The frown was back. "Dashed if I know. I think she's had it away on her toes, and good luck to her. I suspect she won't get far, though. Anthony's determined to bring her back in case the family looks bad."

"The family *is* bad. Though I suppose Her Grace is the best of us."

"Well, she has the advantage of not being born into the family. She has more chance."

She swallowed. "What of His Grace? What was he thinking of, to challenge a younger man more experienced in shooting?"

Victor rummaged among the papers half-buried under his books. "Anthony says the insult could not be overlooked. Read this." He passed over a slightly battered scandal sheet bearing the headline: *Deadly Duel Does for Duke.*

Hera read it while an unpleasant knot began to gather in her stomach. "It says His Grace insulted this fellow's commanding officer first. Colonel Landon."

"His Grace counted the colonel's father, old Sir John Landon, an enemy. And he never kept his opinion to himself whatever the company."

"So basically, he brought about his own death with reasonless prejudice."

"And probably that of the officer he fought, apparently a very well-thought-of veteran of the Peninsular campaign. What a waste."

They sat in silence for a bit, contemplating their once all-powerful and yet always-distant parent.

"I'm glad you're back, at all events," Victor remarked.

Hera nodded. "So am I. But I wish the rest of them would go away."

"They will," Victor said. "As soon as His Grace is buried."

"How can you be sure?"

Victor grinned, a rare mix of humor and malice. "Because I intend to sling them all out."

JUST BEFORE TEA the following day, Hera gazed out of her bedchamber window, wondering a little dreamily if she could simply settle here at Cuttyngs. Victor would let her read what she wanted, do what suited her, and go wherever she liked. Surely that would make up for the awfulness of childhood memories? Not that she had ever realized they were so awful until she began to mix with other people and glimpsed odd moments of family affection and heard of other kinds of upbringings. She had just wanted away from Cuttyngs.

And yet it was pretty here. The oppressive, lingering presence of her father would fade in time with his absence—especially now that the duchess would have free rein at last to do as she wished with the house and gardens. If Her Grace ever came back.

A man was riding up the drive to the front terrace. He wore riding breeches and a dark coat and hat, though he didn't look like any of the neighbors that Hera could remember, and, in any case, they only ever called on invitation. He was probably a lawyer, she decided, although he rode very straight in the saddle, and in her experience solicitors and other men of business were old and traveled in hired carriages. This man was not old.

He swung down from the saddle with the ease of long practice. For some reason, she liked the way he moved—economically, yet easily, like a physically fit man comfortable enough in his own body that he had no need to pose or swagger. Over the last year, Hera had encountered all too many posers and swaggerers and found them faintly ridiculous.

One of the grooms ran around from the stables to take his horse, and the visitor handed over the reins with a brief exchange. Then, without warning, perhaps sensing her observation, he looked upward at the array of windows.

Hera's heart seemed to stop. Not because the gentleman was particularly handsome, although he was pleasing enough in a rugged kind of way. But there was something vital, something curiously intense, about his countenance. Perhaps it was the brilliance of the eyes that suddenly found hers and held her captive, the breadth of his intelligent forehead, or the set of his firm mouth and the way his lips seemed to have an extra upward quirk. It was the face of a man who had seen

much more of life than the country lanes of Cuttyngs, or the fashionable ballrooms of London. This was a man who lived to the full, who
cared.

Fascinated, Hera did not step back to avoid his scrutiny. With a
touch of his hat brim by way of acknowledgement, he released her
gaze and strode out of her line of vision to the front steps.

Hera breathed again. *Perhaps he will join us for tea.*

More likely, he would be discussing business with Anthony or
Victor. As she ran down to the salon where tea was traditionally
served, it crossed her mind to creep farther along the gallery and peer
over the balustrade to the front hall to see if he was there.

Foolish.

And, of course, the caller was not at tea. Only her aunt and Cousin
Anthony joined her, Uncle Hadleigh, no doubt, having retired with
His Grace's brandy. Which meant the visitor must be with Victor, or,
more likely, with Jenkins the steward. Only pride stopped her asking
Anthony if he knew who the caller was. And she would not intrude on
Victor.

In fact, as the afternoon wore on toward the dinner hour, her
powerful impression of the man inevitably faded and became lost in
her annoyance with having to wear unrelieved black. Was there ever a
more depressing color?

After the funeral, she thought, as she made her way downstairs to
the drawing room before dinner, when her father was buried and
everyone else had gone, she would throw off her mourning. No one
would see and blame her except those, like farmers and tenants and
the vicar, who could do nothing about it.

On that happy thought, she walked into the drawing room. A tall
man stood with his back to her, one forearm leaning on the mantel-
piece while he gazed into the flames of the evening fire. He
straightened and turned as she entered the otherwise empty room.
Her foot faltered, for it was the interesting stranger.

CHAPTER TWO

T HE STRANGER SMILED, almost as though he were comforting a frightened child, which infuriated Hera.

"Forgive me," he began gently.

"Why, what have you done?" she snapped.

One eyebrow rose, his only sign of surprise at her rudeness. "Startled you," he said. "His Grace invited me, you know."

Was there a trace of sardonic humor in that smooth voice now? If there was, it was lost in his words. "His Grace?" she repeated, appalled.

"The duke, your brother," he explained.

She felt embarrassed color rise to her cheeks. "I remember him," she retorted. "I don't, however, remember you."

"I believe we met, briefly, on either side of a window. My name is Justin Rivers. I gather you are Lady Hera."

Realizing that she had been rooted to the spot during this slightly ill-tempered exchange—ill-tempered at least on her part—she forced herself to move into the room and sit in the chair usually commandeered by her aunt.

"I am," she said, waving one gracious hand by way of invitation to sit. "What brings you to Cuttyngs, Mr. Rivers? Are you a friend of my brother's?"

She knew he wasn't. Like her, Victor didn't have any friends, for he never went anywhere, and no one came to Cuttyngs.

"I cannot claim so. I am merely a physician." He sat down, and those brilliant eyes caught and trapped hers once more. "The physician, in fact, who last attended His Grace, your father."

"Was he ill?" she asked in surprise.

The eyebrow flew up again. "He was shot."

Her breath caught. Just for an instant she was afraid laughter or some other quite inappropriate noise would spill out. "You attended the duel."

He inclined his head.

"Then you are not a very good physician, are you?" she taunted him. She was appalled by her own manners, but for some reason it seemed very important to conceal his initial effect on her.

"Good enough to be unsatisfied by the duke's death."

"*Unsatisfied?* Do you imagine the rest of us are happy about it?"

"I don't know. Are you?"

It hit her like an unexpected blow, and she could only stare into those brilliant blue eyes. The challenge in them faded into something at once sharper and softer, and then the sound of Victor's uneven footsteps and the click of his walking stick on the floor distracted the doctor, who rose to meet him.

"Good God, Victor, are you joining us?" Hera asked in amazement.

"Rejoice," Victor said flippantly. "I see you've met Dr. Rivers. Was His Grace ill, Hera?"

"Not that I ever saw or heard." Which said nothing. Even when they were both in London, they had lived in different houses and only met very occasionally by accident. "Why?"

Victor sank into the chair at her other side and propped up his stick against the arm. "Dr. Rivers thinks the shot might not have been what killed him."

Hera blinked from her brother to the doctor. "Is the shot not likeliest?"

"The wound was to his shoulder and struck no serious organ," Dr. Rivers said. "Nor did it bleed as it should. In my experience, such a wound, while painful, should not have killed him, certainly not so immediately."

"Dr. Rivers has been an army surgeon for some years on the Peninsular campaign," Victor put in.

Hera nodded, glad to have some of her initial speculations confirmed. "So, you are wondering if he had some illness that caused him to expire of shock? If his heart gave out with the stress of the duel?"

"Something like that," Dr. Rivers said steadily.

"But it doesn't make any difference," Hera protested. "His Grace is still dead."

"It makes a difference to his opponent."

Hera's eyes widened, then narrowed. "You are here on behalf of this officer—Butler, is it?"

"Does that offend you?" Rivers asked.

Hera thought about it. "No."

Just for the barest instant, she thought his eyes smiled, and butterflies soared in her stomach. And then he rose as the Hadleighs and Anthony entered the room, and the moment passed as if it had never been.

DURING ONE OF the more awkward dinners he had ever endured, Justin Rivers hoped he would not be obliged to suffer an evening of Severne company, too. The polite, deadly dull conversation was carried largely by the late duke's sister, Lady Hadleigh, and Mr. Anthony Severne, the duke's cousin, whom Justin already knew because he had been one of His Grace's seconds in the duel.

The new duke, a formidably intelligent but unworldly young man, made no secret of his boredom. His sister, the stunningly beautiful

Lady Hera, only spoke when directly addressed, although her face gave nothing away. At some point, whether by herself or others, her expression had been schooled to a polite mask, which was a pity, for she appeared to have both character and wit. That she had used her sharp tongue against him was understandable. She had lost her father by a barbaric ritual at which he had assisted against his better judgment. The family needed someone to blame, and Justin was blatantly trying to exonerate the culprit.

Not that he was proving very successful. The young duke had surprised him by listening and considering. But not he nor his sister nor his cousin Anthony Severne knew of any illness that might have caused His Grace to fall so suddenly ill that he staggered into Butler's line of fire. Justin did not doubt Butler's word that he had aimed well away from the duke's person. He had known the major a long time, and in some very sticky situations, and a more honorable man he had never met.

He was considering simply asking Lady Hadleigh about her brother's health, when, unexpectedly, the young duke did it for him.

Cutting across a conversation comparing spring weather last year and this, he said abruptly, "Aunt, was His Grace in good health over the last few months?"

Lady Hadleigh frowned at the interruption. "Of course. He was always in good health. Why?"

The young duke did not answer. He turned to his uncle instead. "Uncle?"

"Never complained to me," Lord Hadleigh said vaguely.

"Victor, are you trying to challenge the will on the grounds of His Grace's sanity?" Lady Hadleigh asked. "For I tell you now—"

"Of course I'm not!" the duke snapped. "No idea what's in it, and don't much care either. Unless it declares me illegitimate, of course."

"Victor!" exclaimed Lady Hadleigh, covering up some sound from Lady Hera that sounded suspiciously like a giggle. Intrigued, Justin turned to look at the younger woman, but she didn't notice him. While everyone else's outraged attention was on the duke, Lady Hera subtly raised her glass to her brother. The duke saw and quirked one lip in response. It was an odd moment of understanding between members of an otherwise broken, unfeeling family. No one even knew where the duchess was to inform her of her husband's death.

As soon as the meal concluded, Lady Hadleigh rose. "Come, Hera, let us leave the gentlemen to their wine. I believe an early night would be suitable. After all, there is much to do tomorrow when His Grace comes home."

"Oh for God's sake, Aunt, don't make it sound like he has any choice in the matter," the duke growled.

Lady Hadleigh ignored him, sailing out of the room with Lady Hera obediently behind her. Justin knew a moment of unexpected loss. The girl intrigued him, and without her, he was left in the company of the pompous Anthony, the drunken Hadleigh, and the bored duke. Well, he had brought it on himself by coming here. And he hadn't even learned anything that might help Giles Butler.

Port and brandy decanters were set on the table and the footmen withdrew. Anthony poured himself a glass of port while Hadleigh reached for the brandy, then, after pouring himself a large one, passed the decanter to Justin.

Justin splashed some brandy into his glass. He expected to need it. But at the head of the table, the young duke took a glass of port, downed it in one swallow, and rose awkwardly to his feet.

"I'll bid you good night, gentlemen. Doctor, ring for anything you need. I'll see you at breakfast." With that, he picked up his stick and limped out of the room.

Justin wondered, in a professional kind of a way, exactly what was wrong with His Grace's twisted leg. He sipped his brandy politely, while Anthony rose and followed the duke.

Lord Hadleigh stood and swiped up the brandy decanter. "I believe

I'll retire early, too. Nothing more exhausting than a house of mourning, is there? Good night, Rivers."

Justin smiled with perfect amiability. *Thank God.* He finished his brandy slowly—it was very good cognac—then left also to enjoy a brisk evening walk before retiring. He had been with the army long enough to have developed the knack of sleeping whenever opportunity offered or required. But tonight, he needed exercise to calm the thoughts in his head.

After informing a passing footman that he was going for a walk, and would he please not lock the side door before his return, he set off with only the moonlight to guide his steps.

Although the late duke had not been a likeable man—Justin had found him arrogant, pompous, compassionless, selfish, and downright stupid—he had been too young to die, and Justin was sorry for it. Dueling was a pest on mankind that he had no time for, and he wished to God that Giles Butler had simply refused the duke's challenge. But that wasn't in the nature of the man.

Besides, Justin had seen his face immediately after the duke fell. He was undoubtedly astonished and appalled, because he had fully intended to miss. And Butler was one of the best shots in the regiment of any rank. By every standard, the duel had been a tragedy. There was nothing Justin could do for the duke, but if he could keep Butler's neck from the noose, he would.

The ship Butler had been intending to board for Ostend was due to leave Harwich tomorrow. Justin hoped Butler would be on it. He himself still fully intended to be there to patch up the survivors of however many battles it took to recapture Bonaparte. But he had time. When he had met up with Butler and the others, he had been on his way home to bid farewell to his father and siblings. He should still find time to do that, but in truth, he wasn't sorry to be putting it off for another few days. Family quarrels were…difficult.

Ahead of him was a pleasant glow. A formal rose garden laid out in rigid lines basked in the light of several fixed lanterns. And walking restlessly along one of the paths was the unmistakable figure of Lady Hera Severne.

He stood still, for he wasn't sure she could even see him among the shadows, and he didn't want to disturb her solitude if that was what she wanted. If she did not approach or speak, he would merely turn around and walk away. In the meantime, he watched her, a curiously restless, almost discontented figure in a bright red pelisse. Her movements were quick and graceful, and she did not droop with grief. Instead, she seemed thoughtful, oddly detached from her surroundings and her fellow creatures. Some emotion that was not quite pity tugged at him.

She did notice him, however, for she came to an abrupt halt on the path. He bowed slightly, and just as he prepared to walk silently on, she turned and came directly toward him, so he waited.

"A pleasant evening for a stroll," he observed.

She cast a glance at the sky. "It would be pleasanter to go further, but I didn't think to bring a carrying lantern. Besides, Aunt Hadleigh would have kittens."

He swallowed his laughter. "Well, perhaps it is not good for a young lady to roam alone at night."

"It is not good for a young lady to do anything very much at all." She seemed about to say more, then closed her shapely lips and walked toward a wooden bench on the terrace in front of the roses.

Taking this as an invitation, he sat beside her at a polite distance, half turned toward her with his arm resting along the back of the bench.

"Why did you go to the peninsula?" she asked abruptly.

Surprised, he answered honestly, "Because I thought it would be excellent experience for my career, and I wanted to be useful."

"Were you?"

"Not as much as I would have liked, but I flatter myself I made some difference."

"Were you happy?"

His eyebrows flew up. "What an odd question. Who can be happy among the death and injury of war? And yet I stayed for six years rather than the two I had intended, so I suppose I must admit I had moments of happiness."

"Her Grace, my stepmother, says the ancient plant remedies are as useful as physicians." The glow from the rose garden lights showed the challenge in her bright hazel eyes.

"Her Grace is quite right," he said peaceably. "In many cases. English physicians receive indifferent training and are on the whole too wedded to old and discredited theories. I, however, was educated in Edinburgh."

"Does that make you better?"

"Yes," he said baldly, and was gratified to see her smile. She had a rather lovely smile, quick and fugitive, softening her curving lips and warming her cool countenance so briefly that he might have missed it. Oh yes, she intrigued him.

"Will you go back?" she asked. "To the war?"

"Yes, I'll see it through. After I visit my family."

"Is that where you are going when you leave us?"

"No, I'm going to London first, to speak with your father's physician. I have the permission of His Grace, your brother. Do I have yours also?"

She blinked, as though taken aback, then she gave a sniff of distaste.

"That is your aunt's trick," he said to provoke her, although he wasn't quite sure why.

"I learned it from her," she agreed without heat. "I find it useful to express disdain when I have no idea what to say."

"Yes or no would suffice."

"I see no reason for you to ask," she retorted. "If you have my brother's permission, you do not need mine."

"I don't *need* it," he agreed. "But I would prefer to have it. He was your father, too."

She looked stricken, but not, curiously, with grief. She tore her gaze free of his and stared at the roses in silence. Baffled, he continued to watch her profile.

"It's horrible, isn't it?" she said abruptly. "Regimented into dull rows of one color each, all exactly the same size and shape. It has no charm, no sense of natural beauty."

Justin did not regard himself as slow-witted, but it took him a moment to realize she was talking about the formal rose garden. "I would not have made it quite like that," he agreed. "But everyone has their own idea of what is beautiful."

"Her Grace tried to change it, once—my stepmother's grace, not my mother's—but my father forbade it and had everything put back the way it was."

"Perhaps it was in honor of your mother," Justin suggested, feeling somewhat at sea.

"My parents bore no sentimentality toward each other. My father never noticed flowers of any kind. He was just opposing my step-mother because he could. He was like that, sucking all the joy, all the spirit, out of life."

Shocked by her insight, Justin felt compassion rise in him. He hadn't liked the duke, but it seemed his own daughter hadn't either.

In a distant, almost dreamy voice, she said, "He was cruel to Victor. He never noticed me. And he humiliated my stepmother. He was cold and mean-spirited, and I am glad he is dead."

Yet the eyes that turned up to his were full of shame and guilt and fear. "I am, you see, just as wicked."

Justin saw no wickedness in that face, only a lost child grown to womanhood without a parent's love. Without thought, he reached out and clasped her hand. She wore no gloves and her fingers were cold. "No," he said. "Feelings are not wicked."

She searched his eyes, quite seriously. "Do you really believe that?"

"Of course. Or I would have to condemn myself. I have wished many people to death and the devil. I have even wished to be the cause of their going. And I am a physician sworn to save life."

It won him the faintest, briefest smile he had ever seen, and yet it moved him.

"You are being kind," she said.

"It's expected, despite being against my nature."

Her delightful lips quirked again. "Now I know you are lying, but I thank you for it all the same."

He gazed at his large hand still holding hers and knew he should release her. He didn't. Her fingers were warm now, delicate and soft. And his feelings toward her were no longer those of a physician. His other hand still lay on the back of the bench. With barely any effort, he could drop it to her shoulder, or even brush her elegant neck with his fingers...

Instead, keeping very still, he said, "You are strong enough to choose your own path, you know."

She wrinkled her nose. "Women never do. It is chosen for them. Even men can't always choose. Victor's only desire since he was a boy was to study at Oxford. My father wouldn't hear of it. He was going to go anyway, after this summer, but now he can't because he has responsibility for all this." She waved her free hand liberally to indicate the entire Cuttyngham estate.

"There are ways around such problems, for you as well as your brother."

Unexpectedly, she nodded. "And for you?"

"For me?" he repeated, surprised once more.

"You don't want to go home either, do you? I could hear it in your voice."

An acid comment seemed to burn the tip of his tongue. But he found himself saying honestly, "I do want to go home. And yet I am not looking forward to the inevitable quarrel with my brother."

"Will you win?"

"Yes. But I won't enjoy it. My brother, like my father, is a clergyman. But unlike my father, Philip has ambition. He wants to take a post with the Archbishop of Canterbury, and wishes me to settle at home to keep an eye on my father, who is growing frail. His argument being that I can practice medicine anywhere."

"Can you?"

"Of course. But first, I need to be with the army fighting Bonaparte's return."

Her eyes remained steady on his. "Because it is your duty?"

"They are both my duty," he said. "But my father is one man, surrounded by parishioners who love him. Defeating Bonaparte will not be accomplished without incredible slaughter and injury, and there are never enough surgeons."

"Is that your justification?"

His breath caught on what wasn't quite laughter. "You, my lady, are far too perceptive. Yes, I am justifying a choice I made from instinct. I still believe it to be right, but it doesn't take away the guilt."

Her brow twitched, as though she had caught the connection to her own feelings of shame. "Are you still being kind to me?"

"I don't know." He couldn't really think beyond his desire to touch her. Although determined not to, he let his fingers brush against her bright pelisse. "Is this your rebellion against mourning?"

The smile dawned again, lingering this time. "There is no one to see."

Apart from him. It forced him to release her hand, to rise and stand back from her. "Flatterer."

A short laugh broke from her, a strangely charming sound, husky, almost *rusty*, as though from lack of use. "I didn't mean that, as you well know. You are more real than anyone I have met in a long time."

She rose as she spoke and, giving him no time to bow, began to walk past him. At the last moment, she paused and glanced fleetingly up at him. "Good night."

Before he could reply, she took sudden hold of his arms, stood on tiptoe, and touched her lips to his in the softest, lightest of kisses.

Startled, he did nothing to prevent it, although at least he didn't crush her in his arms and ravish her. In fact, vulnerable as she was, he almost jerked away from her before he realized how unforgivably humiliating that would be. Instead, after the first instant, he parted his lips and kissed her back in the same gentle spirit.

It only lasted a second, a strangely spellbinding moment in time that was unexpectedly sweet and moving and quite inappropriately arousing. Just as suddenly, she released him and walked away, though not before he had glimpsed the bright spots of color in her cheeks. No doubt more of embarrassment than excitement.

He watched her go ruefully and set about a brisk walk to cool his inconvenient ardor.

CHAPTER THREE

WHAT HAVE *I done?* Overcome with shame and embarrassment, Hera rushed upstairs to her own rooms.

It had been a moment of blind instinct, following her own sudden, inexplicable desire to kiss him—for being kind, perhaps, or understanding. Or just for being different from any other man she had ever encountered. For being *him*. She had broken every rule of propriety and modesty. And, sinking onto the window seat of her little sitting room, she came to the unexpected realization that she didn't care. A soft laugh broke from her.

More than that, she didn't believe he minded at all. She had felt the pressure of his lips in return. In fact, her stomach tingled at the memory of it. If he hadn't seized her or taken any advantage, neither had he been revolted. In fact, she suspected he understood perfectly. He was a very perceptive man.

She pulled back the curtain and waited a few moments, until she saw him striding past in the moonlight, making a tour around the perimeter of the house. This time, she didn't want to be seen, so she let the curtain fall back in place, apart from the merest crack. He did not look like a man who was appalled or disgusted or even worried by the behavior of his host's sister. She smiled, because she suspected he took every human frailty, physical or otherwise, in his stride, accepting and understanding. Something she had never even tried to do. She could learn from him.

Except that she would never see him again.

For some reason, that brought more sadness than the death of her own father.

IN THE EARLY hours of the morning, Hera was vaguely aware of a disturbance—carriage wheels and the clops of horses outside, low voices and movement within the house. Perhaps the doctor leaving early in case he encountered the mad Lady Hera again. She closed her eyes and went back to sleep.

When she woke, it was to hot chocolate and the news that the duchess had returned. Both were delivered by her maid, along with the added information that Her Grace had brought with her a strange lady who had lost her luggage.

Intrigued, Hera dressed and went downstairs to break her fast. However, in the breakfast parlor, she discovered only Aunt Hadleigh, Anthony, and Victor making one of his rare appearances at table.

"Her Grace is back," Victor told her at once. "Just in time to play the role of grieving widow."

"Really, Victor, must you speak in such vulgar terms?" Aunt Hadleigh scolded. "Even Her Grace will grieve in her own way."

"Even?" Hera repeated sardonically. "Aunt, just because His Grace disparaged her doesn't mean you should."

"A little respect would not go amiss," Victor agreed, picking up his coffee cup. Over it, he regarded in turn their aunt and uncle and cousin. "In fact, I insist upon it."

Good for you, Victor.

Inevitably, Aunt Hadleigh opened her mouth to assert privilege, but Anthony took the wind out of her sails, saying quietly, "Quite right, Your Grace."

Aunt Hadleigh closed her mouth, though the light of battle remained in her eyes.

Hera changed the subject. "Has Dr. Rivers left already?"

"No," Victor said. "He'll speak to Her Grace before he goes."

"I don't know what the wretched man is looking for," Aunt Hadleigh said. "The officer, his friend, is clearly culpable. At least you will agree with me on that, Anthony. And you were there."

"I was," Anthony allowed. "And I do."

Victor got clumsily to his feet and snatched up his stick. Without a word, he limped across the room, making, as usual, for the library.

>>>><<<<

DETERMINED NOT TO prowl around the house on the off chance of running into Dr. Rivers, Hera decided to go for a ride. No doubt Aunt Hadleigh would object on numerous grounds, including mourning, so Hera had no intention of telling her. Instead, she changed into her riding habit and was hurrying down the main staircase when she saw the easily recognized figure of Dr. Rivers in front of her.

Her heart gave a funny little tumble of pleasure, especially when he glanced around and smiled with conspiratorial amusement as he waited for her to catch up.

"Good morning, my lady. Out of mourning again?"

"No one has yet dyed my riding habit." No doubt because it was an old one that she hadn't worn since before her first Season. "Have you seen Her Grace?"

"I have. And mean to be in London by this evening. Apparently, I can hire a post-chaise at Cuttyngham for speed. I'll accompany you to the stables if you're going now?"

He did not refer to the kiss, and seemed to behave no differently toward her, which was something of a relief.

When they were outside, she asked, "Did Her Grace tell you anything that might help Major Butler?"

He cast her a quick glance, as though surprised she remembered the name and rank of the man who had shot her father. "No. Like you, she had no reason to believe the late duke was not in perfect health."

Hera drew in a breath. "Whatever happens, will you tell the major that neither Victor nor I blame him?"

His gaze captured hers as they walked. "That is generous."

"No. But I believe I trust your judgment over Anthony's."

That seemed to leave him speechless for several seconds. Then, with the stables in sight, he said, "You have no cause to. But I thank you."

The groom led out the big horse she remembered from his arrival, fully saddled, with the doctor's bags attached. Hera walked beside Dr. Rivers, not minding the silence, just absorbing the presence of a remarkable man while she could.

Before he took the horse's reins, he turned to her and bowed. "Lady Hera. I wish you happiness. Thank you for making a difficult visit so interesting."

She couldn't help the smile that flickered across her lips. "A dubious compliment at best, but I accept in the same spirit." She held out her hand. "Goodbye, Dr. Rivers."

He took her hand and bowed over it with perfect correctness. He could not know her pulse was racing. "Goodbye, my lady." Then he released her and swung himself into the saddle. He tossed the groom a coin with a murmur of thanks and gathered the reins before tipping his hat to Hera. With a glinting smile that stirred those butterflies again, he rode off at a brisk trot.

HER GRACE THE duchess was different in some indefinable way that Hera couldn't quite put her finger on. She did not pretend any deep grief that no one would have believed in, but she behaved with perfect dignity and respect throughout the few difficult days that encompassed His Grace's lying in the church, his burial, and even Victor's abrupt and barely civil throwing out of all guests, leaving only Hera, the duchess, and the duchess's newly acquired companion, a mysterious lady of about her own age called Miss Wallace.

Apparently, Miss Wallace had been the reason for Her Grace's unexpected journey. Hera doubted that, though she did not quibble. She could hardly blame the duchess for wanting companionship. A mere couple of years younger than the duchess, Hera had never known quite how to treat her, even before she had chosen to escape her father by going to London with the Hadleighs. It had been a pity in many ways, since the duchess would have been better company for her Season, but the thought of living in the same house as her father had decided her against it. Much to her father's relief.

The duchess had probably never known that her overtures of friendship had warmed her stepchildren. At the same time, they had baffled Hera, who had been glad of her presence and yet still stood aloof. For the first time, she wondered if that had hurt the lonely young duchess and knew she should have tried harder. She had felt only pity for anyone married to her father, yet focused solely on her own escape.

Until she had achieved it and faced the reality of choosing a husband.

Shuddering, Hera said to Victor, "I don't wish to go back to London and the wretched Marriage Mart. Even when mourning is finished."

"Don't, then." After a moment, he looked up from his books. "Is there somewhere else you'd rather be? You know you always have a home here." He must have seen her wrinkling her nose, for he said humorously, "Her Grace will make it pleasanter now."

"But your wife will have her own ideas."

Victor looked around him exaggeratedly. "Did I miss something?"

"It's your duty to the dukedom, isn't it?"

"Marriage and I shall not suit," he said dryly. "Anthony, or Anthony's children, will inherit after me."

She stared at him. "Anthony has children?"

"A daughter, at least."

"I didn't even know he was married!"

"I don't think he is."

"Oh. Well, his illegitimate children can't inherit, and he's not exactly young anymore."

"He's not in his dotage either. Anyway, it makes no difference. Do what you want, Hera. Go where you want. You might even find Her Grace a good companion in your travels."

"She has Miss Wallace now." And in any case, Hera was conscious of an urge toward independence, which would scandalize polite society. She shrugged. "I am in no hurry."

But it seemed the duchess was. Two days after the old duke was buried, she took off again, this time in the ducal traveling carriage that had no coat of arms.

"I'm sorry to leave you again so soon," she told Hera, breezing into her sitting room the morning of her departure. She wore black, and yet her eyes shone with a glow Hera hadn't noticed before. The duchess was beautiful. "But there is something I have to do, and I don't know quite how long it will take me. I shall leave Sophia—Miss Wallace—here as your chaperone for the time being. Be kind to her, if you will, for her life has not been easy. I have asked her to look to preparing the dower house for us to remove to. I'm sure she would value your help if it interests you."

Hera gazed at her. There was a new vitality about her stepmother, as though she had...hope. That was the quality in her that had been crushed since her first arrival here as a bride, younger even than Hera was now.

"Is it because of us?" Hera blurted. "Because I would not drive you out, and neither would Victor."

It was hardly ringing affection, but the duchess smiled as though it was. "No, my dear. I must find my own feet. As you and Victor must, too. I will write as soon as I can, so that you may always find me if you need to."

And with that, she was gone.

From curiosity, Hera accompanied Sophia Wallace to the dower house, which hadn't been occupied for more than a decade.

"I think we need the steward to see to the building," Sophia said. "Do you think Her Grace would like the interior redecorated?"

"I imagine so," Hera said, "though I know nothing of her taste. She was never allowed to touch the main house. I know she hated it, though."

"Do you think she will ever actually live here?"

Hera blinked. "You mean the main house is big enough for her to live separately if she wishes?"

Sophia didn't answer the question, saying instead, "It needs some repairs in any case. Shall we look around, so that we have some suggestions for her?"

It was an unusual couple of hours for Hera in that she was cooperating with someone else on practical matters that had little to do with herself. Sophia was down-to-earth, with an amusing turn of phrase, and Hera actually enjoyed their survey of the house.

The path to the main house ran close to the stables, and as they walked back, they were privileged to see Victor ride home from some outing with Jenkins, his steward.

Hera smiled with pride, for Victor had taught himself to ride only recently. Their father had forbidden it, either from excessive care for the safety of his once sickly son, or in his determination to see his him as a mere cripple and unworthy heir to the dukedom. In any case, Victor had used the old duke's increasingly long absences from

Cuttyngs to learn horsemanship. Hera had taught him the basics before her departure from London. Some empathy for his mounts, gritty determination, and not a little pain had done the rest. Victor now looked very well on a horse and appeared to be in total command of it.

Hera doubted their father ever knew. And for Victor, the freedom he gained was immense—not only to roam the acres that were now his, but freedom from the pity he found intolerable. On horseback, his lameness was invisible.

Dismounting was more of a palaver, but he carried a walking stick in his belt like a sword and used it to aid him.

Once she had changed her dress for tea—it was not black but a summery sky-blue—she decided to beard her brother in the library to discuss the dower house. Of course, it was possible Victor would join them for tea, but he only did so erratically.

He had changed out of his riding clothes, back into his old, comfortable coat and breeches, and now lounged at his usual desk, opening the post that must have arrived in his absence. Hera was pleased to note a faint glow of health in his cheeks, rather than the deathly pallor that had been more normal for him.

He glanced up. "Hera, solve me a mystery. Who is Harriet Severne?"

"Harriet? Must be some distant—" She broke off, suddenly remembering the letter of application she had written the day she had heard of her father's death. Glancing down at the still-sealed epistle in Victor's long fingers, she saw that it was addressed to Miss Harriet Severne, care of His Grace, the Duke of Cuttyngham at Cuttyngs, Essex.

Color flooded into her face. She snatched the letter and sat down with a bump opposite him. "It is I. In a fit of boredom, I applied for a companion's post, but I never truly expected to hear back."

"Haven't you had enough of being a companion to Aunt Hadleigh?" he asked sardonically.

"I was hoping there were more interesting people in the world." She smiled quickly, remembering Dr. Rivers. And Sophia Wallace. And even her own stepmother. "There are."

Victor watched her break the seal and unfold the letter. "But not so interesting that they might employ Lady Hera Severne as some old lady's companion?"

"It seemed unlikely," Hera agreed, skimming the letter, which was hearteningly long. "So I invented Harriet. I meant to warn you, but it went out of my... Victor, they're offering me the position!"

"Who is?" he asked, carefully neutral. "And where are they?"

"Their name is Astley and they are in...Lincolnshire. They want me to assist the lady of the house, a Lady Astley, with some extra duties caring for some unfortunate ward or other. My duties will be light, and I will have leisure time to pursue my own interests. They possess a fine library and gardens, among other things."

Victor shifted uncomfortably. It might have been physical pain, though Hera doubted it. "Do we know anything about these Astleys?"

"No," Hera admitted, casting him a quick smile. "To be honest, that is part of the charm."

"And the risk," he pointed out.

She met his gaze. "You are forbidding me?"

His crooked smile dawned. "Do I look like our late father? There is no point in forbidding you because I know you'll go anyway, if only for the novelty. All I ask is that you wait a few days before accepting, so that I can make inquiries. Neither of us wants you walking into some criminal trap for friendless young women."

Hera, who had never even thought of such a thing, found herself wondering how her even less worldly brother had done so.

"Who would you ask?" she said. "We don't know anyone in Lincolnshire."

"Actually, I think Frostbrook's main seat is there."

The Earl of Frostbrook had been, if not a friend of their father's, then at least an acquaintance. They had shared some kind of alliance in the House of Lords, and His Grace had left the earl a horse in his will. Hera had encountered him occasionally at the most formal events in London and never been sure of him. He seemed as cold and distant as her father, and yet there was odd humor in his remarks and intelligence in his cool eyes. Surprisingly, he had a rakish reputation, but Hera had only ever encountered his formidable formality.

"Wouldn't he wonder why you ask?" she asked.

"I see no reason why he would care. And then there is Dorrick—solicitors know everything. If they don't, they can find out. Will you wait four days, Hera?"

"Of course." To be asked rather than commanded was a form of bliss. Added to the hope of a different, independent life where she could earn money of her own, it brought a smile to her lips and a new spring to her step as she walked to the door.

Victor rummaged in a drawer for paper and reached for his pen. "Hera?"

She glanced back.

"You know you are not obliged to do this or anything else? There is money that will be yours when you are five and twenty, whether or not you marry. And if you are in a hurry, we can try to break the trust to bring it forward."

Hera considered. "Her Grace said something once about serving no purpose, being of no use at Cuttyngs. I felt sorry for her without understanding, but I think I do now. I want to be useful. Not so much to the rich old lady who is employing me, but to the unfortunate ward."

She didn't need to say that the vulnerability this term implied reminded her of herself and Victor growing up in their cold, cruel gilded cage. Victor understood.

⟫⟫⟫⟨⟨⟨

WHILE THEY WAITED for Victor's inquiries to bear fruit, Hera and Sophia went through the dower house, throwing out old and rotted items and planning what could be done with various rooms, what new furnishings and linens were necessary. Hera also prepared to travel, with her older and plainer gowns. None of them were black.

So, when both Lord Frostbrook and Mr. Dorrick, the family solicitor, wrote to Victor that Sir Hugh and Lady Astley of Denholm Hall were an old and respected family in Lincolnshire, providing the same address near the village of St. Bride that Hera had been given, she was immediately ready to set off.

CHAPTER FOUR

S HE TRAVELED BY post-chaise that made good if bumpy time up to Lincolnshire. Hera had never undertaken such a long journey before and was surprised by how tiring she found it. At the same time, the varied scenery interested her greatly, as did the changing accents of the inn staff who served her and changed the horses.

She was still excited about her new post. She suspected Victor had his doubts but was letting her make her own mistakes. But then, she too had doubts about leaving Victor to grapple with his new role alone. For although he was perfectly capable of running Cuttyngs and all the other estates far better than their late father, he was liable to grow even more reclusive during this mourning period, especially without either Hera or Her Grace to bring him out of it.

He had no intention of marrying, and always turned the subject with impatience when Hera tried to bring it up. Not that he should be pressed into matrimony any more than she should, but she suspected his reasons, and they bothered her.

Their father had been unnecessarily cruel, calling Victor sickly, a weakling, and a cripple who was unlikely to live long. In fact, during the blazing row of His Grace's last visit home, Hera had heard her father yell at Victor that he would damned well pay some well-born imbecile to marry him, though he doubted even that would produce an heir. Victor had said nothing about it, but he had been even whiter than usual when she crept into the library to sit with him in the same silent solidarity as in childhood.

It bothered Hera that Victor might believe such nonsense, that he could not see his own good qualities, quite aside from his eligibility and wealth as Duke of Cuttyngham. He was handsome, clever, and witty, and if his humor was occasionally malicious, well, the malice was usually deserved. Beside all of that, a lame leg counted for very little. He just needed the kind of wife who would not be offended when he got lost in his studies and forgot about her for a while.

And then there was Sophia Wallace, meant to be Her Grace's companion, now left alone with him, unchaperoned. Which was odd under any circumstances but might work out for the best. After all, she was a gentlewoman, good company, and not remotely put out either by his lameness or his formidable intellect. She might well be just what he needed...

Hera's speculation was interrupted by the sudden slowing of the carriage. Daylight was beginning to fade, and they had only just crossed the boundary into Lincolnshire. Another hour, according to the postilion, would see her at Denholm Hall. They had changed horses not long ago, so there was no reason to stop unless there was a problem.

The carriage came to a halt amidst a good deal of shouting from the postilions and other people. Hera peered out of the window but could see nothing beyond her own chaise. Without warning, one of her outriders appeared so suddenly that she drew back in alarm before pulling down the window.

"There's been an accident in the road, ma'am," he informed her. "Wheel came off the mail coach."

"Oh dear. Is anyone hurt?"

"Not bad, considering. The coachman managed to slow the horses before it happened. But there's a lady unconscious from a knock on the head. They're asking if we can take her the rest of the way to St.

Bride."

"Well, of course, if we can pass the broken carriage. We have room, and it is not out of our way, is it?"

"No, ma'am. We should get past without any bother, and we go through the village to reach—" He broke off, shuffling his horse back out of the way as a gentleman on foot pushed his way in. Hatless and frowning, he was instantly recognizable.

"Dr. Rivers!" she said in astonishment.

His gaze flew to hers. His frown vanished in a short, surprised bark of laughter. "My—"

Hastily, she cut him off, for she was not *my lady* here. "Were you in the mail coach? I understand a lady is hurt and needs urgent assistance to St. Bride."

"Might she beg a place in your chaise, m—"

"Of course," she interrupted again. Hastily changing seats so that she faced backward, she said, "Bring her here. I have a cushion for her head, and a blanket."

She might have imagined the warmth in his eyes as he nodded and strode off. A few moments later, he reappeared with a lady hanging limp in his arms. Hera placed the cushion for her head, so that they could lay her mostly flat, although her skirts and dainty feet dangled off the bench.

Her face—a charmingly pretty face—was marred by a nasty graze on her forehead. A trickle of blood vanished into her golden hair and the crumpled hat still clinging to it. She looked to be in her late twenties, a matron of the middling sort. Her clothing was good quality without being in the first stare of fashion.

"Will the wound need to be stitched?" Hera asked.

"No, it should heal on its own. I'm more worried that she's still unconscious. She must have struck her head with some force. Your postilion says you're going through St. Bride."

"To Denholm Hall."

His gaze flew up from his patient. "Really? You know the Astleys?"

The injured lady emitted a soft moan, lifting her gloved hand to her head. Dr. Rivers caught it. "No, lie still," he said with gentle firmness. "You're quite safe, although I'm afraid your head will hurt like the devil for a while."

Her eyelids fluttered open. "What happened?" she whispered, staring into his eyes.

"A wheel came off, and you were thrown against the door. This kind lady will take you safely home."

She tried to sit, clutching at the doctor's arm. "Don't leave me, Justin!"

Justin. They were on first-name terms. Clearly, she was more than simply a fellow passenger to him, and the knowledge caused a rush of bleak, unpleasant feeling Hera did not want to sort out.

"Stay with your patient by all means, doctor," she said carelessly. "There is no point in your leaving here just to stand in the road and wait to be rescued by someone else."

He hesitated only a moment, glancing from his patient to Hera, his expression unreadable. "Then I thank you. Give me one moment to fetch my bags, and Mrs. Thomson's."

As he rose, Mrs. Thomson's hand fell limply back on to the blanket and her eyes closed once more. Hera regarded her with interest, recognizing a fellow actress when she met one. For almost two Seasons, Hera had played the part of the perfect young lady, and occasionally the supercilious, slightly rude noblewoman. Before that, she had played whatever part necessary to avoid punishment or parental attention. Only with Victor had she even been herself. And perhaps for a few minutes one evening with Dr. Rivers, who turned out to be a friend, to call it no more, of the prostrate lady now exaggerating her symptoms for his delectation.

Mrs. Thomson did not open her eyes again until Dr. Rivers re-turned, the bags stowed in the space behind the carriage and tied to the roof. He brought only his medical bag inside and sat on the backward-facing bench beside Hera.

"Try to lie as still as you can," he advised his patient. "Though I'm afraid it's inevitable you'll be bumped about."

Mrs. Thomson, who perhaps expected him to be kneeling on the floor by her side, mopping her brow and holding her head steady, blinked at him and bravely said she would do her best.

"Allow me to present you to our savior," the doctor said. There was a hint of laughter behind his gravity that gave Hera some hope that he recognized Mrs. Thomson's exaggerations as well as she did.

However, he wasn't going to think much of Hera's lies, whether or not he chose to keep her secret. She leaned forward hastily, offering her hand to the prostrate lady. "How do you do, ma'am?" she said before Dr. Rivers could utter another word. "I'm Harriet Severne, on my way to Denholm Hall. Do you live in St. Bride?"

The gloved fingers barely touched Hera's. "Just on the edge of the village, Mrs...."

"Miss Severne," Hera said, feeling Dr. Rivers's gaze burning her skin. She tilted her chin to show she didn't care for his opinion.

"Mr. Thomson is Sir Hugh Astley's land steward," Justin said. "Are you a friend of Lady Astley's, *Miss Severne*?"

She was not deaf to the subtle mockery in his voice, though she chose to ignore it. "Hardly, sir. I am her new companion."

"Are you, by God?" His laughter was no longer quite so subtle. "Why do I find that so hard to believe?"

Mrs. Thomson, perhaps piqued by the doctor's attention to Hera, said tartly, "Perhaps because you consider Lady Astley too young to need a companion. Gentlemen never realize that a lady might be lonely at any age."

Hera hid her surprise. She had, in fact, imagined Lady Astley to be elderly, or at least in late middle years. Even though the duchess, only three years older than Hera, had just employed Sophia Wallace in just that capacity. And then gone off on her own, abandoning that companion at Cuttyngs. Something odd was going on with the duchess. But if Hera meant to carry off her deception in the teeth of Dr. Rivers's knowledge of her identity, she would have to keep her mind on her own business, not her stepmother's.

"And what takes you in this direction, doctor?" she asked.

"Family," he replied.

"Justin's father is the vicar of St. Bride," Mrs. Thomson said.

"Goodness," Hera said, before she could help it. "What a strange coincidence."

"In what way?" Mrs. Thomson asked, not without hostility.

Suddenly perceiving all sorts of pitfalls, such as revealing the tendency of her thoughts to dwell upon the doctor, Hera yawned behind her hand to give herself time and mumbled, "Oh, just the oddity of running into acquaintances in unexpected places."

To her surprise, Mrs. Thomson beamed at her, as though Hera had uttered a great wisdom. "Indeed. Like Justin and I meeting on the mail coach after all these years! Just think, when he went away to war, I was not even married."

There was very little to say by way of response to that, and Mrs. Thomson must have realized it, for she closed her eyes and reclined both gracefully and prettily.

"So, you are to be Lady Astley's companion," Dr. Rivers said. "Why?"

"Because she asked, and I agreed," Hera replied.

"Then your family circumstances have altered drastically since we last met?" he asked with what might have been a hint of mockery. "Or doesn't your family know?"

"Of course they know," she snapped, torn between irritation and relief that he had not mentioned the head of the family she belonged to.

"I cannot imagine they approve of such a mad start."

"Which shows how little you know my family," she said sweetly. "My brother is very glad that I choose to be useful in the world."

"*Useful?*" He was gazing at her in open mockery now. "Fetching and carrying for someone who already has a houseful of servants and a family of her own?"

She threw up her chin. "I do not need your approval or your permission for whatever post I take, or for my reasons."

"Of course you do not, but you needn't pretend. If you wished to be useful, there are any number of areas where you could be, among people who truly need the help—the poor, the sick, the crippled, the hungry."

Angry color flooded her face, because it had never entered her head to help such people whose existence she was barely aware of on the periphery of her own. "It is not only the poor who need help," she snapped. "Why, my own stepmother—" She broke off, appalled that she had almost revealed her stepmother employed a companion.

"Yes?" Dr. Rivers encouraged her, his eyes gleaming with mockery, or just sheer entertainment.

Hera waved a dismissive hand. "I shall not bore you with my private history."

"Please do. I'm sure we should not be bored at all."

She eyed him with dislike. "Why are you so opposed to my wishing to be useful to somebody?"

"Because you are not being *useful*, are you? *You are running away.*"

Stricken as much by his attack as by the truth in it, she stared at him. A furious retort stuck in her throat because a lump had formed there, and she had the horrific realization that she might cry. As she tore her gaze free, she encountered the avid observation of Mrs. Thomson, drinking the quarrel in with undisguised glee.

Which at least brought Hera back to her familiar role. She met the doctor's contemptuous gaze with her own. "Not running away, doctor," she drawled. "Running *to*. Lord, isn't this journey tedious?

How much longer, do you suppose?"

Having thus disposed of both her companions with the civil insult, she closed her eyes and pretended to seek respite in sleep.

There was silence in the carriage for some time. Hera had no intention of breaking it, merely allowed the carriage to bump her around, without ever lurching into Dr. Rivers—quite a feat in so small and cramped a vehicle.

"There are few positions suitable to a lady," Mrs. Thomson said, as though excusing her to Dr. Rivers, which infuriated Hera even further. "And Lady Astley is kind."

"But is Miss Severne?" the doctor wondered aloud, with deliberate provocation.

Hera ignored him.

"Justin!" Mrs. Thomson scolded. "How can you even say such a thing when she has taken us into her carriage and saved us from sitting among the wreckage for hours? *You* are being unkind!"

"Physician, heal thyself," Hera murmured, without opening her eyes. She could not be sure, but the faint sound coming from the man next to her might have been a breath of surprised laughter.

She only opened her eyes as the horses slowed to enter the village of St. Bride. Of course, it was dark by then, so she could see very little of it, just a few silhouettes of cottages and a church, and then Dr. Rivers knocked vigorously on the roof and the carriage came to a halt.

"Do you think you can totter up the path, Vera?" Dr. Rivers inquired. "Or shall I carry you?"

Hera, fairly sure what the answer would be, glanced at the doctor to find his sardonic gaze on her face rather than on his patient's, although he switched it in time for Mrs. Thomson's answer.

"Just help me down from the carriage, and I'm sure I can walk on your arm. Otherwise, my husband will think me dead! Miss Severne, thank you so much for allowing us to share your chaise. You have been most kind."

Dr. Rivers had already jumped down and was retrieving bags, while someone hurried up the path from the house with a lantern.

"Not at all, Mrs. Thomson," Hera said graciously. "I am only glad I could help. I wish you a quick recovery from your injury. Good night."

"Good night." Mrs. Thomson smiled as she turned to be lifted from the carriage. The man with the lantern, a harassed-looking individual in a waistcoat, who looked some years older than Mrs. Thomson, joined them. Dr. Rivers was, presumably, explaining the lady's injury to her husband. Hera saw no reason to wait.

She reached out and closed the door herself before rapping on the chaise ceiling. She did not look at the group by the garden gate as the horses began to move once more. Departing without a word to Dr. Rivers gave her a certain amount of satisfaction, at least for two minutes before her heart began to hurt.

JUSTIN, EXPLAINING TO the suspicious Mr. Thomson what had happened to his wife, heard the door of the carriage close and tried to extricate himself with all speed in order to speak to Lady Hera. *Miss Severne* indeed! However, duty compelled him to issue brisk instructions to Thomson about guarding against the ill effects of head injuries, even though he was unsure whether Vera had actually lost consciousness or not. And while he did so, the chaise simply drove off up the hill toward Denholm Hall.

Drat the girl! He could hardly run after it, especially since a startled glance showed him Hera gazing out of the opposite window before she vanished. As though, duty done, she had forgotten all about him and Vera Thomson.

Perhaps she had, ridiculous female. What the devil did she imagine she was doing?

Raising his hat, he left Thomson to take in his wife's bags, collected his own from where he'd left them in the road, and strode back toward the vicarage, fuming, although he wasn't quite sure why.

Because he had been rude to Hera when she was merely feeling her way toward independence from one of the most broken families he had ever come across? Because he had kissed her and expected her to be more sensible of the honor? Even though he was merely a rough army surgeon, younger son of a country vicar, and she the lovely daughter of a wealthy duke.

And why in the world did even this unworldly young lady imagine life as a paid companion would be better than that under her brother's roof? The impression he had gained during his brief visit was that though understated, there was both affection and understanding between the brother and sister. If none of either commodity elsewhere in the family.

She had not even waited to ask him about what he had discovered in London of her father's health. Not that he had learned anything useful at all. He still had no reason for the duke to have staggered into Butler's shot, or for him to have died of the wound so quickly. Illness and death were erratic, of course, and did not always give the convenient warnings a physician would prefer. It was just that something about the duel felt *wrong*.

The whole damned family is wrong! Moodily, he strode up the path through the dark churchyard, taking the shortcut to the vicarage behind it. At last, the familiar sight of home cut through everything else, raising his spirits in spite of himself. And yet, as he lifted the knocker, he was already preparing for the fight.

He did not get it, or at least not at once. His father opened the door himself and stood there beaming, a frail figure with quiet, compassionate eyes, which only partially concealed the formidable intelligence beneath.

"Justin! You're back."

"Just for a week," Justin said cheerfully, carrying his bags into the entrance hall.

Philip, his brother, came out of the parlor. Also smiling. "A week is better than nothing! We were afraid you had gone already."

"What do you take me for?" Justin said irritably.

"Hungry," his father said peaceably. "Come and have some supper."

It was undeniably pleasant to relax back into family, where distant past met present and the more recent past was easily blurred. As Justin was proud of his father and brother, he knew they were proud of him. Once he had thought that pride in him would be a balm to his soul on returning from the war. Instead, it seemed only to emphasize his unworthiness. In spite of the evening's laughter and the pleasure of reunion, there was a distance between them now, one of his own making that he hoped they could not see.

He happily argued philosophy, theology, and politics with his father and brother, and bantered with them and with Philip's wife, Evelyn, whom he very much liked. She made Philip happy, even without the added joy—so far—of children.

He retired late, pleasantly fuddled from the French brandy he had brought on his last visit, and exhausted from his journey and his contradictory emotions, which somehow encompassed Hera Severne as well as his family. Unusual for him, he fell into deep and immediate sleep.

Tonight, of all nights, the dreams came. He woke in a cold sweat, his vision full of blood and death and failure—and then thought he was still dreaming when a firm but gentle hand pushed him back into the pillows and told him to hush.

"Oh, not you," Justin uttered. "Not you, too!"

"Too?" Philip repeated. "Who else has been in your bedchamber this night?"

The lamp flared into life, casting light over the familiar furnishings of Justin's boyhood bedchamber, and the anxious face of his brother.

Slowly, carefully, he slowed his breathing.

"Sorry," he mumbled. "I was dreaming. What is it?"

"You cried out," Philip said. "The same dreams?"

"No," Justin lied, regretting the moment of weakness on his last visit when he had blurted something of the dreams to his brother.

Philip was silent, and Justin closed his eyes. "Going back to sleep. Good night, Philip."

Philip stayed where he was, looming over him. "You need rest, Justin. You need to be at home."

"You mean you need to be in London with a clear conscience," Justin retorted. "It's not quite the same thing."

"No, it isn't," Philip said, clearly stung. "And you need time to realize that you could never save everyone! It was not your fault those men died."

"They didn't all die," Justin said coldly. "I saved some. Which is why I will go back to the army and save a few more. Good night, Philip."

"Justin—"

Justin swore at him, and this time, Philip went.

CHAPTER FIVE

HAVING PAID THE post boys at the front door of Denholm Hall, Hera turned to find a footman collecting her bags, and another waiting to show her into the house.

Although far from the scale of Cuttyngs, Denholm Hall appeared to be a comfortable manor house. She could hardly judge the state of repair in the darkness, but the entrance hall was very fine, and there were lights on everywhere.

An elderly but sedate butler welcomed her to the hall and introduced himself as Simmonds before turning to the thin, slightly harassed-looking housekeeper whom he presented as Mrs. Wyse.

"And this is Miss Figg, our nurse."

A plump, motherly woman of uncertain years, beaming from ear to ear, waddled forward and curtseyed. "Bless you, ma'am, so kind of you to help us! Come along and I'll take you to her ladyship."

Laying aside the slightly odd greeting, Hera followed Miss Figg the nurse—why did they have a nurse if Lady Astley was not the old lady Hera had been imagining?—across the hall and up the staircase to a bright, well-appointed drawing room on the first floor.

"Miss Severne, your ladyship," the nurse announced, with a beaming smile. "I thought you'd want to meet her before I show her to her room.

A couple who had been seated on either side of the fireplace, the gentleman reading, the lady busy with needlework, rose at once. The lady came forward, smiling, a young, fashionably dressed matron perhaps ten years Hera's senior.

"Miss Severne, what a pleasure to meet you. I'm Lady Astley, and this is Sir Hugh, my husband."

Hera curtseyed.

Sir Hugh, a well-made man in his thirties, ambled forward. "How do you?" he said affably. "Hope the journey wasn't too appalling?"

"Not at all—remarkably quick, considering the distance."

"Still, you must be exhausted," Lady Astley said kindly. "Journeys do that to one, even when one sleeps the entire way! Have you dined, Miss Severne? Would a cold collation in your room be acceptable? And we can meet tomorrow to discuss your duties."

"Of course, my lady. It would be very welcome."

"Then I shall leave you to Nurse's tender care and look forward to our chat tomorrow. Good night, Miss Severne."

"Good night, my lady, Sir Hugh." With that, she was led from the room by Miss Figg, who took her up another flight of stairs.

"Does Lady Astley have children?" Hera asked.

"No," the nurse replied with clear regret. "They have not been so blessed, though her ladyship is still young, as I keep telling her!" She cast Hera a surprisingly shrewd glance. "You are wondering why they call me Nurse? Why I am here? Well, I was Sir Hugh's nurse from his birth, and I've got into the habit of taking care of all the poorly in the household. But you'll get used to us in time! That's Sir Hugh's room, and her ladyship's next door. We've put you further along the passage here…" They walked some distance along, then she threw open a door on her left, beaming as though she were bestowing a valuable gift.

And she was, in a way. The room was both bigger and more luxurious than Hera had expected, with a comfortable chair by the fireside and a desk by the window. A lamp already burned on the dressing table, and Miss Figg lit a spill from it with which to light the other candles.

Hera's bags were already waiting for her.

"There's warm water to wash, and the fire's been lit to take off the chill, though you won't want it during the day. They'll bring your supper up directly. And just ring if you need anything at all."

"I will, thank you," Hera murmured. "Good night, Miss Figg."

"Call me Nurse," Miss Figg said, waddling to the door, where she turned. "Oh, I should tell you. There's a staircase at this end of the passage, but it's not at all safe. You should use the main staircase, where we came up. Good night, miss."

As Hera munched her way through the generous helpings of supper, which came with a glass of indifferent wine, it struck her that for a young woman so desperate for companionship, Lady Astley had dismissed her with surprising speed. But then, her husband had been present, and no doubt it was during his absences she felt the need of company.

Hera also realized she had failed to ask Miss Figg about the ward, whose care would be part of her duties. And oddly, the nurse had not mentioned this person when they had been discussing children.

As requested, Hera piled the remains of her meal onto the tray provided and left it outside her door. Then, her head spinning with her new home, as well as with Dr. Rivers and Vera Thomson, she prepared for bed. She did not expect to sleep for some time, but as soon as head touched the pillow, she knew nothing more until a maid woke her, asking if she would like tea, coffee, or hot chocolate in her room before breakfast.

Surprised by yet another courtesy, Hera chose coffee and asked the maid where she should go to break her fast. Armed with directions to the breakfast parlor on the ground floor, she set off half an hour later and found Lady Astley alone at the table.

"Ah, Miss Severne, good morning. Do help yourself from the sideboard and come and join me. Did you sleep well?"

"Excellently, thank you. Everything is most comfortable."

"Oh, good, because we do want you to feel at home here."

Hera sat down with some eggs and toast and fresh coffee and found her employer watching her with apparent pleasure.

Lady Astley stirred. "As I said in my letter, your duties will not be in any way arduous. Mostly, it will just be accompanying me on morning calls and being with me to receive others. My husband spends a good deal of time away in Lincoln and York and even London, and I find solitude grows quickly dreary. You said in your letter of inquiry that you ride, so we must find you a suitable mount so that we may ride out together too. How is your needlework, Miss Severne?"

"You mean embroidery work rather than mending? No one ever called it more than fair," Hera admitted. "Of course, I was taught, but between ourselves, I find it tedious."

Lady Astley laughed as though Hera had been deliberately witty. "Everyone has their own accomplishments," she said with a trace of smugness. "Mine is needlework, and I do enjoy it. But perhaps, since you have a delightful voice, you could read to me while I work? I should enjoy that."

"So should I," Hera said, crossing her fingers in her lap with the hope that Lady Astley's reading preferences were more than improving religious verses. "What about meals, Lady Astley? Would you like me take them with you or in my own room?"

"Oh, with us, of course! Whether or not Sir Hugh is present, you are clearly going to be an excellent companion at dinner."

"Does your ward also join us for meals?" Hera asked.

Lady Astley set down her cup with odd deliberation. "No. No, he does not. Mostly, he will be no trouble to you at all... But I'll take you to meet him after breakfast. It's a lovely day, so he'll be in the garden, I expect."

"I look forward to it. How old is he, ma'am?"

Lady Astley blinked. "Oh, he is not a child, just a poor unfortunate it is our duty to care for. He is not mad," she added hastily, "nor dangerous in any way. He is just extremely...*odd* and cannot cope with normal life. He is also often ill and needs simply to sleep until he feels better. But you will see for yourself after breakfast. Though perhaps I should show you around the house first..."

After breakfast, Lady Astley duly guided Hera about the house, showing her the public rooms and formal rooms, including the fine library she had been promised. "You must treat the house as your own and use these rooms whenever you wish. Except for Hugh's study—this is his study. He spends a lot of time there. We shan't disturb him. Now, shall we fetch our bonnets and go into the garden?"

Obediently, Hera collected her bonnet and cloak from her chamber, and walked down the main staircase to the front hall. She wanted to throw wide the front door and explore, but it seemed impolite not to wait for Lady Astley.

She occupied the time by examining the pictures on the walls—a portrait of a fierce old man in the previous century's ornate fashion, including a powdered wig, a few pleasant landscapes, and another portrait of a gentleman with his small sons. The younger child, probably only two or three years old, was climbing on his father's knee. The larger, of perhaps ten or eleven years, sat on the floor, curiously but definitely apart from the others, smiling, with his arm around a hound.

"What a charming portrait," she said, as Lady Astley approached from the staircase.

"Yes, I rather like it."

Hera peered a little closer at the older child with the dog. "Is that Sir Hugh?"

"No, that's Hugh's older brother, who sadly died only a few years after the likeness was taken. Hugh is the climbing baby! He doesn't care for the picture, but I hung it here anyway. Shall we go out?"

Obediently, Hera turned and followed her employer out the front door. The countryside was pretty, mostly flat farmland stretching for miles, dotted with animals and cottages and hamlets. Water winked somewhere in the distance.

Lady Astley pointed out the village of St. Bride. "It's a brisk half-hour walk, but most pleasant on a fine day. I thought we might go this afternoon, if the rain stays off. These are our formal gardens."

They were delightful. Terraces, lawns, and flowerbeds stretched down in gentle slopes. An ornamental fountain graced the central terrace, and water glinted in a pond on the bottom lawn.

"It's delightful when we entertain," Lady Astley said. "We have had wonderful afternoon parties here, and in the evenings, we set lanterns all over and our guests can spill out from the covered terrace."

Hera thought of the lights her mother had always ordered be lit around her own formal rose garden, a tradition which had been followed until the present, although she imagined Victor or the duchess would change it now. For one thing, the Cuttyngs garden lacked this charm.

Most of Cuttyngs lacked charm.

Lady Astley pointed out the overgrown maze, which could be entered by a gate from the formal garden, or from the side of the house. "We have not done anything with it yet, but it might be fun to retrieve it, don't you think?"

Beyond it was an orchard, and around the next corner, what seemed to be another walled garden. Lady Astley walked up to an almost hidden, ivy-covered door and unbolted it, leading the way inside.

It was indeed a garden, bounded by walls and large trees. But there was nothing formal about this space. It was a riot of color, surprising and splendid, broken by erratic stone paths, swirling about like waves on a rocky shore.

Seated on a stone bench, sewing in the sunshine, was Nurse Figg. Some distance from her, a gardener crouched, pulling up weeds and throwing them into a bucket. Nurse Figg spotted Lady Astley and Hera almost at once, and beamed as she heaved to her feet, her work still in her hands.

"Good morning! Mr. George, look who is here to see you!"

Hera glanced about with interest, but no one sprang out from behind a tree or rushed across the crazy paths to greet them.

"Mr. George!" Nurse called, and again, "Mr. George. Mr. George."

As though finally annoyed by the constant repetition, the gardener rose to his feet and turned to face them. A smile dawned and he ambled toward them. He wore no hat or coat, just a thick calico shirt and a plain woolen waistcoat, without a cravat. Grass-stained breeches, still retaining traces of soil, narrowed into grubby but decent leather boots. Although his sightly wild brown hair was graying at the temples, he seemed at first to have a younger face. Only as he came up close to them did Hera see the weathered lines that placed him probably in his late thirties at least.

"What do you think?" he asked without greeting, waving his hand to encompass the whole garden.

"Very fine," Lady Astley replied.

"Unique," Hera said in awe, "and incredibly colorful. Did you design all of this?" She didn't know whether she should call him sir, or if he truly was just a gardener.

"Designed, dug, planted, and maintained," Mr. George said with a hint of pride. "I like it."

"So do I," Hera said. "Very much."

"But I have forgotten my manners," Lady Astley exclaimed. "Miss Severne, this is George. George, my new companion, Miss Severne, who will be delighted to spend time with you. She would like to be friends."

"Would she?" George regarded Hera, not with humor, precisely, but with a hint of skepticism. "Why?"

Lady Astley looked both appalled and flabbergasted. For Hera, the question might not have been well mannered, but it was eminently reasonable.

"I like gardens," Hera said, almost with surprise. "At my old home,

I was never allowed to work on them, but I'd love to help you, if I may."

George looked alarmed. "Help?"

"It's a large area to maintain. Obviously, I'd only do what you tell me, and you would make sure I'm doing it correctly so that I don't spoil anything."

The anxiety faded a little from his eyes. "Perhaps. If you truly want to." He pulled a watch from his waistcoat pocket. "Tomorrow," he decided. "I have to get on now, or the morning will be gone. Good day, Miss Severne. Caroline." He bowed quite elegantly if distractedly, and strode off back to the flowerbed he had been weeding.

"You see, he is not worldly," Lady Astley said apologetically. "But gentle and completely harmless. I think you struck just the right note, did she not, Nurse?"

Nurse Figg nodded sagely. "He likes her."

Hera was not quite sure how they could tell, but she let it go, obediently following Lady Astley back the way they had come. Through the open door in the wall, Hera glanced back over her shoulder at the amazing garden, then the door closed and Lady Astley slid the bolt home. For some reason, a little shiver passed through Hera, as though someone was being locked in their room.

"Is that all he does?" she asked. "Garden?"

"Lord no. He likes to read, too, but everything has to happen in a strict routine or he becomes…upset."

Hera glanced at her. "How upset?"

"Only a very little," Lady Astley said with a smile. "We accommodate him, and if it makes him ill, we have medicine. It all works very well, but he does need constant care, and it is too much for poor Nurse when Hugh and I go away anywhere. But I think you and Nurse would manage admirably between you."

Hera began to wonder if the odd but apparently amiable George was to be her primary duty.

"Have the rest of the morning to yourself," Lady Astley said. "I daresay you will have letters to write to your family to assure them you have arrived safely. Join me for luncheon and then we can walk into the village, where I have a few calls to make."

LADY ASTLEY'S FIRST call was on the Miss Pinktons, a pair of genteel spinster ladies, presumably fallen upon hard times, since they resided in one of the cottages on the Denholm estate. Although small, the parlor was very comfortable, a fine if slightly worn Turkish carpet on the floor, well-upholstered chairs for visitors, and elegant ornaments displayed on the mantelshelf. The ladies twittered like little birds, delighted by Lady Astley's attention. It struck Hera that her employer, while clearly kind and amiable, liked to play the bountiful lady of the manor, bestowing a basket of early strawberries upon them.

"You will come to dinner on Thursday evening, will you not?" Lady Astley said. "The Hailes will be there, and the Jewels, and the vicar and his son, of course."

"Oh, we shall be delighted, Lady Astley, so kind…"

The next visit was to Mrs. Thomson on the edge of the village. Her face lit up as she welcomed Lady Astley into her house, although her expression slipped a little when she glimpsed Hera behind. Her house was larger than the Pinktons', but less well appointed. She had a maid who brought tea, and she conversed politely.

Hera asked after her injury, now carefully hidden beneath her hair, and she pronounced herself quite recovered, although she did regale Lady Astley with a dramatic version of the mail coach accident.

"Oh, and you'll never guess who was also on the coach and so much help to me! Dr. Justin Rivers, the vicar's younger son! He has come home for a little again, although he says not to stay."

"That is odd," Lady Astley said, "for Mr. Philip Rivers told me his brother would set up his practice here! Perhaps he has changed his mind."

"It will be something to do with that monster, Bonaparte," Mrs. Thomson said shrewdly. "No one can make plans while he is loose!"

Mrs. Thomson also received a basket of strawberries, although the steward's wife was not invited to the dinner party.

The final basket was for the vicar. Hera, her stomach already churning with emotion after the mention of the Rivers family, steeled herself to meet the doctor's contempt once more.

But when they were shown into the vicar's parlor, they were welcomed by a man she did not know. With a little surreptitious scrutiny, she could see a resemblance to Dr. Rivers in the shape of his eyes and his face, but his expression was quite different, and there was nothing remotely sharp or sardonic about his pleasant voice.

"This is my companion, Miss Severne," Lady Astley said. "Miss Severne, Mr. Philip Rivers, the vicar's son, who is a clergyman in his own right."

"How do you do, Miss Severne?" There was civility but not a great deal of interest in his voice. "My wife will be down directly, and here is my father, delighted to welcome you."

An older, frailer gentleman with gentle eyes came into the room, greeting Lady Astley with clear pleasure and accepting the strawberries with gratitude before he passed them to the waiting maid. When Hera was introduced, he seemed both surprised and interested, and welcomed her to St. Bride with a pleasure that seemed genuine.

"I believe you are currently enjoying the company of your other son, also?" Lady Astley said as she sat down. "What a pleasant reunion for you all!"

"Indeed," Philip said with a slightly fixed smile. "Justin has gone up to see old Sam Smith, who is in sadly constant pain."

"Is Dr. Rivers quite fixed in St. Bride now?" Lady Astley asked. "I know you were both hoping he would set up a practice here. Indeed, we all were! A physician closer at hand would be of enormous benefit."

"He feels a strong duty toward the soldiers currently gathering to face Bonaparte," the vicar said with pride. "As you know, he was a surgeon with the Peninsular army for some years."

Philip's lips had tightened. It seemed to take some effort to keep silent, but fortunately, his wife came in and the moment passed in greetings and introductions to Hera.

"Severne," repeated Mrs. Rivers. "Are you perhaps some relation to the Duke of Cuttyngham?"

"Only very distantly," Hera said.

"I was so shocked to hear about his death. Our condolences to all your family."

"Thank you," Hera replied uncomfortably, for she read curiosity in the younger clergyman's wife. A Severne hiring herself out as a companion was odd enough, but Hera, in her lavender and gray grown, was clearly not even in mourning. "It is not a close connection." Not in one sense, at least.

Mrs. Rivers seemed to be quite a worldly and ambitious woman, no doubt for her husband, but her interest in Hera brought home all the inherent dishonesty of the position. Hera had not envisioned having to actually lie and now wished she had changed her surname as well. Which, of course, was merely another form of dishonesty.

She was very glad when, after making sure the vicar and his family would attend her dinner, Lady Astley rose to take her leave. But there was no time for relief to settle, for the parlor door opened during their farewells and Justin Rivers himself walked in.

"Ah, Justin," the vicar said, clearly pleased. "You have not met Lady Astley, have you? My younger son, ma'am, Dr. Justin Rivers. Justin, Lady Astley, Sir Hugh's wife."

Lady Astley graciously offered her hand and a smile. "I believe you were with the army when we were married. And we missed you on your last visit to St. Bride. How do you do, doctor?"

Dr. Rivers bowed correctly over her hand. He had not even glanced at Hera, though he must have suspected her presence, even before Lady Astley waved one hand toward her and said, "My companion, Miss Severne."

"Miss Severne and I have met before," he said, turning his sardonic gaze on Hera. "Indeed, it was she who rescued Mrs. Thomson from the mail coach accident."

"Rescue?" Lady Astley repeated in surprise. "I had not realized the accident had been so serious."

"I was not involved in it," Hera said hastily, "merely took up Mrs. Thomson and the doctor in the chaise because she was injured."

"Chaise?" Mrs. Rivers looked impressed, though for some reason Lady Astley seemed disturbed. "You traveled post to take up your position?"

"I expect Miss Severne's family insisted," Dr. Rivers murmured.

Hera cast him a look of dislike. "I had a little money put by."

But Lady Astley had moved on, hoping she could count on Dr. Rivers's presence at her dinner on Thursday. He thanked her civilly, and she smiled as she made for the door, Philip and his wife at her heels to see her off. Hera followed behind, as a modest companion should—though to her annoyance, Justin decided to escort her.

"So how do you find the life of a companion so far?" he murmured.

"Pleasanter than the life of a debutante," she replied. "I never had the chance to ask you last night if you learned anything from His Grace's physician."

Justin sighed. "No, though he seemed to imagine he was teaching me about medicine."

"Then you had a wasted journey."

"Not entirely. I also called upon one of the seconds who has some of the same doubts as me." He murmured something under his breath as they came to the front door and the end of any privacy of conversation. "I'll walk up to Denholm this evening," he said. "Unless your duties are too intense to free you."

"Like yours?" she retorted, and walked away without a word, keeping her farewells for his brother and sister-in-law.

CHAPTER SIX

"SHALL WE HAVE tea with George?" Lady Astley said brightly when they re-entered the hall. "That way you may get to know him better. I would very much like to go with my husband to Lincoln on Friday, though I shall not unless you are happy being in charge of George."

Hera blinked. "Does he need to be kept in charge of?"

"Very lightly, and very seldom," Lady Astley replied with a smile, whisking off her bonnet and handing it to the butler. "But the possibility remains. Nurse will be with you, of course."

George was discovered in a room on the second floor, which seemed to have been turned into a cross between a study, a library, and a sitting room. It overlooked his "secret" garden and was lined with books and cupboards. An upholstered chair had been set by the fireplace. Nurse Figg sat there, knitting, although she rose as soon as they came in, beaming her usual smile of welcome, and went to sit instead on a stool in the corner.

George occupied the large desk in the middle of the room, surrounded by notes and lists, bound books and old newspapers. He was writing busily and didn't appear to notice them come in, which gave Hera time to take in the rest of the room—which, for some reason, reminded her of the garden, with little pathways between piles of books and plants.

"Good afternoon, George," Lady Astley said brightly. "We've come to take tea with you."

"I can't stop for tea," George said.

Lady Astley blinked. "But you always stop for tea."

"Not today. I have to finish this for Hugh."

"Oh, but Hugh would not like you to miss tea." Lady Astley sounded so shocked that George looked up at last, indecision clear on his face.

"Would he not?"

"Of course not," Nurse said heartily. "You stop for tea, Mr. George. Look, Miss Severne is joining you, too. You find the ladies somewhere comfortable to sit." With that, she stuffed the knitting in her work basket and sailed out of the room.

George put his pen carefully in the stand and stood up. After removing a potted plant from the small table by the window, he dragged the armchair and his desk chair to it before snatching up a stool that had been buried under other things. By then, a footman with a large tray had arrived and set out what he could on the table. George waited politely until both ladies were seated before taking the stool.

"What are you working on?" Hera asked him.

"Numbers," he said. "They always have patterns. Like flowers."

"I never thought of them like that," Hera admitted.

"Most people don't. I like them. Thank you," he added, accepting a cup of tea from Lady Astley. He seemed to have perfect manners, and he spoke like a gentleman, even though he dressed like an outdoor servant. Hera had gathered that he was the son of some dependent thrust onto the Astleys' responsibility, but if so, he had learned a great deal, despite his oddity.

"What do you do with the numbers?" Hera asked, after she had sipped her tea and helped herself to a cucumber sandwich.

"Oh, don't ask," Lady Astley begged. "You won't understand the answers, which are long and difficult and make my head spin."

"No, they don't," George said, contradicting her for the first time in Hera's presence, although it was said very mildly. "You are clever. Is she not, Miss Severne?"

"You must not ask Miss Severne such things. She will feel obliged to say yes in case she hurts my feelings! But I think Miss Severne is clever too."

"And pretty," George observed, his eyes resting on Hera. "I expect you'll get married."

"Not today," Hera said, and won an unexpected smile from George. Despite his air of untidiness and rough grooming, he had a singularly sweet smile, charming and humorous and infectious.

Lady Astley led the conversation, however, about the weather and the garden and whether there would be rain in the next few days. It reminded Hera of stultifying small talk in London, so she was not surprised to see George's eyes glaze over, as though his brain had returned to his number patterns. However, while his mind clearly wandered, his mouth made the correct civilities. If he was mad, it was a very odd kind of insanity.

He rose with alacrity as soon as Lady Astley did, clearly eager to be relieved of the company, although he did say, "Come again." And his gaze seemed to be on Hera while he did.

"I will, thank you," she replied, and followed Lady Astley from the room. She heard the chair being dragged back across the room to the desk.

"He likes you," Lady Astley said in a tone of relief, "which makes everything so much easier."

Nurse Figg, appearing from nowhere, beamed at them both and re-entered the room. As though her charge could not be left alone even for a moment.

HERA HAD ABSOLUTELY no intention of walking in the gardens that evening on the off chance that Dr. Rivers might really pass for a chat. He could make a morning call like everyone else, if he had something to say to her, and it did not sound as if he did. They could discuss the duel, perhaps, when he came for dinner on Thursday.

She dined with Sir Hugh and Lady Astley, and although she hadn't truly been looking forward to even more small talk about the weather, she was pleasantly surprised. They discussed many things, from literature to the Congress of Vienna, and Bonaparte's escape from enforced exile on Elba to take back France. She was sure such discussion would have interested their ward, but perhaps they did not wish to agitate him with anything too deep and disturbing. On the other hand, judging by the quantity of books in his room, he was no stranger to literature, mathematics, or botany.

They treat him like a child they are teaching, she thought suddenly, *not a grown, educated man*. However, she had only been here a day, and presumably they knew their ward rather better than she did.

After the meal, the ladies repaired to the drawing room. "Your evenings will normally be free," Lady Astley told her. "Unless I need you, of course, in which case I shall tell you well in advance. You will join us for dinner on Thursday, I hope?"

"Thank you," Hera replied, trying desperately not to wonder if Dr. Rivers would bother to come.

"Excellent. Then from now, this evening is your own."

It sounded a little like dismissal, so Hera asked, "May I borrow a book from the library?"

"Of course you may!"

"Then I shall bid you good night."

Hera spent a very pleasant hour in the library, earmarking classical texts for perusal, so that she could at least hold her own with her brother when she next went home. In the meantime, she took a travel book and a Gothic novel from the shelves and was preparing to retire to her own chamber when the boot boy came in with the coal scuttle.

"Oh, I'm just leaving," Hera said. "You don't need to light the fire for me."

"Looks like it's all laid anyway," the boy said cheerfully. "Never mind. Message for you, miss, from the doctor who's the vicar's son. He's in the maze."

She blinked. "Why?"

The boy shrugged and grinned. "Waiting for you, miss."

In high dudgeon, Hera fetched her cloak and left the house by the side door nearest the maze, swiping up a lantern as she went. Opening the gate, she marched inside and almost cried out when a figure loomed up in the darkness.

Fortunately, her lantern showed her Dr. Rivers before she did more than stop dead with a lurching heart.

"Good grief, are you *trying* to scare away what's left of my wits?" she demanded. "Or just ruin my reputation?"

"Your wits seem perfectly in order, judging by your scolding tongue. As for your reputation, Jim the boot boy won't tell. His family and mine have a history. Besides," he added with a gleam of mockery clear in the lantern's glow, "I thought you despised such conventional thinking."

She sniffed, before she remembered how much the gesture annoyed her in Aunt Hadleigh. "Not when it loses me a position that I find congenial and interesting."

"*Interesting?*" he said in clear amusement.

"Interesting," she snapped. "And of my own choosing. I know you think both I and my position are trivial and pointless, but this *is* my choice, just as going to Brussels with the army is yours, whatever your family says. I do not give you leave to judge me, for you have no reason and less right."

He stared at her, the lantern light playing over his frowning brow and his lean face. Rather to her surprise, he took her arm and began to walk. "You are quite right," he said mildly. "I apologize. Your bolt from your brother's house to this one makes no sense to me, but that is my fault, not yours. And for what it's worth, I never thought you remotely trivial, let alone pointless."

She glanced at him with suspicion, expecting some sarcastic remark to follow.

"Don't be embarrassed," he said kindly. "It's hardly a fulsome compliment, though I could make you one of those, too."

"Please don't trouble," she said icily. The warmth of his hand on her elbow shifted, drawing her arm through his. She pretended not to notice. "Also, please don't get us lost in this wretched maze!"

"As if I would. I knew the way out when I was ten years old."

"You played up here as a child?" It shouldn't have surprised her. She just couldn't imagine him as a child. "With Sir Hugh?"

"Yes, sometimes, though he was closer to my brother Philip in age. All the village children would play up here occasionally."

"And you're still invited to dinner."

"Are you?"

"Yes, as it happens." And she was looking forward to it now. She hurried into speech once more. "Who was the second you spoke to in London? My cousin Anthony? Or Lord Frostbrook?"

"Frostbrook. He says the duchess spoke to him about much the same things."

"Her Grace did?" Hera said, lifting a surprised eyebrow. "You spoke to her at Cuttyngs, did you not?"

"I did, which was why she asked Frostbrook what he saw. The more he thinks about it, the more he believes I am right, that the duke collapsed into the path of Butler's pistol ball. But neither of us have any proof and can find no reason for him to have done so. Tell me, does the duchess have any reason, any motive, in proving the duke did not die in a duel?"

Hera frowned. "Like what?"

"I don't know. She seemed worried about Butler to me."

"We're all worried for Butler," Hera said wryly. "We know what His Grace was like. Neither Butler nor anyone else could have forced a quarrel upon him that he did not want. I may not have been present, but I'm as sure as I can be that His Grace did the forcing. He didn't believe in opinions other than his own. And yet, he is dead."

"The one indisputable fact in the whole tragedy. Frostbrook also reminded me of something I noticed at the time and then forgot. Someone else was present at the duel."

"Does that matter?"

"Duels are a male preserve because they are considered too violent for ladies' delicate sensibilities. And they are fought with as much secrecy as possible because they are quite rightly illegal. Present at this one should have been only the two principals—your father and Major Butler—each with two seconds, and myself for medical emergencies. But someone else was watching from the trees some yards away. A woman. A lady, I think. Do you have any idea who she might be?"

She stared at him. "Perhaps she lived nearby and was curious about the disturbance. Perhaps she was also staying at the inn. Are you asking me if she was my father's mistress?"

A faint smile chased across his lips and was gone. "I would not expect you to know such a thing. Frostbrook says she was not, that to his knowledge your father had no current mistress."

"Less insulting for Her Grace, I suppose."

"I doubt this woman has anything to do with the wretched affair," he said with a sigh. "I only ask because two of your family members were at the inn. I hoped if I could identify the woman, she might know something about the duke that would help explain his death. Could she have been anything to do with either the duke or your cousin Anthony? She seemed quite young by her posture, although she was too far away for me to make out her features."

Hera began to shake her head before a memory came back to her.

"Anthony has a daughter, according to Victor. She may be illegitimate, for none of us have met her. Nor her mother. I suppose your mystery lady could be one of them, although I doubt either would be able to help you to assess his grace's health." She glanced at him. "What will you do now?"

He shrugged. "Take the fight to Wellington, I suppose. He thinks well of Butler, and of Colonel Landon, whom Butler was defending. On the other hand, he doesn't like his officers dueling, which is eminently sensible. As if there aren't enough ways to die in war without adding to them out of it."

"Did you say that to Major Butler?" she asked, wishing the young man had listened.

"And to your parent."

Unexpected laughter shook her. "I would have liked to see his face. No, actually, I wouldn't. Where *is* Major Butler? He has not been arrested, has he?"

"Hopefully, he is in Brussels and trusting Wellington doesn't arrest him there." He caught and held her gaze. "What will you do, now you have arrived here?"

"Stay, for the time being. The Astleys' ward is an interesting man."

The doctor's eyes flew up. "Man? Not a boy?"

"No, I would say he is in late thirties, perhaps even forty, although sometimes he looks younger. But I'm not supposed to talk about him. I think he embarrasses them."

"Why? Is he simple?"

"No, I suspect he's very clever. But he is also rather strange."

"Perhaps I should come and visit this ward."

"I don't think the Astleys would like that," Hera said regretfully. "I suspect you're not supposed to know he's there."

He cast her a look of incredulity.

"Seriously," she said. "I should not have spoken of him to you."

"Then why did you?"

"Because it's he who actually makes my position interesting," she admitted. "He and the books and the free time. And I shall have my own money. I only mentioned him because..." *Because even though you're annoying, I trust you, and for no good reason I imagine we are friends.* "Because the words slipped out," she said hastily. "I owe Lady Astley my loyalty, so please don't say anything to anyone else."

"Everyone else must know about him," Dr. Rivers argued. "You cannot hide a grown man loose about a manor house."

He wasn't really loose, of course. He was always with Nurse Figg, and the door into his garden was bolted... Was his sitting room locked, too? She shook her head briskly. She should not have begun the Gothic novel.

"All the same, I would rather you did not bring him up in conversation with anyone. Including your family," she said.

"Very well."

She let out a breath of relief. "How is your family? I gather they know you intend to go to Brussels. Does your father mind?"

"Lord, no. It's Philip who minds. My father and I have both told him to go to London. I don't intend to be away for years, and my father will survive quite well without either of us for a few months. Admittedly, he's a little frail, but he's hardly in his dotage."

Hera thought about it. "Maybe there's another reason Philip doesn't want you to go."

"Such as?"

"Such as he doesn't want you to die."

He scowled. "Why the devil should I die?"

"Oh, for heaven's sake, you're going to *war!*" she exclaimed. "You may not actually fight, but you are bound to be close to battle all the time. I imagine he's afraid you've used up all your luck on the peninsula. Maybe your father's afraid, too."

He stared at her. She was sure his lips parted to make some blistering rebuttal, but in the end, he closed his mouth in silence. He kicked the hedge at his side and veered right. "I wonder if you are perceptive or imaginative."

"Which are you?" she retorted.

"Oh, perceptive," he said with mock gravity. "I am a scientist and accounted very sharp."

"Very grumpy," she corrected him, and he laughed.

"Well, I am in good company."

"I am not remotely grumpy."

"No..." He came to a halt, gazing down into her face. "No, I can never quite make up my mind *what* you are. Why did you kiss me?"

Heat rushed into her face. She just hoped he would not see it in the dim light. "Because you had been kind, I suppose," she muttered.

"Not grumpy?" he teased.

"Not then. In any case, it is not gentlemanly of you to bring it up. It was a moment of impulse and meant nothing."

"It must be my turn, then?"

She frowned in confusion. "Your turn?"

"For a moment of impulse," he said, lifting her hand from his arm. Neither of them wore gloves, and his touch was suddenly electric. He raised her hand to his lips and softly kissed her fingers. Then he took her other hand and kissed that, too. "Meaning nothing, of course."

"Of course." She meant it to be airy and dismissive, but her voice shook, and instead of pulling free, she let him turn her hand and softly kiss the inside of her wrist. Warm pleasure soared through her veins, almost frightening her in its intensity, and yet she was afraid to breathe in case he stopped.

A smile, faint and rueful, lurked on his lips. Releasing one of her hands, he reached up and brushed a strand of fallen hair from her cheek. The skim of his fingertips caught at her breath.

"The trouble is, you mean a great deal, though I don't know why or how. You should go in before you are missed."

With a little gasp, she tugged her hand free. "How? You've lost us in this wretched ma—" She broke off as he reached past her, so close that she smelled his soap, sandalwood and spice, and opened the gate. The gate where she had first come in.

"Good night," he murmured.

"Good night," she replied carelessly, whisking up the lantern and walking away. He could not know that her heart drummed and her stomach burned with strange new feelings, or that her mind wrestled desperately with everything he had said and done.

It was only later, as—after retrieving her chosen books from the library—she reached her own bedchamber and sank onto the bed, that the idea came to her.

Had he been *flirting* with her?

It was not at all like the heavy-handed admiration or even the more practiced flattery she had encountered in London. In fact, it was almost as if he did not want to like her and did anyway. She smiled at the thought, because she felt rather the same toward him. A friend who flirted was not unpleasant at all. In fact, he was rather exciting.

IT SEEMED SHE had only just fallen asleep when she woke again to the sounds of scraping and scratching above her. So far as she knew, the servants all slept in basement accommodation, so it couldn't be them moving about. Mice under the attic floorboards? She didn't want to think about that, so she pulled the covers over her ears and tried to ignore it. Something metallic clanked on the floor above. A few moments later, something creaked, like an unoiled hinge, then, after a second, came the sound of a hastily closed door, more scraping, and quick footsteps.

Human footsteps. Certainly not mice.

Hera pushed back the covers and sat up. Who on earth could be in the attic at this time of night? How did anyone even get up there?

Nurse Figg had said the stairs were damaged and dangerous…

A rush of voices like whispers reached her. Imagination? Her heart was beating fast with alarm. She could not throw off the feeling that something was wrong, that someone was in danger.

Fumbling, she lit the candle at her bedside and wrapped herself in her dressing gown. She lifted the candle and padded across the cold floor to the door. Beyond it, the passage was in darkness, causing her to hesitate. Then, with a deep breath, she went out into the passage and crept along toward the damaged stairs at the end. The door opposite the steps stood open to reveal a flight of narrower stairs going upward. Someone *was* up there.

She raised her candle higher, and just then heard a woman's voice murmuring. It sounded like Nurse Figg, irritated but not remotely distressed.

She must sleep up there, away from the other servants, Hera thought in relief.

Laughing at herself, she crept back the way she had come and went back to bed.

CHAPTER SEVEN

I N THE MORNING, Lady Astley went off to consult with Cook about the dinner party menu for Thursday evening, leaving her companion to her own devices. Accordingly, Hera took herself to George's garden. She had to unbolt the door in the wall to get in, but as soon as she did, she saw George busily weeding a different section of the garden.

As before, Nurse sat knitting on a bench. She beamed at Hera over the top of her work. Hera smiled back and walked forward to join George.

"I can't talk today," he said without looking up. "I have too much to do."

"Have you? Perhaps I can help, and then you won't have too much to do."

George looked up quickly, as if he had expected his visitor to be someone else—one of the servants, perhaps, or Lady Astley. "Good morning, Miss Severne."

"Good morning. What would you like to do?"

"Can you pull out the weeds without harming the flowers?"

"Oh yes," she said, with much more confidence than she felt. She had never weeded in her life before. "Then we can talk as we work. If you like."

He spared her a glance as she knelt down at the opposite side of the flowerbed and pulled on her gloves. "Do you *want* to talk to me?" he asked in surprise.

"Of course! If it wouldn't annoy you."

His sweet smile dawned. "Oh no. You have a kind face. Not all beautiful women do."

He returned to his work, and after her initial surprise, she found a weed among the flowers and dug it out by the root with her trowel, just as he did.

"Are we in a great hurry to finish the weeding?" she asked.

"No, just to finish the numbers. So I need to be done with the garden early."

"Ah, I see," she said, just as though she did. "Why are you in such a rush for the numbers?"

"I'm not. Hugh is."

She let that go. For the next hour, they both weeded, sometimes talking, sometimes enjoying a silence that grew oddly companionable. Perhaps Hera was growing used to him, because by the time he stood up, she thought he was conversing much more naturally, rather than just by question and answer, and odd, staccato statements.

"Are we finished weeding?" she asked.

"For today. One is never truly finished." He gave a formal little bow. "Thank you for your help, Miss Severne."

"My pleasure, sir! My parents would never let me garden at home, so I'm thrilled by the opportunity."

"You'd probably enjoy planting more," he said, "but you're here at the wrong time." He didn't quite wander off. There was far too much purpose in his stride. But with a pair of Nurse's scissors, he marched smartly from flowerbed to flowerbed, cutting one bloom from each, and when he was finished, he presented the whole to Hera with a shy smile.

"Oh! Thank you," she said, quite touched. "What a beautiful riot of color. I shall put them in a vase in my room."

He looked pleased. "I have to go. But you can come back tomorrow, if you like."

"I would like," she replied. "Thank you."

He bowed and strode up the curving paths to the French door into the house, moving so quickly that Nurse was taken by surprise. She jumped to her feet, grabbed her basket, and trotted after him with her knitting still clutched in one hand.

Hera followed them more slowly. The glass doors led into a plain, clearly little-used salon. After closing them behind her, she walked out into the hall, in time to see Nurse vanish, panting, up the back stairs. Not the servants' stairs, but the apparently damaged ones that Hera had been warned not to use.

"Mr. George, wait for me!" Nurse gasped in the distance.

So he had gone up the same dangerous staircase.

JUSTIN FOUND HIS father where he expected to, in his study, composing his sermon for the coming Sunday.

The vicar smiled a distracted welcome and carried on writing. Justin watched the movement of his pen without really seeing it. His father reached for the open Bible, no doubt to find some reference or other, and paused an instant as his gaze fell on Justin.

The vicar thumbed through the pages until he found what he wanted and then hastily wrote it down before he said, "What is worrying you, Justin? Your friend's duel?"

"Yes," Justin admitted. "Though I doubt there is anything more I can do about that except express my concerns to Wellington. If he'll let me." He stirred uncomfortably, for he had come to glean his father's view and wasn't quite sure where to begin. "Do you have much to do with the Astleys?" he asked abruptly.

"Of course. Why do you ask?"

"Because they have invited us to dine. Do they do so often?"

"A few times a year, especially when they have guests from London."

"Do you like them?" Justin asked.

"The London people? Most of them."

"Good, but I meant the Astleys."

"They are very pleasant and generous."

"I don't remember Hugh being very pleasant at all. When we were children."

"Well, he is a little worldly, perhaps, but that is no bad thing with an estate to run and tenants to care for. I have never found him malicious."

"Not when things went his way."

His father smiled. "Well, most things seem to go his way these days. Materially speaking. What do you have against him? Apart from boyhood squabbles?"

Justin shrugged. "Nothing. I'm just curious. Why does Lady Astley need a companion?"

His father sat back, regarding him thoughtfully. "Is this about Miss Severne?"

"What makes you think so?" Justin asked irritably.

"There is clearly something between you."

"Clearly?" Justin repeated in dismay.

His father laughed. "To me, my boy, to me. Who is she?"

"If I told you, you'd never believe me. Who is Lady Astley?"

His father blinked. "One of the Renfields, I believe—old Yorkshire family. In fact, I'm told she met Sir Hugh during the York Season."

"Do they have children? Adopted children? Wards?"

"Not to my knowledge." His father's voice was amused, although his vague eyes had sharpened.

"Then the two of them lived alone at Denholm Hall until Miss Severne's arrival?"

"Apart from the servants. What is this sudden interest in the Astleys?"

Justin sighed. "I wish I knew. I seem to be collecting mysteries."

His father gathered his papers together. "Do you *really* believe the Duke of Cuttyngham did not die of being shot?"

"No, I don't *believe* it, though there are indications. I *want* it to be true so that my friend is not accused of murder."

"And because you could not save him," his father said gently.

Justin sprang to his feet, turning his back to his father as though gazing out of the window, although he saw nothing but pain, his own and his many patients'.

"You can't save them all, Justin."

Justin drew in a breath as though that would control the unbearable failures. "He was one I could and should have saved."

"And since you can't save him, you'll save Giles Butler?"

Justin's smile was twisted. "Something like that." He turned back to his father. "He wasn't even a very nice man, the Duke of Cuttyngham. He was insulting and condescending, adamant and stupid, and from all I can gather, he treated his wife and family appallingly. But he should not have died."

His father sighed. "I know better than to remind you that it was Butler who shot him, not you. By all means, look for the truth, but whatever that is, Justin, the duke's death is not your fault. None of the deaths you have seen are your fault or your failure."

It was unbearable. He closed his eyes as though that would hide him, hide his grief, his mourning for every patient he had lost. The rest of the world never saw that. He took damned good care they should not. But his gentle, unworldly father had never been the rest of the world. Neither had Philip, the prying, know-it-all big brother…

He swallowed the lump in his throat. "Then I shall just claim the successes."

"You should," the vicar said. "For they are considerable."

Justin waved that away impatiently and threw himself back into his chair. "You don't think I should go back to the army, do you?"

His father didn't answer for several moments. Then he said, "I want you to follow your heart and your mind, as you always have. But I fear many more people will die before Bonaparte is put back in his box. You cannot save them all."

Justin forced a smile. "And I am not the only surgeon. You don't need to worry for me, Father. I believe I have found a quite different lost cause to torment myself with."

⇛⇛⇚⇚

IN THE MORNING, Hera went out riding with Lady Astley.

"George was not in his garden this morning," Hera observed as they trotted out of the stable yard. No groom was to accompany them. "Is he well?"

"Oh, yes. He has given priority to his 'numbers' today. If he finishes, whatever that means, he will go in the garden later instead." Lady Astley cast Hera a smiling glance that was oddly sharp. "He does not frighten you, does he?"

"Goodness, no! He seems a very gentle man."

"He is," Lady Astley agreed with obvious relief. "But some people are afraid of him just because he is different."

"Well, we're all different," Hera said with a hint of ruefulness. "Though I confess I have never met anyone remotely like George before."

"We are very fond of George," Lady Astley pronounced. "And very protective."

"How do you come to be responsible for him?" Hera asked.

Lady Astley laughed. "Oh, that is a long story! But you will be comfortable when Hugh and I are away on Friday?"

"Of course."

"Good. If this works well, perhaps Hugh and I might risk going further afield, one day soon. Even to London! Let's go through the woods to the river. It's a beautiful morning, is it not?"

It was indeed. Hera breathed in the fresh wood smells, loving the dappling of the sun through the trees and the joyful singing of the birds. As they emerged from the wood, she even enjoyed a short gallop over open country before she realized Lady Astley was not with her.

She slowed, twisting around in the saddle and saw that the other horse was merely walking, favoring one of its front hooves. Hera turned her mount around and rode back.

"He went lame suddenly," Lady Astley said with some annoyance. "Can you see what is wrong?"

Hera dismounted and went to her, stroking the horse's nose before she bent to examine its hoof. "The shoe is loose. How far are we to the blacksmith?"

Lady Astley wrinkled her nose. "Further than we are from home. How annoying! I wanted to show you so much!"

"Never mind. You had better dismount. You can ride my horse instead, while I lead yours back to the stables."

"Oh, no, we shall just walk back together and lead both the horses. At least it is a pleasant day for a stroll."

Lady Astley chose a different path through the woods that was, she said, more direct. Certainly, it was busier. They passed an old man and a donkey heading for the village, met a couple of young girls going in the opposite direction. And then, like a stab in the heart, Justin Rivers walked over the rise toward them, with Mrs. Thomson dangling from his arm, a basket in his other hand.

"Good morning, doctor! Mrs. Thomson," Lady Astley said warmly.

Although the steward's wife was dressed rather prettily, with curling ribbons on her bonnet, the doctor wore what looked like an old coat and breeches, and no cravat. Hera would have liked to disdain him for such ungentlemanly attire, but in truth he looked handsome and beguilingly casual, and she found it hard to look away from the strong brown column of his throat.

Mrs. Thomson curtseyed, blushing. Why would she blush?

Dr. Rivers bowed. "Are you taking the horses for a walk?" he asked humorously. He had barely glanced at Hera.

"Alas, we were attempting to take them for a gallop," Lady Astley replied, "but my mare has loosened her shoe somehow, and now we must go back. Which is annoying on such a fine day. I had been hoping to show Miss Severne all our sights. Where are you two going?"

"Oh, I'm hoping to entice my husband for an al fresco luncheon," Mrs. Thomson replied, indicating the basket Justin carried.

"And I am just walking," Dr. Rivers said apologetically. "I'm afraid my brother and I played on Denholm land too much as children—as did Mrs. Thomson!—and I don't seem to have lost the habit of wandering your acres at will."

"Well, we shan't accuse you of trespass!" Lady Astley said gaily. "You must walk wherever you wish."

"I should hurry on, or I will miss my husband," Mrs. Thomson said hastily. She glanced at Dr. Rivers, as though expecting his continued escort.

But Justin only smiled and bowed and offered the basket. "Enjoy your luncheon, Vera."

There was nothing for her to do but accept the basket with a murmur of thanks and walk on past the horses. Hera wondered if she had truly meant to share luncheon with her husband or with Dr. Rivers.

"Allow me to take the mare to the blacksmith for you," Justin offered.

"Well..." Lady Astley hesitated, then suddenly beamed. "No, I have a much better idea! I shall take both the horses back to Denholm Hall, and you, doctor, shall show Miss Severne some of our sights. I have a few things to do this afternoon, but I shan't need you before tea, Miss Severne."

"Truly?" Hera asked, catching her eye, knowing she must not mention George. "Are you sure you can manage?"

"Oh yes. The horses are placid beasts. Enjoy a pleasant walk!" And, taking the reins from Hera's hand, she walked on down the path, leading both horses without apparent difficulty.

Hera watched her go for several moments.

"You are frowning," Dr. Rivers observed. "Is it my companionship you object to?"

Deliberately, Hera smoothed out her frown. "No. I was wondering why Lady Astley wanted a companion. She seems to keep finding reasons to shuffle me off. Perhaps it will be different when Sir Hugh is away."

"Or perhaps she doesn't want a companion for herself but for this ward of hers."

"It is possible," Hera said, "though I haven't seen him this morning either."

"Well, enjoy your freedom. Isn't that why you accepted the position?"

He had begun to walk, wandering off the path, and she kept pace while casting him a quizzical glance. "Is that why you laugh at me? Because people don't take paid employment to gain free time?"

"No. I know there's more to it than that," he said quietly. Taken by surprise, she stared at him, and he smiled fleetingly. "I laugh at you because I like you."

Color flooded her face. Beneath it, she was ridiculously pleased, but she retorted, "You laugh at people you like?"

"Well, I laugh *with* them, though they may not always see that. Don't you?"

She thought about it. "I don't think I ever laugh much. Except with Victor occasionally."

"Not with friends?"

How to answer that? She took a deep breath and decided on honesty. "I don't really have friends. We were never allowed to play with other children—being so immeasurably above our neighbors. By the time I met young ladies of my own age, I had nothing in common with them. Mostly, they think I am rude."

"Mostly, I suspect, you have rivals," he corrected her wryly. "But I imagine the young men have more reason to pursue the beautiful daughter of a duke."

She grimaced. "The well-dowered daughter of an influential duke. Although that influence has gone. Unless Victor decides to pursue politics, of course, although I have never known him to show interest in much that happened since the Renaissance."

He smiled. "You are an unworldly pair. Like my father, though in a different way. He sees only the good in everyone. And you, I think, have seen only the worst."

"You mean my family? That is probably true! Although Her Grace is good. I never knew how to be friends with her, but I like her. Do you know, her name is Rosamund? I have never heard anyone use it."

He took her hand and drew it through his arm as he had done last night. She was almost sorry she was wearing gloves today.

"Don't think sad thoughts today. Instead, let me tell you a funny story about the dog and the goose who guarded our camp through most of Spain…"

Unexpectedly, she was swept into the world of army camps and energetic young men with free time on their hands between marching and fighting. She was fascinated and entertained and laughed out loud several times. She could almost see the characters he spoke of, not just officers and men, but Spanish noblemen and peasants, a French countess, camp followers, and officers' wives who followed the drum, too. She interrupted with eager questions and listened avidly to the answers.

At some point, they had emerged from the woods and were now walking along a lane between fields. Occupying one was a flock of wooly sheep and little lambs bleating and jumping. The other appeared to be fallow, although a man was repairing the dry-stone wall around it.

"You must find everything tediously tame back in England," she said. What she meant was, *you must find me tedious.*

As if he knew that, he caught her gaze, his eyes excitingly warm. "No. I find *you* remarkably intriguing. For example."

She flushed. "I can't imagine why, so I suspect you are being polite."

"Entire regiments would laugh themselves silly at the very idea."

The man replacing the stones on the wall straightened and pushed his cap to the back of his head, nodding to Justin and Hera.

They nodded back, then Justin halted and looked again. "Joe? Joe Wilkes?"

The man's eyes widened in quick suspicion. He stared, then his jaw dropped almost comically. *"Justin?"*

Justin thrust out his hand, and Joe Wilkes shook it enthusiastically, grinning from ear to ear.

"Amazing what the cat drags in," Joe exclaimed. "Never thought I'd see you again!"

"Never thought I'd see you either. I heard you'd gone south."

"I did. Came back when my old man passed away."

The smiled died from Justin's face. "I'm sorry. I didn't know."

"No reason why you should. You were out of the country, I gather. Bet you have some tales to tell!"

"One or two. As will you. But where are my manners?" Justin turned to Hera. "He...Miss Severne. This is my old friend, Joe Wilkes. Joe, Miss Severne, who is Lady Astley's companion."

Joe snatched off his cap and bowed jerkily.

"How do you do," Hera said politely.

"Ma'am. Come by later, Justin, and meet my wife."

"Wife!" Justin repeated in amazement. "When did that happen?"

Joe suddenly frowned, a look of anxious sadness sweeping over his eager gaze. "Four years ago, but maybe wait until the little one's better. Jenny won't like us wakening her."

"What's wrong with your little one?" Justin asked quickly.

Joe shrugged miserably. "Fever. Sore head. People say it will pass, or not, when it's ready."

"Then maybe we should go now. Have you forgotten I'm a doctor, Joe?"

"Not forgotten, it's just..."

"You have a different doctor?" Justin asked.

"Of course not!" Joe said with curled lip. "There's been no doctor here since old Bailey curled up his toes, and he wasn't much use before that either! But—"

"Then you'd better let me see her, hadn't you?"

CHAPTER EIGHT

A S THE VICAR'S son, Justin was undoubtedly a gentleman. As a tenant farmer, Joe Wilkes was just as clearly not. But with the unconscious egalitarianism of children, they had been friends, and neither, it seemed, had forgotten that. Joe introduced his comely wife with some pride, and Justin treated her with the same kind of friendliness he accorded Lady Astley.

While welcoming Justin as her husband's friend, she showed clear signs of hostility at having to entertain a lady, too.

"I know, I'm the last thing you need when you're worrying about a sick child," Hera said. "But I can sit quietly in the corner or obey simple instructions as necessary."

Jenny blinked and then let out a breath of laughter. "I'll make us tea." She lowered her voice. "Is he really a physician?"

Hera nodded soothingly. Although, actually, she had no idea how skilled Justin was with children. Perhaps she wouldn't mention the army surgeon part until later…

But in truth, she needn't have worried. He spoke softly to the crying, fevered child, made her laugh when he listened to her heart, and made her stick her tongue out and say, "Ah."

"Her throat is a trifle inflamed," he told the anxious parents. "I'll make up a 'magic' potion for that and send you something to relieve the fever as well. She should be right as rain in a day or so, and if she isn't, you know where to find me."

"In the tavern," Joe said dryly.

"Exactly. Thank you for the tea!"

Justin strode out, obliging Hera to trot to keep with him until he noticed and deliberately slowed his pace. "Sorry. I'm just glad to have met Joe again, and to be able to help."

"I know," she said, smiling.

After a little while, he said abruptly, "I could do good here. There is no doctor for miles. Perhaps I should stay."

"Instead of going to Brussels?" she asked.

His lips quirked. "No. After Brussels."

"I thought so. There are worse places to be. Will you have enough patients, though, to maintain a practice?"

"If I can include a few rich ones," he said cynically.

"And your father is here, and your old friends."

He turned his head to her. "And you? Will you still be here in two months or a year or however long it takes to oust Bonaparte once more?"

"Does it matter?" she asked.

"Unless you want to hide forever."

"You mean deceive."

"There is an element of deceit," he pointed out.

She shrugged. "It's second nature to me. I seem to have been deceiving for most of my life."

His brow twitched. "I think you were surviving."

"Perhaps," she said doubtfully.

"Would you like to know what I think?"

"I don't know."

"I think you wanted to find out what and who you were without the weight of other people's expectations or coercions. You wanted to know what you were capable of. It's an eccentric route to self-discovery but safer than traveling up the River Nile or disguising yourself as a highwayman."

Something leapt in her, catching at her breath. He laughed and threw one arm around her shoulders. "Your eyes sparkle at the very idea. I don't advise highway robbery, but exploring might be fun."

As she was hugged briefly to him, his arm strong, sheltering, and thrilling, some other longing soared, too, something both physical and emotional. Whatever confused motives had brought her to Denholm Hall, she knew it was merely a step to another phase of her life.

"*The world's mine oyster,*" she quoted, smiling, "*which I, with sword, will open.*"

"That's my girl."

His words as much as his closeness spread heat through her veins. The movement of his hip against her as they walked thrilled her, and suddenly the pleasure was at once too intense and not nearly enough. Besides, it was entirely improper.

She broke free and began to run, because she could not be still, and when he loped along beside her, she laughed with sheer happiness.

THAT NIGHT, SHE again woke to faint scraping sounds in the attic above. Nurse, presumably, was restive again. Why did she sleep in the attic, anyway? For privacy? Perhaps there was no suitable accommodation left in the basement. Or was it to be nearer George?

George. Where did George sleep? There was no bed in his "study."

She made a note to find out, for it was something she should know if she was meant to be in charge while the Astleys were away from home.

She closed her eyes to ignore the faint noises and go back to sleep. But a few moments later, her eyes snapped open again. The sounds were very faint, but came now, she was sure, from the passage outside her door—a gentle rustling, like clothing, and soft footfalls coming from the direction of the attic door.

Nurse, on her way to make herself a hot drink? Afraid to use the so-called dangerous stairs, which Hera had seen both her and George climb before? She raised her head and peered toward her bedchamber door. No light shone under it as the wanderer rustled softly by.

Why would anyone walk about a house like this in the dark? The Astleys were well able to afford candles. Wax candles at that. No smell of tallow ever seeped into the main part of the house, even from beyond the baize door to the servants' hall and kitchens.

Oh, no, is she sleepwalking? The possibility entered Hera's brain with a thud. One of the maids at Cuttyngs had walked in her sleep and fallen down the stairs and broken her leg. His Grace had dismissed her, choosing to believe she had some tryst with a footman instead.

Such casual cruelty. Even now, it drove Hera from her bed in panic to prevent another accident. She paused only to light a candle and snatch up her robe before hastening along the dark passage to the main stairs. There was no sign of Nurse on the stairs as Hera hurried downward, but over the banister, she glimpsed a faint light, like a candle's glow, moving along the gallery.

It brought Hera to a halt, for a sleepwalker was unlikely to light a candle. A door clicked gently open, and the light vanished. Hera hesitated. No one appeared to be in danger. This really was none of her business now. But her curiosity was too thoroughly aroused for her to return to bed and sleep.

With sudden determination, she descended the rest of the stairs and walked toward the last position she had seen the light.

Eventually, she found it, a pale, glowing line beneath the library door. Taking a deep breath, she lifted the latch and went in.

The lamps and several branches of candles were lit, making the great room almost cozy in the resulting glow. In one of the large armchairs, glancing up from the book in his lap, sat George, in a very fine, voluminous brocade dressing gown.

He rose immediately, although he did not drop the book. In fact, he kept his finger on the page to keep his place.

"George? What—"

He waved one agitated hand to hush her. "Close the door before we're heard."

Hera hesitated, then obeyed and moved further into the room. "But what are you doing here in the middle of the night?"

"Well, I don't get to come very often during the day, and I expect I'll be ill again soon."

Anxiously, she scanned his handsome face, which was still somehow boyish despite his years. "Do you feel unwell?"

"No."

"Then what makes you think you will be ill? How can you tell?"

He shrugged. "I often am, after the numbers."

She frowned. "You work too hard on the numbers and make yourself ill?"

"Probably." He looked around rather vaguely and waved her to a chair near his. She leaned her hip on the arm as he sank back into his own chair.

"Maybe you should give up the numbers if they make you ill?" Hera suggested.

"I like the numbers. So does Hugh."

"Then…maybe you need to work on them a little less? More slowly, perhaps?"

"Maybe," he said, meeting her gaze before his eyes slid away again. "You don't want me to be ill."

"Of course I don't."

A smile flitted across his lips. "Then perhaps I won't be."

"George," she said with sudden unease, "you don't *make* yourself ill, do you?"

"I don't think so. It's probably the numbers." His gaze strayed to the book on his knee. His fingers stroked it idly, and he reminded her suddenly of Victor. Only Victor would just start reading if he wanted to, whoever was in the room with him and however rude it made him appear. George was not so ill-mannered.

"Would it be better to take the book up to bed with you?" she asked.

He sighed. "Probably. I like to sit here sometimes, though. On my own."

"I'm sorry I disturbed you," Hera said, and meant it.

But George gave her one of his sweet smiles. "Don't be. I like your company."

Then whose didn't he like? Figg's? It was she who was always with him. He didn't seem to see anyone else, except Sir Hugh and Lady Astley occasionally. He must be appallingly lonely.

He sighed and rose to his feet. "I'll take the book up to bed, and perhaps I won't be ill."

He began to turn down the lamps and douse the candles. Hera helped him until there was only her bedchamber candle and one other. He must have waited to light it until he was far enough away from any of the bedchambers.

She handed him his own candle. "That is a very handsome dressing gown," she said.

"Yes, I like it, though it was my father's."

It was such an odd way to phrase it that she opened her mouth to ask more. But he laid his finger on his lips as he softly opened the door. He led the way back toward the main staircase, and they climbed silently together. Upstairs, he glanced at Sir Hugh and Lady Astley's doors as they passed them, as though nervous the pair would see the lights. But he seemed to be too much of a gentleman to insist they blow out the candles.

They walked on past several guest chambers to her own half-open door, where she paused and mouthed, "Good night."

He grinned and inclined his head. She went in and closed the door, without shutting it tight. An instant later, she heard a breath and, when she peeked out the door, saw that he had indeed blown out his candle. But she could make out his darker figure moving to the end of the passage, past the last bedchamber door.

Where on earth…? A door opened and closed softly. The attic door. He and Figg both slept in the attic? On impulse, she picked up her candle again and walked to the end of the passage. She was sure she could make out the faintest light beneath the attic door.

And then she heard the snores coming from the last bedchamber, the one that shared a wall with the "dangerous" staircase. Somehow, she recognized that the snores were in Nurse Figg's "voice."

Giving up, Hera padded back to her own chamber and went, finally, to bed.

IN THE MORNING, as new theories about George began to swirl around her mind, she was glad a closer connection seemed to have been formed over his secret visit to the library. She felt she was actually helping him, in companionship if nothing else.

That was part of the happiness with which she greeted the day, throwing the window wide to gaze out across the peaceful fields to the water glinting in the far distance. The rest was largely to do with Justin Rivers.

She had liked talking to him. She was intrigued by the natural way he had greeted his childhood friend and gone to his aid. And she had liked watching him minister to the sick child. Somehow, she had imagined his bedside manner would be too brisk and abrasive and would probably frighten her. But again, Hera had misjudged him.

Even when she had run from the sudden, overwhelming intensity of her feelings, he wasn't shocked or even disapproving. He had merely run with her, catching her hand in places to help her over difficult ground. Once, he had snatched her around the waist and swung her over a narrow stream. It had been childish and fun and full of laughter, and they had ended up leaning against the same broad oak, gasping for breath and grinning at each other. The warmth in his eyes had been even more exhilarating.

He likes me, she though now in wonder, no longer even seeing the view. *He is my friend.*

She had never had a friend before.

It warmed the blood in her veins, made it hard to stop smiling as she all but ran downstairs to breakfast. For once, Sir Hugh as well as Lady Astley were in the breakfast parlor. He appeared to be in excellent spirits, working through a large plateful of sausages and bacon and eggs. And Lady Astley's constant good humor had spilled into excitement, as she looked forward to the dinner party and to her expedition to Lincoln with her husband.

"George tells me he likes you very much," Sir Hugh said genially to Hera. "Which bodes very well, very well indeed. As long as you remember the rules and make sure he is kept as quiet as usual while enjoying only his usual pursuits, everything will go splendidly. And, of course, Nurse will be there."

"What rules?" Hera blurted, before she realized Lady Astley's anxious gaze was upon her.

"That he should not be excited, ever, by encountering people he is not used to. Which is anyone other than myself, Lady Astley, Nurse Figg, and now you. Did Lady Astley not explain this to you at the outset?"

"Well, yes, she did," Hera said hastily. "But I had not realized the advice was quite as strict as to be rules. My fault entirely."

A frown had formed on Sir Hugh's brow. "You do know he is to be brought down from his sitting room using only the back stairs which lead almost to the green salon and the French windows to his garden?"

Hera blinked. "Nurse told me the stairs were dangerous and I should never use them."

Sir Hugh muttered something below his breath.

"It's what we tell the servants," Lady Astley said, "to keep them from blundering into George and upsetting him. But Nurse was told that does not include you. I think she is jealous. You will have to speak to her, Hugh."

Sir Hugh grunted. "She's getting too old," he said testily. "On the other hand, George is used to her, and she to him, so in matters of health, Miss Severne, please do refer to her. Otherwise, just keep to the strict routine and all will be well."

Having brought the discussion to a close with this pronounce-ment, he pushed his plate away and rose to his feet. "Excuse me, ladies, I have matters to attend to."

"And so have I." Lady Astley beamed, pouring herself a fresh cup of tea. "With all to be ready for this evening's dinner, and then travel tomorrow!"

Apparently, none of Lady Astley's duties of the day needed a com-panion. She had an excellent lady's maid and housekeeper and a full complement of servants. It all fed Hera's growing suspicion that she had been engaged primarily for George rather than Lady Astley.

Accordingly, as her ladyship bustled off, Hera finished her toast and coffee and went in search of George. As expected, she found him in his own garden, with Nurse sitting and smiling on her usual bench. She did not look jealous in the least. But then, Hera had never sensed anything in her character except outward good nature.

"Good morning, Nurse," Hera said, passing her as she went to join George at one of the round flowerbeds. "Good morning, George."

She knelt opposite him, expecting one of his sweet, conspiratorial smiles, after their meeting in the library last night. But he took a moment to look up at her, and he wasn't smiling at all.

"Good morning, Miss Severne," he mumbled, and returned to his work. But his hands lacked the quickness she had seen before. They seemed sluggish.

"Have you broken your fast, George?" she asked.

He nodded.

She waited for further information but received none. "Shall I help you?"

"If you like, yes. It is hard work today."

"It seems to be," she agreed, picking up a trowel. "Are you well, George?"

"I think so," he replied.

But he did not seem well. His movements were sluggish, and when she peered at his face, there was something different about it, though she could not put her finger on what. He weeded in silence for a time, and she made light comments that rarely won more response than a nod.

Then he sat back. "I'm tired. I believe I'll go inside."

He rose to his feet and ambled off toward the French doors, abandoning his tools where they lay. Nurse jumped up and waddled ahead of him. Concerned, Hera followed, catching up with Nurse on the back stairs.

"Oh, no, miss, you shouldn't be coming this way!" Figg exclaimed.

"Yes, I should," Hera said, keeping her gaze steadily on the nurse, who flushed slightly and dropped her eyes. Taking that as acceptance she was caught out, Hera asked, "What is wrong with him this morning? Is he ill?"

"No, just tired," Nurse replied, comfortable once more in familiar territory. "He gets like this sometimes, but he'll be fine in the end. We know what to do. He'll have an extra sleep now and be right as rain. Don't worry, miss. Sir Hugh and her ladyship wouldn't go away and leave him if they weren't certain he was fine."

Thoughtfully, Hera returned to the garden and tidied away the tools in their box. Then, since the time appeared to be her own, she went for a walk.

CHAPTER NINE

AFTER MUCH INTERNAL debate, Hera chose the dark burgundy evening gown that she had not yet worn at Denholm Hall. Aware that she wouldn't even be thinking about it had Dr. Rivers not been one of the invited guests, she almost dressed exactly as she had every evening since her arrival, just to prove Justin's presence made no possible difference to her.

Eventually deciding the prettier gown would better honor her employers, she put on the burgundy and twisted and wrestled her way to all the fastenings. Then she brushed her hair into the usual, severe style she adopted without her maid and regarded herself dubiously in the glass.

On impulse, she loosened a few pins and softened the dragged-back look into a swept-up one. She thought it looked better, although whether it would stay that way was anyone's guess. Annoyed with herself for caring, she scowled at the glass, then marched out of her chamber.

On impulse, she went first to George's study. She had not seen him since this morning in the garden, and she worried about his health. But the room was empty. He wasn't in the garden either. Emerging a moment later, she all but ran into Nurse.

"He's not there," Hera said. "Is he well?"

"Oh, yes, miss, just resting!" Nurse beamed and sailed on into the room with her duster and polish.

Why do the maids not clean in George's room when he isn't there?

Because the household had its own way of doing things, just as Cuttyngs had, often driven by habit and custom rather than good sense. There was no mystery to it. She had to stop imagining herself in one of Mrs. Radcliffe's hair-raising Gothic novels.

The chairs in the drawing room had been rearranged to accommodate the expected guests, and a footman hovered by a tray of sherry glasses. He offered the tray to Hera as soon as she entered the room, and she took one without thinking. Discovering the gaze of both Astleys upon her, she wondered if she should have asked their permission first. Was the paid companion not meant to drink sherry in company?

Fortunately, there was no one else here to see, so she went immediately to the sofa beside Lady Astley.

"Should I abstain?" she asked, lifting her glass a little to show what she meant.

"Good grief, no. John would not have offered if you weren't meant to have it! Is that a carriage, Hugh? Our first guests have arrived!"

There was something almost childish about her delight in her own dinner party, and judging by his tolerant smile, it appeared to be her husband's pleasure to indulge her.

First to arrive were their neighbors, Mr. and Mrs. Jewel and their adult children. Hera made way for Mrs. Jewel on the sofa beside Lady Astley and endeavored to melt into the background. However, after the first introduction, the two younger Mr. Jewels began immediately to compete for her attention.

Suspecting this had more to do with brotherly rivalry than with admiration, Hera wondered how to fend them off, for their mother was clearly displeased and would inevitably blame Hera for seeking their attention. In her old life, she would have simply told them they bored her and sent them away, but a mere companion could not be so rude to her employer's friends. And they had only been in the house five minutes!

By the time the Miss Pinktons arrived, the young men were still focused on her to an embarrassing degree. When the elder elbowed the younger out of the way and stood improperly close to her, Hera had had enough.

She met the teasing, challenging gaze of the elder son with a contemptuous one of her own, then looked to the younger and back.

"You are aware, are you not, that I am merely the companion?" she said clearly, yet so haughtily she might have been announcing her royal connections. Her voice cut through a momentary silence like glass.

She was aware of several heads swiveling toward her, and young Mr. Jewel all but leaping backward so that he got tangled up with his brother. At the same time, the Rivers family walked into the drawing room, which at least provided a distraction.

Hera used the opportunity to move away from the Jewel brothers and hover near Lady Astley once more, like a good companion.

"Dare I say good evening?" murmured a familiar voice in her ear.

Her gaze flew to Dr. Rivers, who was looking severely handsome in evening dress. There was a smile of both amusement and such understanding in his eyes that her heart seemed to tumble into her stomach. And it wasn't even unpleasant.

She swallowed. "I never realized before how helpful rank can be," she said, trying to quell her indignation.

"Or a ferocious chaperone."

"I have cause to be grateful to Aunt Hadleigh after all."

His lips quirked and he moved on, allowing her to greet the vicar with a curtsey.

Dinner was announced shortly afterward. Naturally, Hera went in at the bottom of the order, escorted by the youngest and slightly chastened Mr. Jewel.

"I'm sorry about earlier," he said disarmingly as they walked to the dining room. "Good manners were defeated by silly rivalry."

"They were, rather." *And not even for any prize you really want or would be allowed!* She smiled faintly. "But I shall forgive you this time."

The youngest Mr. Jewel turned out to be pleasant if callow company. Despite being around her own age, he seemed much more juvenile. Which was odd, for her upbringing had been of the most sheltered. She frequently found her attention wandering further up the table to Justin, who was seated between Miss Jewel and the elderly Miss Pinkton. She was pleased to see he appeared to devote as much attention to the elder lady as to the younger, who was certainly doing her best to flirt with him. Although, judging by the girl's occasional blank smiles, she did not always understand his remarks.

Occasionally, she wondered what George would have made of the company, and how he would have conversed. She had not seen him since the slightly worrying encounter in the garden. She hoped he was feeling better. In fact, when the ladies left the gentlemen to their wine and Lady Astley asked Hera to fetch her shawl from her bedchamber, she used the time to also go in search of Nurse.

With Lady Astley's shawl over her arm, she found Nurse in George's sitting room, having a comfortable rest in the armchair by the fireplace. Of George himself, there was no sign.

Nurse smiled and heaved herself to her feet. "All well, miss? What can I help you with?"

"I just came to see how George is. I thought he would be here."

"Gone for an early night, miss. Best thing for him. I'm sure he'll be right as rain in the morning."

Hera peered at her more closely. "Then you are not worried for him?"

"Bless you, ma'am, no. Everything's quite normal for Mr. George. He often has a down day or two and then is quite happy again after a good, long sleep. You go and enjoy your evening."

Feeling vaguely dissatisfied, Hera left again and returned to the drawing room.

Here, the ladies had arranged themselves becomingly around the room, not just for comfort, but to leave space for the gentlemen to sit beside them when they rejoined the party. Hera delivered the shawl to Lady Astley.

She took it with a faint smile of thanks but did not interrupt her conversation. Hera took up a place behind her, close enough to come easily when summoned, but not so near that she could overhear the conversation. This was something she seemed to have absorbed unconsciously from other paid companions at the few country houses parties she had attended. And from observing the duchess's new companion, Miss Wallace.

It was, Hera reflected, quite a lonely life, where one was tolerated in a society one was never quite part of. It could also be humiliating and downright cruel, although neither the Astleys nor their friends had offered her any such insult.

In fact, after a few moments, Lady Astley turned her head. "Miss Severne, you play the pianoforte, do you not? Perhaps you would indulge us with a little gentle music while we talk?"

It was an unusual request. In Hera's world, music was played by virtuosos for the entertainment and delectation of guests. Or by debutantes showing off their accomplishments to prospective husbands. In both cases, the audience was expected to listen. However, Hera, relieved to have something to do, was quite happy to be ignored while she did it.

Accordingly, she moved over to the pianoforte—a rather fine instrument she had noticed before but never played—and sat down. She did not trouble searching for music, but simply began to softly play various pieces she had learned since childhood. Where certain passages had grown vague in her memory, she improvised until she found herself back on firmer ground.

Soon, she was only vaguely aware of the hum of feminine voices behind her. The knowledge that no one was listening was even comfortable.

"What normally happens when you play in drawing rooms?" Dr. Rivers said at her elbow, almost causing her fingers to jump off the keys. As it was, they slipped a little, although she doubted anyone but Justin noticed.

She recovered and continued to play while she spoke distractedly. "Some ambitious gentleman will insist on turning the pages of the music I never read, and my performance will be greeted as something extraordinarily gifted rather than the tinklings of an occasionally above-average amateur. There are advantages in being the daughter of a duke."

"But you judged it all lies?"

"Mostly."

"Being ignored is better?"

"Infinitely. You will draw other people's attention to me."

"You want me to go away?"

"Not yet. George sleeps in the attic while his nurse sleeps in the bedchamber I thought was his. I think he is locked in at night and has learned to pick the lock just to sit alone in the library and read. Now, you may go away."

"Thank you."

She knew the moment he turned from her and wasn't in the least disheartened. In fact, she found herself smiling at the keys, because she knew he wasn't remotely offended. She had heard the breath of laughter in his voice.

Since the gentlemen were now in the room, she brought her piece to a gentle end and rose. No doubt it was time for the unmarried female guests to show off their skills. Catching Lady Astley's eye, she received a nod of approval that she had done the right thing, so she took up her old place behind her employer.

As expected, the three young, unmarried ladies were called upon to entertain. Hera clapped politely after each, although the last reluctant performer was so poor as to be almost comic, a fact of which her parents were blissfully unaware. Hera caught Justin's eyes, and for an instant the wicked laughter she saw there almost undid her. She had to look hastily away again.

"Bravo," Justin's brother Philip said as soon as the piece was finished.

"Perhaps another?" Justin suggested.

Hera choked, and Lady Astley looked positively alarmed, but fortunately the tea service arrived, bringing the musical part of the evening to a natural conclusion. Hera became occupied in ferrying cups and saucers from Lady Astley to her various guests and offering plates of elegant little sweet and savory treats.

The evening was drawing to a close, and Hera became conscious of a restless disappointment that there had been no real opportunity to talk to Dr. Rivers. She recalled their first meeting at Cuttyngs when he was the barely tolerated interloper—a gentleman, perhaps, but only just, and certainly not of the rank that normally came to Cuttyngs. Now, at Denholm Hall, there was still a social gulf, but this time she was the humble one.

What nonsense we create for ourselves...

At last, it was time for farewells, and Hera dutifully followed the Astleys down to the doorstep to wave off their guests. Most remembered to say goodbye to Hera. Both Jewel brothers even shook her hand by way, she suspected, of apology, although there was a spark of genuine interest in the eyes of the younger. What would her father have made of such a prospective match? What would Aunt Hadleigh say?

They would both have curled their lips in contempt because the Jewels had no great wealth, position, or political influence. Hera had always been expected to make not just a decent match but a brilliant one. The duke had not been pleased when she sent the second of his two preferred suitors about their business. He had made it plain she would be expected to take the third. No further refusals against his wishes would be tolerated.

And then he had died.

For a moment she felt sorry for the loss of a life without laughter or love. She wondered what he had cared about beyond status and the ambition to maintain his own at all costs. It made her shiver as she kept the fixed smile on her face, exchanging curtsies and nods with the Rivers family. The vicar took her hand kindly.

So did Justin, bowing punctiliously and murmuring below his breath, "The maze in an hour." And then he ran down the steps to the ancient carriage, leaving her to wonder if she had imagined the instruction.

⫸⫷

LADY ASTLEY SEEMED very content with her party. "I believe everyone enjoyed it. Thank you for your support, Miss Severne. And now, with an early start tomorrow, I shall retire for the night. We plan to leave at first light."

She crossed the hall toward the stairs, Sir Hugh following with a slight bow.

"You still plan to go tomorrow?" Hera blurted. "Do you know that George is not well?"

She did not see their eyes swivel and meet, but she was sure it happened before Sir Hugh turned back to her. "He is just having one of his quiet periods. It is a pattern with him. There is nothing to fear, Miss Severne. Nurse understands him perfectly well. If he wishes to sleep, then leave him to it, but we would be grateful if you were available to keep him company in the garden if he wishes to be there, and perhaps to read to him. He seems to enjoy your company, and we have every faith in you. Good night, Miss Severne."

"Good night," she murmured behind them, still frowning.

When she went upstairs, the lights were all out. And though she walked to the very end of the passage, there was no one in George's sitting room. There was no light shining under Figg's door. Judging by the energetic snores, the nurse was sound asleep.

On impulse, Hera tried to pull open the attic door and found it locked. So she walked back to her own chamber, wondering why she was so uneasy.

She really did want to talk to Dr. Rivers this evening. There was no point in pretending to herself that she would not go to the maze as she was so insolently commanded.

So, about an hour after the guests had departed, she left her room once more, with only her bedroom candle to guide her downstairs to the main side door. She had to slide back the bolts and hope that the servants really were in bed and wouldn't shove them home again before she returned. From her candle, she lit the lantern at the side door and covered it with her scarf so that it emitted less light. Then she made her way to the maze gate, which opened for her as though by magic.

She gasped as warm fingers closed around hers, taking the lantern from her. She knew it was Justin from his scent, even before she peered up at him. As he set it down, the lantern cast shadows over one side of his face, making it smooth and mysterious on one side, sharp and handsome on the other. It caught at her breath, and he paused, his eyes locked to hers.

She felt his arm at her back, drawing her further under the over-growing hedge.

"Don't look at me like that," he said.

"Like what?" she managed.

"As if you are"—his lips curved and straightened again at once—"happy to see me."

"Of course I am. I need to know what you want and can't afford to spend time waiting for you."

"Waiting for me to do what?" he asked softly.

"Turn up," she replied.

"Not kiss you?" he suggested, warm laughter in his eyes that was not quite teasing.

Heat swept through her, depriving her of breath. There had to be a clever retort to such impudence, but all she could manage was a slightly shaky "No!"

"Are you sure?" His gaze moved deliberately to her lips, and her heart turned over. His arm at her back hardened, drawing her closer.

"Perfectly sure," she said hoarsely.

"Pity," he said, his arm already loosening.

In panic, she snatched at his lapel. She didn't know why. She didn't even mean to, but abruptly she couldn't bear to be any further away from him than she was now. She did not want to lose that warmth in his eyes as he gazed at her, or the sensual promise in the curve of his mouth.

Now it was his breath that caught, his voice that wasn't quite steady. "May I?"

Her fingers clutched convulsively, tugging. And then he bent even closer and kissed her mouth.

She had never imagined such sweet, physical tenderness in a man, such emotion surging through her from one kiss. But then the kiss did not stop. His lips moved, all silk and fire, parting hers, caressing, coaxing, and she melted into him. She slid her arms around him, holding him at first to stay upright in this wondrous assault on her senses, and then simply to pull him closer.

She marveled at his strength, the complexities of his hardness and gentleness, and her own galloping desires, suddenly so intense that they frightened her. Gasping, she pulled back from the blinding kiss, seizing his face between her hands—though whether to fend him off or caress it, she could not have said.

"Why?" she got out, both a plea and a demand.

"I told you before. I like you."

"Why?" she repeated helplessly.

He took hold of her wrists and kissed them, one after the other before placing her hands behind his neck. He was no longer smiling. "Because you are quick and curious, honest and unafraid. Because there is a kindness and empathy in you, and a kind of strength that I value all the more because I have no idea where you can have learned these things." His thumbs brushed her cheeks, the corners of her mouth. "Because you are just a little damaged and vulnerable, and so beautiful you make me ache in places I didn't know existed."

He bent and kissed her again, caressing her face, her hair, her neck, while she hung astounded and almost helpless in his arms. She wasn't sure she liked to be thought of as either damaged or vulnerable, but she could only return his kiss with fervor and delight.

This time, it was he who broke it. "I didn't mean to do or say any of this."

"Do you regret it?" she asked, wondering in panic what the pain of that would feel like.

"God, no."

She smiled at the vehemence of that and pressed her cheek to his. He held her close against him for a long time, and that was wonderful, too. He drew in a long, slow breath that echoed through his body to hers, and then he began to walk, though he kept one arm around her, and snatched up the abandoned lantern.

"Tell me about this George."

CHAPTER TEN

REALITY SEEPED IN, which was probably just as well. Hera's skin still tingled from his caresses, and her happiness felt curiously, bewitchingly physical. But it was all too sudden, too overwhelming, and George worried her.

"I have the feeling I was engaged more as a companion to him than to Lady Astley," she said. "They told me he was not mad but spoke of him as if he were childlike. Mrs. Irwin, our housekeeper at Cuttyngs, had a nephew like that."

"Does George look…different to most people?" Justin asked.

"No. Apart from the fact he does not dress like a gentleman, he looks very well. And I don't think he is childish at all. He seems to sleep in the attic, locked in. But he managed to escape the other night, for I found him in the library, and he was reading Herodotus—and not in translation, either. His sitting room is full of books, on botany, largely, but also other sciences and mathematics, with a sprinkling of classics. He speaks bluntly, but not in a childlike or uneducated manner."

"A mere eccentric? Then why do they hide him in the attic?"

"I think his oddness embarrasses them. He is always guarded by Nurse Figg. She was Sir Hugh's old nurse."

"I remember her," Justin said.

"And when he leaves his own sitting room, she smuggles him

down a back staircase no one else is allowed to use, into a room that is used for nothing else. It has French windows into his garden, which he maintains lovingly in its distinctive pattern. The garden door to the rest of the grounds is kept bolted on the other side. In fact, I wouldn't be surprised if isn't locked, too, except when Nurse is expecting someone. Then, when George is finished for the day, he is taken back to his sitting room. He eats all his meals there, never with the family."

"Do they have nothing to do with him, then?"

"Oh, yes, they visit him. Sir Hugh even seems to enter into his number obsession, understands whatever pattern George sees or makes. I haven't got to the bottom of the number story, but he works very hard on it, so hard that it seems to make him ill afterward. He told me he is nearly always ill after he finishes. And I think he is ill again."

"What makes you say so?"

"Well, the other night in the library, he was his normal bright, charming self, conspiratorial in a humorous kind of a way because he had escaped. The following morning, he was listless, complaining of a headache, as though he were sickening for something. Nurse seemed to recognize the signs. So did Sir Hugh and Lady Astley. They seem to think it is part of a normal cycle for him, and I should not worry."

"But you do."

It wasn't a question, and she cast him a quick smile. She liked walking like this, tucked into his body with his arm warmly around her as they strolled.

"Yes. It was as though he were going through the motions in the garden but was really too tired to be bothered. His headache clearly troubled him; his movements were sluggish. He even *looked* different."

"In what way?" Justin asked, and she could somehow hear his frown in his sharpened voice.

She thought about it. "His eyes," she said at last. "His eyes were different, although I don't think I could tell you exactly how. Do you think he is dangerously ill?"

"Probably not, if it is so familiar to the Astleys and to Figg. But I would like to see him, all the same. Something is wrong here."

She let out a sigh. "I was afraid I was making drama out of nothing. The trouble is, Figg won't allow you to see him. We're not even supposed to talk about him. I could probably overrule Figg and take you anyway, swearing you to secrecy... But then I'd be sent away, and I should worry even more about George. Especially when you leave the country. When are you leaving?" she finished anxiously.

"Soon," Justin said in a distracted sort of way. "No... I should not barge in and turn everything upside down. If he gets worse and you believe his very life might be in danger, send for me anyway. In the meantime, I think we should try to find out exactly who this George is. Where did he come from? Why are the Astleys responsible for him? And why is his presence so secret?"

"You said it could never be kept from servants, that there were bound to be rumors."

"I do appear to have been wrong. My father knows nothing about him. Neither do any of the servants I've encountered in the village—the Astleys' or anyone else's."

"The servants are nearly all old," Hera said. "I suppose they must be ferociously loyal to the family. And help keep the younger footmen and parlor maids away from what they are not meant to see. But Cook must know, and they must see Nurse taking his meals from the kitchen, unless it is all very well timed." She frowned. "And I think it is. Justin, is this not a very elaborate conspiracy just to keep an embarrassingly odd relative out of the public eye?"

"Yes." After a few seconds' thought, he glanced down at her, moving his hand on her cloaked shoulders. "Are you cold? Do you need to go back inside?"

She shook her head. She didn't want ever to go back inside, not without him. Foolish. And entirely impractical. "What is my purpose to the Astleys, then? Just to make friends with George and keep him happy? They seem genuinely pleased that he and I like each other."

"Then at least his welfare matters to them. Hera, what did they ask for? In the advertisement you answered?"

"A companion for a lady residing mostly in the country. A lady of good birth, education, and placid nature."

"Placid!" He grinned, and the whiteness of his teeth glinted in the upward swing of the lantern.

"Placid," she said. "It said the duties would be light, with generous remuneration and free time. And they asked for replies with details of family background and education."

"And what particular nonsense did you spout in your letter?"

"The truth," she said with dignity. "Leaving out my connection to the dukes, of course. I said I was an orphan of independent spirit with no one depending on me and that I found myself in the position of having to make my own way in the world. I told them that although I had no experience, I had an excellent education."

"You made it sound as if you had no family at all."

"No, I didn't," she argued, although she supposed it could have been so interpreted. "In any case, I didn't really expect to be engaged, because I had no experience or references."

"But they took you on anyway," he said slowly. He stopped and turned toward her, his hands on her shoulders. "I want you to be careful, and observant. And I think I will begin the habit of calling every day."

"But the Astleys will not be here. They are going to Lincoln to-morrow and won't return until at least the day after. Why? What is it you fear?"

He relaxed, though he pulled her to him in a quick hug. "Nothing. I am looking for excuses to see you."

She smiled, liking the feel of his rough stubble against her cheek. "Because you like me."

His lips brushed her temple. "I do," he said ruefully. "I seem to have forgotten you are a duke's daughter." He released her. "Come, I'll take you to the exit."

He led her by the hand, which was still a pleasure, although she missed the greater closeness. She didn't like that he had remembered her rank, that to the world, their difference in birth separated them from all but superficial friendship. What did she want from him, anyway? No one had ever affected her as he did. He understood her, laughed at her, admired her, kissed her…

A sudden longing to know him pierced her heart. For his past, his beliefs, his ambitions, were not clear to her at all. Only his present, the part of him that spoke to her.

"Justin?"

He glanced down at her, and the words seemed to stick in her throat. In desperation, she pulled his hand to her cheek and her throat loosened.

"I like you too," she whispered.

He did not slow down, although his breath seemed to hitch. He brushed his fingertips against her cheek, and then he drew her hand to his lips and kissed it once. "You should not," he said, "although I'm selfish enough to be glad. Good night, Hera."

He closed her fingers over the lantern and opened the gate. She flitted through and returned to the house, churned up, troubled, and yet overwhelmingly glad of whatever it was she shared with Justin.

SHE WOKE LATER than she meant to and hurried to wash and dress in time to wave off the Astleys, but it seemed she was too late, and they had already gone.

"Left at the crack of dawn," Mrs. Wyse said when Hera ran into her on the stairs. "Shall I just have Nurse bring your breakfast up?"

Hera paused. This was the first indication she had had that any of the other servants were aware of George's existence. She hadn't mentioned his name, of course, but there was no other reason for Nurse to be involved in Hera's breakfast arrangements.

"Yes. Yes, perhaps that would be best. Thank you."

Hera returned upstairs and walked along the passage to George's sitting room. It was empty. Hoping this meant he was better and already in the garden, she went across to the window, but there was no sign of him outside either.

Hera left again. At the attic door she paused and tried the latch. It was locked, as she expected it to be. Frowning now, she marched over to Figg's door and knocked sharply. When she got no reply, she simply threw open the door, and was immediately assailed by a stench remarkably like the tap room of an inn, except somehow sharper, and with no tobacco.

It caught at her breath, caused her nose to wrinkle involuntarily. An empty bottle sat on the bedside table; another beside it was half-full of some clear liquid Hera doubted was lemonade. Figg was not there.

Furious now, she strode from the room and closed the door on the smell as she made for the attic door. She had raised her hand to knock loudly, even if it brought the entire household, when the door flew open and a very flustered Nurse Figg all but fell through. The force of her breath could have knocked out an army.

Her cap was askew, her hair tumbling out from under it. But worse than her unusual unkemptness was the fright in her bloodshot eyes. Nor did she even try to hide from Hera.

"I can't wake him," she wailed. "He's really, really ill!"

The nurse's fear was catching.

"Show me," Hera instructed her, and all but pushed Nurse back inside.

With surprising speed, the older woman launched herself up a wooden staircase and then through another door into George's sleeping quarters. Here again were books and plants, though in lesser quantity, and in any case, Hera hardly noticed for the still figure in the large bed.

Her heart jumping with fright, she went and sat on the side of the bed, seizing his hand. "George! George, wake up—it's morning. Time for breakfast. And I do believe the garden needs you."

Neither her voice nor touch elicited any response.

"Is he dead?" Nurse whispered hoarsely.

Hera could feel no certain pulse in his wrist. She bent over him and, with unspeakable relief, felt a faintest breath against her ear. "No, not yet. Send someone as fast as possible for Dr. Rivers at the vicarage. Can you do that, Figg, or must I leave him to do it myself?"

"No, no, I will," she wailed. "But I can't say it's for *him*!"

"For the love of God, just bring him. I don't care who you tell the servants it's for, but he must come here *now*!"

Hera was in danger of becoming hysterical, so tried to swallow back her fury. But at least Nurse was already clattering back down the stairs. Hera returned her attention to George, patting and slapping at his hands and cheeks and speaking to him alternately sharply and softly. Neither had any effect.

Eventually, she rose, looking for water, and found another room through a narrow door. Here, she found evidence that he had been sick. But at least there was fresh water in a large jug, which she poured into the clean bowl and carried through to the bedchamber, along with a few clothes.

Carefully, she bathed his hands and face. She didn't know whether it was good or not that she could smell no gin on his breath. No bottles lurked in the vicinity, either. At least if he had been dead drunk she would have been more or less sure he would wake up again eventually.

Nurse did not come back. Hera hoped she had the sense to send someone who moved more quickly than she, that she was merely lurking downstairs to bring the doctor straight up.

⇶⋘

OVER BREAKFAST, JUSTIN asked his father and brother what they knew of Sir Hugh Astley's ward.

"I didn't know he had one," the vicar said in faint surprise.

"Never heard of anyone," Philip added.

"Aren't there cousins or distant relatives?"

"I suppose a cousin might have had children and died," Philip said doubtfully, "leaving them to Hugh's guardianship."

"But Hugh has never spoken of it?" Justin asked.

"He rarely speaks of anything to me. Last night was the first time I've been in his company for years." Philip's smile was lopsided. "He has other fish to fry these days, and he seems to be very good at it."

Justin regarded him over his coffee cup. "Meaning what?"

"Meaning since Sir Cuthbert died, the whole estate has vastly improved. Denholm Hall is in excellent repair. Most of it has been recently redecorated, and her ladyship is never short of new gowns. She has two carriages and excellent horses. The servants are better paid than anyone else's, and the tenants' cottages are in much better condition than before. The land has been vastly improved, every new farming method tried out. And on top of that, I believe Hugh has been very lucky on the Exchange."

"For which you need some money to begin with," Justin mused. "Did he inherit some secret pot from his father, then? Or does the money come from his wife?"

"I really have no idea." Philip stared at him. "It's not like you to care."

Justin smiled.

"It's like him to be curious, though," their father pointed out. "What is on your mind, Justin?"

110

Justin sighed. "I don't really know. You don't suppose old Sir Cuthbert had a by-blow or two, do you?"

"That is not a proper discussion for the breakfast table," Philip said primly.

"Why not?" Justin looked around him exaggeratedly. "Your wife is not here to be offended, and I'm sure Father is more aware than most of the sins of men."

"Well, if Sir Cuthbert had any illegitimate children, I never heard of them," the vicar said mildly. "He always seemed devoted to his lady wife, and they only had the two children. Arthur, who died when he was about thirteen or fourteen years old, and Hugh."

"I suppose you buried Arthur?" Justin said with a hint of apology.

"I did. His parents were devastated, but he had always been a sickly boy, and inevitably succumbed to one of the putrid sore throats that visited the neighborhood every couple of years."

Another barely formed theory crumbled. But then, it seemed to him that George was more likely to come with Lady Astley—a brother, perhaps, an uncle or cousin who needed looking after but who embarrassed her. She seemed to like things to be beautiful and perfect, though when Justin thought about it, Hugh had been like that too as a boy.

"I don't suppose," he said, trying another tack as his father rose to go about his day's work, "that you ever heard rumors of a stranger staying at the hall?"

The vicar paused, looking thoughtful, and Justin began to hope he might be about to learn something useful. Then his father said, "Actually, I don't recall anyone ever staying at Denholm Hall until Miss Severne came. Though the Astleys were always hospitable, it was only ever locally."

Frustrated, Justin poured himself more coffee and tried to think who else to ask. Philip said something to him that clearly registered somewhat late.

"Sorry?" Justin said, catching his brother's expression.

"I said, you seem quite taken with Miss Severne at the hall."

"So would you be if you could flirt with impunity," Justin retorted.

"Defend with attack," Philip mocked. "No, it seems to me you are beginning to see the attractions of home."

"I have always known the attractions of home," Justin said irritably, well aware where this was leading. Clearly, his thinking time was over, so he put down his cup and stood. "I also know my duty. I *will* be back, but not until the war is over. You must follow your own duty also, Philip. Our father will still be here."

"You hope!" followed him out of the door. Philip still liked to have the last word, even when verbally annihilated, but Justin's mind had already moved on. He would go into the village, stop at the tavern to see what he could learn, then walk up to the hall, talking to whomever he met on the way. And then he would call at Denholm Hall and ask for Miss Severne.

It would be unusual and not quite proper for a single, unchaperoned lady to receive him, but he had the cover of his profession, and something about her situation bothered him. In fact, he was downright anxious for her.

Even that, he admitted, was tangled up with his growing obsession. He should never have touched her, let alone kissed her, and never, ever like *that*! But the feel of her, the taste of her, her utterly generous response, had overwhelmed him. He was behaving like a first-year university student shown favor by the tavern maid, and Hera was so far from any tavern maid that his behavior made him blush with shame. And intense, burning desire to repeat it and so much more besides.

He wanted her away from Denholm Hall, without really knowing why. Certainly, he would have no access to her in her own world, if she ever went back, but here...

"Dr. Rivers!"

He had turned out of the churchyard gate and into the main street toward the village square when he was stayed by the sound of his name being urgently shouted. And realized it came amidst a clatter of horses' hooves.

He turned in surprise to see one of the Astleys' grooms astride a very fine black gelding, holding the reins of another, fully saddled mount. They pulled up as he turned toward them.

"Dr. Rivers, you're needed urgently at the hall! Will you please come at once? Miss Severne's been taken real bad!"

The blood sang in his ears. The world seemed to stop.

And yet somehow, without any conscious volition, he said, "Give me a moment to fetch my bag," and he was running back into the vicarage. Within a couple of minutes, he had secured the bag and vaulted into the empty saddle. The stirrup leathers were too short, but he didn't care.

CHAPTER ELEVEN

IT WAS A short ride on horseback to Denholm Hall. The very fact that the groom had brought him a horse for speed terrified him as to Hera's condition. At least the exercise, the blast of cold wind in his face, helped his brain to work again.

"What is the problem?" he shouted to the groom as they rode side by side. "Was there an accident?"

"I don't know, sir. Old Nurse, Miss Figg, just sent me for you, says Miss Severne needs you urgent. Miss Severne being her ladyship's companion."

By then they were at the gates and riding up the drive. The groom indicated not to follow to the front door, and led him up the track at the side of the house that led to the stables.

Justin recognized the plump woman wringing her hands by the side door. Figg, Sir Hugh's old nurse. She had been considerably younger when she had come to drag Hugh in for tea, or tell the boys off for noise or fighting, but her round, good-natured face was instantly recognizable.

And he thought he understood something else. In normal circumstances, in an emergency, the groom would have dismounted to let Justin ride the horse speedily to his patient, leaving the groom to walk back. But in this way, the groom could make sure he entered by a particular door, and that Nurse would be the one to take him to Hera.

His stomach tightened unbearably. What in God's name had happened to her? If he could not heal her, if they had hurt her, heads would roll, literally. And none of it would bring her back. No anger or regret in the world, no skill or effort or willpower ever brought any of them back.

He all but threw himself off the horse, leaving the groom to catch the reins and lead it on to the stables while he strode over to Nurse. To his relief, she wasted no time, leading him up across the hall to a back staircase. The "dangerous stairs" Hera had told him about?

"Thank you for coming, sir," Nurse said humbly. Now he was closer to her, he could see that she was not nearly as neat as he remembered. Her hair was escaping from a cap that sat askew on her curly head. There were stains on her apron. And she smelled of gin.

"What has happened?" he asked grimly.

"You'll see," she said, wheezing up the next flight.

"Is Lady Astley still in the house?"

"No, sir. She and Sir Hugh left early. They're going to be so angry with me for letting this happen."

"Letting what happen?" he snapped.

But she was standing on the top landing, breathing so hard that Justin feared she would be his next patient, and either she didn't hear him or chose not to answer. Instead, she pointed to an almost hidden door facing a long, carpeted passage.

The attic? They had put Hera in the attic where the mysterious George was all but imprisoned? With dread, Justin strode past Nurse and wrenched open the door. He ran up the stairs two at a time and all but threw himself though the door at the top.

Hera, neat as a pin, sat on the edge of a large bed, bathing someone's forehead. As he barged in, she dropped the cloth and sprang to her feet with such joy and relief on her face that he was speechless.

She ran to him, not to embrace him as he needed, but to grab him by the hand, tugging him toward the bed. "Thank God you're here!

We can't wake him, and I didn't know what to do! He has hardly any pulse, but at least he is breathing. Isn't he?"

Again, years of emergencies let him act as he should. While his whole being sagged with relief that Hera was not the patient, his legs carried him past her to the bed, where he sat and searched for the pulse in the man's throat. It was faint, but there.

"He's alive," he said. "What happened?"

"Nothing. Nurse couldn't wake him this morning, and neither could I. I made her send for you. At some point before I came, he was sick. And he barely moves, Justin, but he did make some sounds once, as though he is distressed or in pain..."

While she talked, he examined the mysterious George. There were no obvious signs of injury to his head or body. He drew up an eyelid and let it fall. Then he sniffed the man's breath.

"What medicine has he had?" he asked.

"I...I don't know. Where is Nurse?"

"Here," Nurse said, shuffling into the room.

Justin repeated the question.

"Just his usual," Figg replied a little hoarsely.

"Which is what?"

She licked her lips. "In the cabinet beside you, sir."

He opened the cabinet door and found a bottle, labelled by an apothecary. He unstopped it and sniffed. Then he caught and held Nurse's frightened gaze.

"How much did you give him?" he asked steadily.

"His usual dose, sir. Three drops in a little ale."

"When?"

"Last night, sir, at bedtime."

"Which was when?"

"He went early, so about six yesterday evening."

"Try again," Justin said with an edge of harshness. "How many times, exactly, did you dose him with three drops?"

Figg's hand shook as she rubbed her forehead. "Maybe twice," she whispered.

"You don't remember, do you?" His tongue lashed her with contempt. "You were too drunk."

"He was restless!" Figg said. "Had a sore head!"

"I'm not surprised if you've been dosing him with laudanum all day yesterday and all last night."

"It wasn't all last night!" Figg all but wailed.

"Only because you were too drunk to wake up. Go and clean yourself up. You reek of gin, and you're no use to anyone in this state."

For a moment, while he turned back to George, she stood in silence, though he didn't think she was crushed.

"Nurse," Hera said, low, and Figg's feet shuffled toward the door. "Open your bedroom window."

"Yes, miss," Nurse whispered, and went out.

"They give him laudanum?" Hera said, sinking down on the bed beside him. "Why?"

"I can see no reason. His chest is clear, and unless there is some internal problem I'm unaware of, he is not in pain. I would think they're merely keeping him quiet."

"Infamous," Hera said intensely, a world of horror and compassion in her voice. She stared at him. "The Astleys must know. It must be on their orders."

"I suspect they wanted him quiet during their dinner party. And with their departing the next morning, Nurse began to celebrate her freedom early. She was too drunk to recall when or how often she'd dosed him. But if he was just sleeping, he wouldn't disturb her."

"She's with him all day, every day," Hera said slowly. "It must irk her. It certainly irks him. Will he live, Justin?"

"Yes, this time. But it's as well he was sick."

She was silent for some moments. "Victor won't take laudanum anymore, even when his leg and hip pain him terribly. He says it's habit-forming."

"It is. Highly."

Her eyes were huge in her pale face. "And they give it to George all the time!"

"Not all the time," he said. "You said he looked different only from yesterday. The drug enlarges the pupils of the eye. I suspect that is what you saw, along with the change in his manner to sluggish and uninterested. They were making sure he did not disturb the household while they had guests." He frowned. "But you say he is never loud or violent, so I cannot see the point."

"He is always ill after he finishes the numbers," Hera said slowly. "And he believes he is working on them for Sir Hugh. I took that with a pinch of salt, believing Sir Hugh was merely humoring him. But could there be some purpose in the numbers? Something Hugh needs from him?"

"You told me George is well read and clever... Perhaps we should look into these numbers, and whatever else he does with his time."

George moved his head, groaning.

"Is that good?" Hera asked, fright standing out in her fine eyes.

"He's beginning to wake up. And he's not going to feel well." He picked up the laudanum bottle again and all but tossed it to her. "Pour this away, if you please. If he needs anything to help him cope, *I* shall give him something. Can you arrange for lots of drinking water, weak tea, and toast?"

"Of course." She jumped up at once, as though massively glad to be able to help in some way.

"Hera?"

She glanced back.

"You did the right thing to send for me. Figg could have killed him before the Astleys came home, without even meaning to."

THE SHEER RELIEF of Justin's presence, as though everything would now be well, stayed with Hera throughout the morning, even through the awfulness of realizing what had been done to George. It also allowed her to relax enough to wonder and observe who else was part of the conspiracy.

The housekeeper for sure. Mrs. Wyse had materialized at the foot of the "dangerous" stairs, almost miraculously, as Hera descended, and promised to bring up the items requested immediately.

"Mrs. Wyse," Hera said. "Are you aware that Nurse is too partial to gin?"

Mrs. Wyse hesitated, then nodded. "It's only when Sir Hugh and her ladyship are from home, and we can't possibly get rid of her. She has been with the family forever. Besides, she has a hard life, poor old thing. To be frank, Miss Severne, it's why her ladyship needed a...companion. Someone else with authority who would be loyal." She smiled, with a hard edge behind it. "And you are loyal, are you not, Miss Severne?"

Hera raised her brows. "Utterly, Mrs. Wyse. Are you?"

"Of course." Color seeped into the housekeeper's face, though what it signified, Hera didn't know. She realized her own first loyalty was to George, even though it was the Astleys who paid her. God knew what Mrs. Wyse meant.

Two hours later, Justin joined her in George's sitting room, where she was gazing out of the window upon the amazing, swirling garden, while rain pattered against the window, blurring the view but never spoiling it.

She glanced up at once. "How is he?"

"A little better," Justin replied. "Weak and shaky, with a vile headache and stomach pains. But he drank some tea and ate some toast and has finally fallen asleep again. But he might well suffer more pains and fever as the drug wears off completely."

"I thought you would call me! Did he not mind you being there? A stranger?"

Justin sat down on the window seat beside her. "No... That's the odd thing. One of the many odd things. He looked puzzled to see me, but not upset. Yet his eyes followed me all the time, and then, as if pleased with himself, he said, *Justin*."

Her eyebrows flew up. "Then he knows you! He can't be someone belonging to Lady Astley after—" She broke off. "Or he heard me call you Justin when we thought he was asleep."

"Either is possible," Justin agreed. "We should find out more when he wakes again. I'd better stay until then, in case he is difficult. And to make sure Figg and whoever else is in charge of his medicine know that he can have no more laudanum, except any prescribed by me. I don't suppose you know where it's stored?"

"No, but I suspect Nurse feels guilty enough to tell us."

The window seat was not particularly wide, and although they didn't quite touch, she was very aware of Justin's closeness, his bodily warmth, and the faint, tantalizing soap scent she always associated with him. To stop herself thinking so inappropriately of last night's melting kisses, she looked out of the window instead.

He followed her gaze. "Is this his garden?" he asked, standing up to get a better look.

"Yes. It's unique, isn't it? Such a riot of color among all those swirling beds and paths, and yet somehow it is all perfectly symmetrical."

Justin nodded and gazed at it for a long time. "It isn't just symmetrical," he said after some time. "It's made up of patterns that repeat, like the overall shape of a leaf repeated in all its individual parts. Every corner, every small swirl of his garden, is made up of the same pattern as the whole."

She twisted around, kneeling, and saw, finally, what had always just eluded her before. "So it is! How...incredibly, precisely beautiful. He told me he likes patterns, but I never realized how much."

"There are patterns all over nature, over every science if we look

120

for them. It's mathematical."

She glanced at him. "You mean his numbers?"

"Possibly. He certainly has an amazing mind. Who would addle that with laudanum?"

"Perhaps seeing all those patterns tires him out?" She wanted to think well of the Astleys, even now. She could live with their making mistakes for the best of reasons.

"Perhaps." Justin did not sound convinced. He moved away from her, prowling around the bookshelves that lined the walls, then over to George's large desk. He glanced at the rows and rows of figures on his innumerable pieces of paper, then at the books and newspapers open on the desk.

His gaze grew fixed. He flipped through the pages of one book, frowning.

"What is it?" Hera asked, standing and walking over to him. "Can you tell what he's been doing? Does it make sense?"

"Not to me, or at least not precisely... This is a bound volume of stock prices on the Exchange. With newer ones in the news sheets." He lifted his eyes to hers. "Apparently Hugh has been making a lot of money since his father died."

"Because George has studied where to invest? *That* is his numbers work?"

"Part of it, at least. But everything around the hall and estate is looking so much better now, as though Hugh had adopted the best and newest practices. And yet he is not interested in agriculture. And Thomson is not a man of innovation."

Hera sank into the chair. "George? It's all George?"

"It would explain why they don't send him away to some institution when they're so embarrassed by him. They need him."

"But that's...iniquitous!"

"Especially when they keep him drugged with laudanum in between making use of him."

"Oh, surely it's not as bad as that?" she said anxiously.

"I don't know," he said, throwing the book back down on the desk. "I think we need to speak to George. Whoever he is."

>>>><<<<

LATER IN THE afternoon, when the sun was out, drying the morning's rain, Hera walked out into George's garden in the hope that he would join them for tea. She dragged out a little table, the chair Nurse often sat in, and a couple of others, then went to the kitchen to order tea.

There was still no sign of Figg, but again, Mrs. Wyse intercepted her. "Is Dr. Rivers still here?" she asked.

"Yes, thankfully."

Mrs. Wyse said no more, but brought out tea, with little sandwiches and scones, and then went back inside. Hera paced the garden somewhat anxiously, wondering if she should go up to George's room, but Justin seemed to think it would be best if he provided any help George might need.

And indeed, after another few minutes, they appeared together. Although he looked rather shaky and white as a sheet, George walked unaided out into the garden.

Relieved, Hera hurried toward them, smiling. "Good afternoon! I asked them to bring tea out here, since the weather has turned fine again."

George smiled back a little wanly. "Miss Severne. I was afraid you had gone. Hugh and Caroline have."

"They will be back tomorrow or the day after," Hera said. "Come and sit. You have been too unwell to work."

He cast an anxious glance at the last flowerbed he had been working on, but in the end, he sat, as though obedience was too ingrained in him. She felt a spurt of mingled pity and anger at that, although it was also convenient at this moment.

"This is Nurse's chair," he observed at last as Hera poured him a cup of tea. "Where is Nurse?"

"Resting," Hera replied. "She isn't very well either."

He cast her an unexpected look, suddenly resembling the most congenial of her governesses. "Has she been at the gin again?"

"You know about the gin?" Hera blurted.

"It stinks," George said mildly. "Worse than brandy. Tastes nasty, too."

"You've tried gin?" Justin asked in clear surprise.

George wrinkled his nose. "Wanted to see what the fuss was about. I like a nice, dry port, but I don't really care for the rest."

"Does Hugh share a glass of port with you?" Justin asked.

George shook his head. "I have a glass in the library occasionally." His gaze swept over Hera, and he smiled.

"When you escape?" she said. Then, as he looked suddenly alarmed, "Don't worry. Dr. Rivers knows, and he won't tell a soul. Because he's a doctor, he won't tell even Sir Hugh or Lady Astley anything you don't want him to."

"You're a doctor now," George said, after a long pause. "You must be very clever."

"So must you. All the numbers you work out for Hugh."

George nodded. He looked incredibly tired, and his hand trembled as he lifted the teacup to drink. "I like numbers and patterns. There are patterns everywhere, if you look."

"Like your garden," Justin said. "You based the design on patterns in nature."

George beamed at him. "I did. No one's ever noticed that before."

"How many people have seen the garden?" Justin asked gently.

"Five. Six, counting you. You must be the cleverest. Or the most observant."

"How long have you lived here at Denholm Hall, George?" Hera asked.

His gaze slid away from Justin, but he didn't look at her. "I don't know. I don't remember anywhere else."

Was it a fib? She could not be sure. She didn't think he would lie, but she did sense evasion. She smiled. "I don't even know what to call you to introduce you to Dr. Rivers here! What is your surname?"

A smile flashed across his face and vanished. "It isn't as easy to trick me as you might think. I never break my word."

Distressed, Hera exchanged glances with Justin. Someone had made him promise to hide his identity. Presumably Sir Hugh or Lady Astley. But why? He never met anyone.

Except now.

"I don't want to trick you," she said. "I just want to know who you are."

"George." His gaze moved past her to Justin. "Am I better now?"

"Getting better," Justin replied. "You are frequently ill, I'm told."

George nodded. "Usually for longer. I'll ask for you next time, too."

And Justin wouldn't be here. He would be chasing Napoleon Bonaparte across France.

"Do you know what makes you ill?" Justin asked.

George sighed. "The numbers. I concentrate too hard."

"Do you think so? This time, I think Figg gave you too much medicine by accident. I don't think you should have any more of that medicine."

"What about when I get ill?" George asked.

"Perhaps I could leave a better medicine with Sir Hugh."

George nodded. "I don't really know much about medicine. There hasn't been time."

"You read up on many different things, judging by your books."

George nodded. "I read quickly. I understand it and see patterns."

"And that helps Sir Hugh?" Justin asked.

"Yes. I like to help."

"He is lucky to have you as his friend," Hera said, and won one of George's sweetest smiles.

He had drunk a cup of tea and nibbled a sandwich while gazing across the garden and up at the sky. He did not appear discontented, merely pale and exhausted.

"Shall we take a walk?" Justin suggested. "Just around the garden, and you explain the patterns and the flowers to us."

Obediently, George stood up and waited, as though to follow behind the others. It may have been habit or listlessness. At a glance from Justin, Hera took George's arm and urged him forward. He seemed surprised but not displeased. Justin ambled along beside them, asking occasional questions.

Then they went back inside and upstairs to George's sitting room.

"Do you always feel like this when you are ill?" Justin asked.

George, seated in the armchair, appeared to think about it. "Sometimes I just sleep and sleep. I have terrible dreams and fevers. Sometimes I can't stop thinking about things as though my brain goes too fast, but it doesn't always make much sense when I'm better. Sometimes I don't seem to be able to understand anything at all. That is frightening."

For someone who lived so much inside his own mind, it must be terrifying.

"I should go home," Justin said at last. "My family will wonder what has become of me. But I'll call back tomorrow and see how you are, if you don't mind."

George's eyebrows shot up. He wasn't used to being asked if he minded anything. "I like to talk to you," he said to Justin.

"And I to you," Justin said with a quick smile. He stood up. "Now, I just need to speak to Nurse before I go."

Hera never discovered exactly what he said to Figg. But she appeared in the sitting room looking as neat as a new pin and smelling of nothing except soap. And when Hera checked, the nurse's bedchamber was aired and pleasant, with no sign of any bottles.

Hera's only quarrel with her came in the early evening, when George had retired to bed, exhausted, but eagerly looking forward to tomorrow and feeling better, which Justin had assured him he would.

On impulse, Hera walked to the end of the passage and discovered the attic door locked. She swung around toward Figg's, ready to do battle, and discovered the nurse in her bedchamber doorway, looking both frightened and defiant.

"He's always locked in," she said. "Sir Hugh's orders—which, with respect, miss, you got no authority to overrule."

"In this case, I do," Hera said coldly. "For the sake of George's health. Think, Nurse. What if he had been taken ill while you were unconscious in your room? I couldn't have opened the door! What if there is a fire? What if he is ill again? He cannot escape, and no one but you can let him out or anyone else in."

"But I ain't touched a drop today!" Nurse protested. "Nor I won't, neither. Gave me a proper fright this morning. It's the custom, miss, makes him safe, stops him wandering all over the house, even *out* of the house and coming to grief. Think how Sir Hugh would feel about that!" She smiled with triumph at her hit, then hastily dropped her eyes in pretended submission. "Mr. George don't mind, and it's for the best."

"It's monstrous," Hera said intensely. "We shall most certainly take the matter up with Sir Hugh and Lady Astley when they come home, but until they do, the doors will remain unlocked. Now, are you going to give the key when I ask, or do I have to make enough fuss to draw the entire household?"

Nurse stared at her in horror. "You wouldn't!"

"I would."

"You'd lose your place."

"I am prepared to. Are you?"

Without a word, Nurse took a bunch of keys from her apron

pocket and slapped them into Hera's hand, hard enough to hurt. She wheeled around into her room and shut the door. It wasn't quite a slam, but it came close.

Hera unlocked the attic door. Though, of course, George could have got out anyway if he had wanted to. The whole idea of imprisoning him was repugnant to her. She quickly found out that Nurse's other keys fitted George's sitting room door, and the doors into and out of the salon that led to his garden. She suspected the final, larger key was to the outer garden door, which Lady Astley had unbolted on their first visit.

They really were determined to keep George a secret. And against all the odds, they had succeeded. A lot of care and planning had clearly gone into it. For example, none of the rooms with windows overlooking George's garden were in use, apart from George's own sitting room, and perhaps Nurse's room.

Somehow worse was Hera's feeling that this system was so established that it operated like an oiled machine. Nothing had ever gone wrong until this morning. And even then, no one else in the household had become aware of George's existence. The only other person who knew was Justin, and he would leave soon. God knew when, or even if, he would return.

Her stomach tightened painfully on that thought. A feeling that might have been loneliness swept over her like a tide.

She lay awake for a long time, listening to the silence and thinking.

CHAPTER TWELVE

IN THE MORNING, everything seemed to be more or less back to normal. Hera found George in his sitting room, having breakfast, while Nurse sat in the corner, knitting.

He greeted Hera with a smile, and she joined him at the table.

"What would you like to do today?" she asked him.

He looked so surprised that her heart ached. No one could have asked him that for a very long time. But it didn't upset him, despite Nurse's warning head shake in the corner.

"Gardening," he said after due consideration. "Even if it's raining. And I'd like to talk to you and Dr. Rivers. Maybe he could teach me about medicine."

"I expect he could." It was interesting, Hera thought, that he referred to Justin by his surname in Nurse's company. Yesterday, he had called him by his Christian name, and heard Hera do so, too. It showed a certain worldly awareness that no one seemed to credit to him.

As Nurse stood up to accompany them, Hera went up to her. "You don't need to come, Nurse. I know you are tired and have no time to yourself, but there is no reason why you should have to be with him at the same time I am. I'm sure that's one of the reasons I'm here. No gin, mind you, but you deserve a rest."

Expressions chased each other across Nurse's face—gratification, suspicion, fear of being supplanted, perhaps—but in the end, she dropped a curtsey. "Thank you, miss. So long as we both stick to the rules, Sir Hugh will be happy. Only…only don't let that doctor talk out of turn."

The idea of stopping Justin from saying exactly as he chose was laughable. Somehow, Hera kept her face straight and assured Nurse gravely of the doctor's discretion.

In the garden, George clearly had a plan to follow. Leaving him to set out his tools by his chosen flowerbed, Hera went to the outside garden door and unlocked it, before walking back through the house and round the outside, to draw back the bolt on the other side of his garden door. It was a symbolic gesture, for the gardeners must know perfectly well they could not pass this way. And George showed no signs of even thinking about bolting. But the idea of imprisoning him any longer was abhorrent.

"Can I help?" she asked, going back to join him. "Or will I just get in the way?"

"No, you can weed that side," he said distractedly, then paused. "That is, I'd be grateful if you would. I don't seem to use manners anymore."

But then, no manners were employed toward him either. He was treated like a child, supervised by a children's nurse, and told exactly what to do and when. The routine might have comforted him, but she doubted its unchanging nature was actually good for him.

"We all forget sometimes," she said lightly, kneeling down where he had suggested. "I always wanted a garden of my own. But my parents would never let me interfere. I was never even allowed to get my hands dirty."

As she chatted, he gradually began to offer questions or comments in return. If his own conversation tended toward the lecturing, particularly on plants, he was nevertheless interesting. And it seemed to her that the more they conversed, the less obviously odd he became. Or perhaps she was just growing used to him.

After a couple of hours, the outside garden door creaked open and a collie dog appeared, ears pricked up with interest, closely followed by a leash, with Justin on the other end. He looked at ease and in command, as he usually did, causing butterflies to soar in Hera's stomach. What was it about him that his mere presence brought her such powerful, instant happiness?

George sat back on his heels. "Justin." He sounded pleased, as if he had not even noticed the dog, which appeared to be a lively young pup. With lots of suppressed energy, it danced at the end of the lead, never straying from Justin's side, but clearly desperate to explore.

Hera rose to her feet, dusting off her skirts, before holding out her hand to the dog, more to cover the flush of pleasure caused by Justin's approach. The dog galumphed excitedly, licking her fingers and wagging its bushy tail until it seemed in danger of coming off. Though it clearly wanted to jump on her, it didn't.

"Meet my father's newest rescue project," Justin said wryly. "His name is Wag, for obvious reasons. He was about to be got rid of because Carter said he was untrainable. He probably is with sheep, but he's good as gold walking to heel. Mostly."

She could leave it no longer. Slowly, she raised her gaze to meet his. A wealth of understanding, subtle and yet fierce, lurked in his eyes. A faint, teasing smile played on his lips. Lips that had kissed with such passion that even remembering caught at her breath. She could not help the smile that began to curve her own lips.

Then Wag lunged so suddenly that Justin was taken by surprise. The dog hurled itself past Hera straight at George, who still knelt on the ground, although he had laid down his trowel. Instinctively, both Justin and Hera moved to intervene in case the dog's friendly lunge upset him.

But then Justin caught her arm to stay her, because it was too late. Wag had jumped, both front paws on George's chest, and George, quite unruffled, was rubbing the dog's ears. Wag licked his nose and tried to climb with his back legs onto George's knees. With a shout of laughter, he put his arms around the dog and hugged him.

Justin laughed too, but Hera's amusement froze on her lips as a flash of memory struggled up. She found herself staring at George's delighted face, while the world faded and she barely heard the conversation.

"I'd let him loose to play," Justin said, as though somewhere in the distance, "but I suspect he'd cause havoc among the flowerbeds."

"We can go over to the terrace and tie him to the door handle with a long piece of string," George said.

"Good idea. You find the string." As George trotted off, Justin turned his gaze back to Hera and immediately frowned. "Hera? What is wrong? What is it?"

"I know who he is," she blurted. "He's Hugh's brother Arthur."

AN HOUR LATER, when Nurse had come to fetch George for luncheon, Hera all but dragged Justin through the hall.

He went tolerantly, largely because he was foolishly happy to be dragged anywhere by Hera. Since his father had performed the burial service for young Arthur Astley, he did not see how George could possibly be the same person. Although admittedly, he might be about the right age.

She pulled him to the front of the hall and halted, pointing to a portrait over one of the reception room doorways. The familiar figure of old Sir Cuthbert stared haughtily back, while a small child of about three tried to climb onto his knee. The child must have been Hugh, because an older boy of perhaps ten crouched on the floor beside them, with both arms around a large dog. Arthur—Sir Cuthbert's heir who, tragically, had only lived another couple of years after the portrait was painted.

"It's the pose," Justin said. "Very like the way George greeted Wag. But it doesn't mean anything, Hera."

"It does," she insisted. "Look at Arthur's face. *Really* look."

He did, though largely to humor her. Children could change hugely as they grew to adulthood, and at first, he saw no similarities at all between the ten-year-old Arthur and the almost forty-year-old George. George's face was longer and broader-boned than this child, who was smiling far more widely than George ever did.

And yet perhaps there was *something* about the boy's smile, some personal, almost secretive pleasure. As though he didn't understand either the painter or anyone else and knew they didn't understand him. And the eyes...the eyes were the same shape as George's, like fat almonds, and their expression...

His breath caught. "Damn. It could be. Pardon my language."

"Easily. Did you not know him then? He knows you."

"I was only three or four when he died. I don't recall ever seeing him, and I don't see how he can recognize me!"

"But you could recognize Sir Hugh from the younger child in the painting."

Justin was about to deny it, but there was, in fact, a great deal of the older Hugh in the pampered child, so sure of his father's affections that he would climb on him despite the fearsome expression. He had the family eyes. Like George's.

The sound of a footman's approach had him muttering beneath his breath before he dragged Hera back down the hall toward the salon used to get out to George's garden. He shut the door and swung on Hera.

"How can it be possible?" he demanded. "Arthur died. My father led the funeral and comforted the family in their grief."

"It could have been anyone in the coffin. Or even a pile of earth."

"But he was Sir Cuthbert's heir! They must have had a doctor out to treat him, to pronounce him dead."

"Who was the doctor here then? Is he still in the village?"

Justin racked his brains. "No. Not if it was Dr. Watling. He retired and went to live near his daughter in Yorkshire, before Dr. Bailey came. My father will know old Watling's direction. But *why*? Why would his own father have him declared dead and hidden in the house? It makes no sense."

"Perhaps your brother will remember him?" Hera suggested. "At thirteen, he might have been becoming difficult. He must always have been odd."

"And frustration can make children behave badly," Justin said, pacing the room. "Sir Cuthbert was an old martinet, very proper. He would not have liked an *odd* son... And old Lady Astley would have been dead by the time Arthur died. Or was meant to have died."

He flung around to face her, and was almost distracted by her beauty, by the intensity and trust in her expression. He wanted to hold her and keep her safe. Forcing himself to concentrate, he said, "This would have to have been a massive conspiracy! Not just Hugh, who could only have been six or seven years old when his brother died, but the upper servants would have had to be involved at the very least. And how would they have kept his presence quiet? An adolescent boy, already frustrated and behaving badly, would have been well nigh impossible to silence, let alone hide."

Her brilliant eyes held his. "Laudanum?"

He stared back, then shook his head emphatically. "Impossible. Not for years on end! He would have been hopelessly dependent on the drug, if not dead. As it is, I'm surprised there are not more signs of dependency since we've withdrawn it." He frowned. "Unless..."

"Unless what?"

He began to pace again. "Unless they just gave him it occasionally, a few days at a time to make him calm while he got used to his new life."

"In the attic!" Hera cried indignantly.

"Hush. Yes, in the attic, and the sitting room, with Nurse to super-vise. With his father and brother to visit, as many books as he could devour, a private garden to design and maintain. Anything to keep his mind busy and his body almost healthy. With occasional days drugged into silence when anyone visited or, perhaps, when the family went away, so that Nurse didn't have too much to deal with. The other servants are nearly all people I recall from my youth, who must be incredibly loyal or simply stupid."

"Mrs. Wyse the housekeeper knows," Hera said. "And she helps make sure the other servants don't."

He turned back to face her, troubled and disgusted. Also…angry. "If this is true, it is…"

"Monstrous," Hera supplied. She shuddered. "Dear God, and I railed at *my* father."

"Who seems to have done much the same thing with his own wife," Justin pointed out before she could begin to feel guilty. His own conscience pricked him. "Actually…"

He came toward her and took her hand, drawing her to one of the chairs that was obviously pulled regularly in and out of the garden. "Come and sit down." She sat, and he stood gazing down at her for a moment. He could not bear to hurt her further, but she was no more a child than George was, and he had to tell her. "I had a thought about your father yesterday, while I was helping George. I don't like it any more than you will. But if your father was the healthy man he appeared to everyone, including his physician, and he did collapse and die before the shot, then there is the possibility of poison."

She blinked up at him. "*Poison?* How could that even be possible?"

"Oh, it's possible. Something put covertly in his coffee, or his flask, or his food. Unlikely, I grant you, but very far from impossible."

"But why?" she demanded. "Who? Major Butler, to avoid fighting him?"

"Hardly," Justin said. "Butler is used to facing the might of the French guns and cavalry charges!"

"And wanted to get back to them, I daresay, as much as you do."

She had a point. "It isn't Butler's way," he said with certainty. "Besides, after the challenge, there was no further contact between the principals. They didn't share breakfast before going out to try to put holes in each other. In fact, poison is more often a female's weapon, and I find myself thinking again about that woman I saw watching the duel. I need to write to the duke's seconds, to see if they know who she is, or if they saw what his grace ate or drank before the duel."

He broke off abruptly. "I'm sorry. I wanted you know my thoughts, but this is neither the time nor the place. You have enough to worry about. Especially if what you suspect about George is true. I hate your being here alone."

"Why?"

For some reason, the question took him by surprise. "Because if Sir Hugh has carried on the charade you suspect," he said sharply, "imprisoning his own brother, whose inheritance he has usurped, and making him work for the fruits he and his wife enjoy, they are vile and dangerous people. And I do not want you anywhere near them."

Unexpectedly, she stood up and kissed his cheek, smiling. His heart melted, while the rest of his body sprang to full awareness. Having surprised him, she tried to dance away from him, but he was too quick, catching her in his arms and kissing her mouth with great thoroughness. God, she was sweet, and how the devil he was going to leave her...

He forced himself to end the delicious kiss. Her eyes opened with a flutter. They were warm and clouded with the passion he had aroused, and he had never wanted anything more than to take her to bed. For a long, long time.

Only, one did not take dukes' unmarried daughters to bed. Certainly not in the middle of the day in the house of a stranger...who might just be a particularly nasty thief and fraudster. His stomach tightened again with anxiety. If they were right in their guesses, then the house and estate and wealth were all George's.

Then she laid her cheek against his chest, and his throat dried up. All other thoughts fled his head. There was only the wonder of this young woman, vulnerable and trusting in his unworthy arms. He had only wanted to flirt with her, to show her that romance and marriage might not all be bad. And now, it seemed, they were both captured in a mazelike emotional tangle of his own making.

Worse, he liked it.

And she was still the duke's daughter and he the grumpy physician.

He swallowed. "We should follow George."

Her fingers tightened on his arms. "One more second," she whispered, and his heart broke into tiny pieces.

CHAPTER THIRTEEN

LEAVING HERA TAKING luncheon with George, Justin took the dog back to the vicarage, where he enjoyed his own midday meal with his family.

"Philip, do you remember Arthur Astley?"

"Not really. I vaguely recall seeing him occasionally up at the hall, but he didn't play with us. He was too much older, I suppose."

"Did he ever play with anyone?"

Philip stared at him. "What an odd question."

"I don't believe he did," their father said, helping himself to a slice of bread. "Sir Cuthbert was very protective of his dignity."

"Or his oddity?" Justin asked.

His father smiled gently, forgiving as always of human nature. "That too, perhaps."

"When Arthur died," Justin said, "I don't suppose you saw his body?"

Philip stared at him.

Their father put down his knife. "No. Justin, what are you about?"

"I'm not quite sure. Do you have Dr. Watling's direction?"

HAVING WRITTEN TO Dr. Watling and left his letters at the inn to be collected, Justin walked back up to the hall in the late afternoon, to discover that Sir Hugh and Lady Astley had just come home. Their carriage was being trundled around to the stables.

Justin needed to know about Arthur's death before he could start throwing accusations at Hugh. But in common humanity, he had to speak to him about George, whoever he turned out to be. For this reason, never one to shirk a challenge, he entered by the front door.

"I've just come to see my patient," he told old Simmonds, the butler, discreetly, mindful for Hera's sake of avoiding combat. "I imagine Sir Hugh will not wish to be disturbed so soon after his journey, but if he can spare me a few minutes by appointment, I would be grateful. I'll speak to you again on my way out."

He strode off toward the back stairs, giving Simmonds little chance to object. But then, Justin suspected he knew exactly who the real patient was.

Sounds of laughter drifted from George's sitting room, making Justin smile, and not just because he loved to hear Hera laugh. It was one of the things George needed more of in his life. Giving George the respect he was due, and rarely received, he knocked on the door.

There was a distinct pause, perhaps while Hera urged him to speak.

"Enter," George said hesitantly.

He looked worried as Justin walked in, though his frown immediately cleared. "Justin! Did you bring Wag?"

"Not this time. He might not be welcome in the house." Justin met Hera's gaze. She sat in the window seat, a smile trembling on her lips, her cheeks slightly flushed—because of him, he hoped.

"Hugh is home," George said.

It was hard to tell if this worried or pleased him. "I know. I saw the carriage. Has he been up to see you yet?"

"Not yet," George said. "But it will be teatime soon. Sometimes Hugh or Caroline come for tea. Will you have tea?"

"Probably not today," Justin said. "But I think I should talk to Sir Hugh about your illness and your medicine, if you permit?"

George's brows flew up in astonishment, as if he had never "permitted" anything in his life. "Will it help?"

"I hope so."

George nodded, which Justin took as permission.

"Nurse is with them," Hera said ruefully. "I expect to be summoned directly."

George turned an anxious gaze upon her. "They won't send you away, will they?"

It would, in Justin's grim opinion, be the best thing to happen.

"I'll tell them how much you helped me," George added. "And Dr. Rivers."

Justin sat down, gauging from George's eyes and his movements how much the drug still affected him. Some people seemed to resist dependency more than others, though he had no idea why. George appeared to be one of those.

"Sometimes you call me Justin," he observed. "How do you know my name?"

George ambled over to the window. "You must have told me. Or perhaps it was Miss Severne. What's your Christian name, Miss Severne?"

She almost said, "Hera." Justin could tell by the stricken look in her eyes. And she seemed incapable of saying Harriet, which was the name she had decided upon.

"Perhaps it wouldn't be so proper to use it," Justin said smoothly, "until you have been longer acquainted. Do you feel well, sir? As though the illness has quite gone?"

"Mostly," George said. "Talking helps my head feel less wooly. I don't like to be wooly."

Justin said, "You told me once that you thought the work you do with the numbers made you ill. Why do you keep working on them if that is the case?"

"To help Hugh," George said in apparent surprise.

"Then you do it by choice?" Justin asked. "Even though you believe it makes you ill and gives you a wooly head in the end?"

"Yes," George said.

"Why?" Justin only just managed to keep his voice casual.

"It's all I can do to help." George reached for a book on the nearest shelf and opened it, probably to end the discussion. "I will always help Hugh if I can."

Because he is your little brother, and in your own way you have always looked after him. The knowledge both touched and infuriated Justin, and he was suddenly quite sure that Hera was right, that George *was* Arthur, who had been disinherited, cheated, imprisoned, and exploited by that little brother he was still looking after.

Nurse waddled in without knocking. Both Justin and Hera frowned at her, for they were trying to introduce a climate of respect in which George was treated like the adult he was. He seemed to respond to it. On the other hand, he ignored Nurse's entry.

She looked smug, which boded ill for Hera's position and for Justin's chances of effecting a better life for George.

"Sir Hugh wants to speak to you in his study, doctor," she said, a hint of malice in those oh-so-amiable eyes. "Simmonds will show you where it is."

"I remember where it is." Justin stood up. "Sir Cuthbert told me off in there often enough." He could not risk looking at Hera, although he was aware of her hopeful, anxious gaze fixed on him as he left the room and went to fight for George.

The butler was waiting for him in the front hall and conducted him to the study where, in fact, he had been summoned only once in his childhood.

"Dr. Rivers, sir," Simmonds intoned before bowing and withdrawing, closing the door behind him.

Sir Hugh looked tired and a little flustered, which made him appear more pleasantly human as he rose from behind his tidy desk and leaned across to shake hands with Justin.

"Rivers, how are you? Sit down. Glass of sherry?"

"No, thank you." Justin sat. "I'm grateful you found the time to see me when you must be weary after your journey, but I think it's important you know what occurred while you were away from home."

Sir Hugh looked grave. "With George, yes. It is I who is grateful you were there and available to see to him. Miss Severne is not yet used to his ways and is inclined to panic."

"It's as well she did," Justin said. "Or he is unlikely to have survived."

"Oh, come, Rivers, you overdramatize the—"

"Actually, I don't. On the contrary, I have more experience than I would like on the use and misuse of opium. It is excellent pain relief, but it is a powerful drug with many unpleasant effects. Too much can kill. Even in small doses, it is highly habit-forming, and dependence can cause all sorts of problems, many of them equally lethal. Fortunately, your ward shows no signs yet of such dependency, but the dose he had received during the night almost killed him."

Hugh was clearly not used to being lectured. The flush seeping into his cheeks held as much anger as embarrassment. Justin pressed his point home.

"Dosing him with laudanum to keep him quiet, when he is already perfectly balanced, is damaging. Leaving him in the charge of someone who is so drunk she can't remember how many times she's dosed him already verges on the criminal and is, frankly, the height of stupidity."

"Drunk?" Hugh's rising fury was distracted by the word. He stared at Justin with astonished consternation. "Miss Severne was *drunk*?"

"Of course Miss Severne was not drunk!" Justin exploded. "It was she who sent for me! When I arrived, Nurse Figg reeked of gin, so badly that I suspect she began the evening before you left. She had no idea how often she had given him his medicine, medicine he never needed in the first place. A brisk walk in the fresh air would have done his headache more good. The laudanum just makes it worse."

Hugh closed his eyes. It was a relief to Justin that he had clearly had no idea about this. It gave him hope that Hugh would cooperate in some changes.

"I didn't suspect she went to such lengths," Hugh muttered. "We knew she had begun to tipple a little, of course. We didn't begrudge her. She has been with us for so long. She was my nurse, as you probably know, so I could hardly turn her out. But we employed Miss Severne to oversee—"

"Without explaining the real nature of her duties," Justin said, almost between his teeth. He took a deep breath, recalling that he wanted Hugh's cooperation. "Of course, how you deal with Nurse Figg is your own business. My only concern is with my patient. And in his regard, I have several recommendations. I will put them in writing before I leave St. Bride, but for now, this is my urgent…advice."

He had almost said *instruction*, which would certainly have put Hugh's back up.

"No more laudanum. He does not need to be sedated. He needs more stimulation. More people to talk to, greater distances to roam. He needs to be treated like the highly intelligent adult he is. He is no danger to himself or anyone else. He is an eccentric, not a lunatic. In fact, I have found him to be of a gentle disposition and a brilliant mind. Don't crush him, sir—let him blossom."

His plea was heartfelt, though designed to appeal to Hugh's better nature. Justin knew he could never reverse all the wrongs in a day, but he hoped to sew some seeds, to make a beginning.

And indeed, Hugh regarded him consideringly, mulling over his words and, no doubt, their implications. He gazed away, out of the window, leaned back in his chair, and sat forward again, frowning.

Gradually, the frown smoothed away, and he regarded Justin once more.

"I have to thank you for your thoughtful care of my ward in my absence. Indeed, I apologize for the necessity. After all, although you may be a physician, you are not *his* physician, or mine." Hugh smiled, as though to rob the words of any offense. "I shall take your opinions into careful consideration."

Justin's heart sank. In other words, Hugh would do nothing. "At the very least, don't destroy a remarkable mind." He held Hugh's gaze and added, "A mind I know you value."

Hugh's eyes widened almost imperceptibly as he grappled with what Justin might know or suspect. But he must have grown used to concealment over the years, for the next instant, his impersonal smile was back.

"You have been in the village a week, Dr. Rivers, and met my ward only yesterday. When is it you plan to leave again? Tomorrow? The day after?"

"Probably the latter."

"Then, with respect, you must allow the judgment of longer acquaintance with the facts to stand."

Justin stared at him. "You are imprisoning him, to call it no worse."

"I am not. I am caring for a troubled man who is my ward."

"Is he?" Justin asked, and won several seconds of silence. "I would be interested to see the legal documentation of that."

Hugh smiled. "But you have no right to do so. I hope you are not going to suggest anything that would not only be slanderous, but laughable."

"Such as?" Justin inquired, but he was gazing into Hugh's eyes, and the implacable hardness there took him by surprise. It sent an icy chill down his spine, for he read there quite clearly that Hugh would never allow what he had won to be taken from him. There was nothing he would not do to keep the wealth and status he thought his by right, and no consideration of right or wrong, no person, would ever get in the way of that.

Justin had lost. He had never had any chance of winning. Another patient he had failed. But that was not the whole point.

Hugh smiled. "I cannot tell. Your brother explained to me that you have been overset by the men you lost in war. I cannot have you interfering here. I trust I am clear?"

And there it was—the subtle, humiliating insult, the threat to his livelihood, should Justin decide to settle here after Bonaparte's defeat. He should be angry. Perhaps, one day, he would be. For the present, he had learned more than enough of Hugh and his ruthlessness.

Justin smiled and rose to his feet. "Crystal clear, Hugh. Sadly, however, you do not exert the kind of control you imagine. Not outside this house and your own family, at any rate. I have given you my best advice, and I would strongly advise you to take it. For now, I'll bid you good day."

He sauntered out, aware at least that Hugh was so glad to see him go that he made no effort to stand and ring the bell for him to be escorted out. And since the hall was quiet, Justin loped silently across to the "dangerous stairs" and leapt up them two and three at a time.

At the top, he knocked on George's sitting room door, but was already opening it as a distracted "Enter" drifted out. George appeared to be lost in a book from which he didn't look up. Nurse Figg smiled at him from her corner. There was no sign of Hera, so Justin simply closed the door again and marched along the passage.

He knew which door was hers, for George had told him very early in their acquaintance when Justin had been examining the lingering effects of the laudanum, gauging what he knew and observed and deduced. Again, he knocked perfunctorily and walked in before he even heard the sound of her voice.

She had been reaching for the door handle and now stood right in front of him, her eyes wide with astonishment, her skin flushing rather delightfully with her outrage.

"Justin! I… You…you can't come in here!"

He brushed past her, kicking the door shut. "I'm a physician. Propriety scarcely applies. Besides, we won't be long. Where are your bags?"

"Bags?" she repeated.

"Trunk, valises—I can scarcely recall what you arrived with, but you have to pack them up. We're leaving."

"Leaving?" In her shock, she kept repeating his words, which clearly irritated her. Visibly, she pulled herself together. "Sir Hugh and Lady Astley have only just come home. They won't be going—"

"You," he interrupted. There was no time for social niceties. He needed her to be safe *now*. "You are leaving with me. I'll take you to my father for tonight. Evelyn, my sister-in-law, is there, so it's perfectly respectable. From there, we can discuss how to get you home. Where are your bags? Do you need to send for them?"

"No, but—"

He strode across to the wardrobe and flung open the doors. He had drawn out the small valise, and was reaching to the top of the cupboard for the larger one he had spotted there, when she found her voice, sounding as bewildered as she looked, but perfectly strong.

"Justin, stop! What are you doing? I am not going anywhere."

He spoke with peremptory impatience, so urgent was his fear for her. "Hugh will do nothing for George, change nothing, admit nothing. I saw it in his face. He will do anything to protect what he has. *Anything*, Hera. You are not safe here."

Both valises lay open on the bed, and he began to drag her clothes out of the wardrobe. But when he turned, arms full of clothes, she marched up to him, snatched them from him, and hurled them back into the wardrobe in a heap.

"Stop," she commanded, her voice harsh. "You are irrational and hysterical, and I am staying here."

It was like a slap in the face, both shaming and infuriating. Somewhere, it was even funny, although he was nowhere near that place yet. He took a deep breath, hoping she could not see the color he felt rising under his skin.

"Actually, I am neither," he said more reasonably, "though I may have failed to explain myself adequately. I spoke to Hugh. He will change nothing for George and warned me against interfering, using threats no gentleman would employ."

"He warned *you*. Not me. They engaged me primarily to care for George, and from here I can change things a little at a time. I won't allow them to give him any more laudanum, and I shall—"

"How do you propose to stop them?" he interrupted. *"You can't.* And I will not be here to pick up whatever might be salvageable."

Now she looked as if he had slapped her. She had forgotten he was going away.

Her eyes widened. "You are just walking away from George?"

"No. You are."

"I most certainly am not!"

Justin wanted to close his eyes and begin again. He was going about this all wrong, acting on instinct and the need to protect her. And all she saw was desertion. The disappointment in her eyes cut him to the heart.

He tried again. "Hugh needs to protect himself against the knowledge we have. He thinks you have no family, are of no account to anyone. If he suspects I know who George is, he must suppose you know, too."

She laughed, a harsh, unnatural sound that grated on his ears because it was full of as much hurt as contemptuous amusement. "And you think he will do away with me? Who would look after George then?"

"You'd never know, would you?" he said.

She stared at him. "You are trying to frighten me."

"I hope to God I am succeeding."

Her chin lifted and his heart sank. "You are not. You insult me by the effort, which should be beneath both of us. I will stay with George."

This time, he took several breaths. "I am going abroad, Hera. I will not be here. Even in the short time I have left, I will not be allowed to see George again. You will be isolated in this house."

She met his gaze squarely, and he read the odd little spark of dark amusement in her eyes. "I have been isolated all my life. Go, if you please. I would rather not be compromised by your presence."

"Hera, stop being ridiculous!" he said, goaded into the final foolishness. He even took a furious step toward her, and she fell back against the wardrobe door in alarm. Almost instantly, her fear was drowned in challenge, but dear God, one was as bad as the other. Did she really imagine he would, that he ever *could*, hurt her?

Her doubt of him felt like betrayal, adding to the failure of his persuasion, his failure to George. He could not stay in her presence any longer. He needed to leave. And yet even as his legs carried him to the door, his heart cried to stay just one more moment.

He couldn't do that to her. He had made her afraid of him.

Appalled, he tore open the bedchamber door, and somehow remembered to ensure that the passage was empty before he stepped out and closed the door behind him. The latch fell into place like the final nail in a coffin.

CHAPTER FOURTEEN

HERA CRIED HERSELF to sleep that night. Somehow, discovering Justin was not the man she had believed him to be was worse than losing him, worse than rejection.

At some point during the night, though, she realized her contempt was not entirely justified. He had always intended to go abroad. It wasn't his fault she had forgotten, had made assumptions that one patient would keep him here when many more awaited him once battle was joined. But that he could assume she would just walk away when he told her was unforgiveable, as was his high-handed behavior and his final, threatening advance, as though he would carry her out over his shoulder, regardless of her will.

All that was infuriating enough. But that he should then just walk off without a word…

Anger was better than loss, better than the loneliness that threatened to rise up from her toes. She had thought there was no one like Justin. And there wasn't, not for her. And now she'd discovered even Justin wasn't like the idea she had formed of him. *Her* Justin wouldn't have abandoned George or commanded her to do so in such a high-handed manner. He would never have imagined she would simply walk away from the responsibilities she had taken on for payment and now felt so keenly. That in reality he assumed she would simply abandon George hurt beyond belief, because it showed he thought so little of her.

Just like her parents, her aunt, and everyone else she knew. With the possible exception of Victor, and she was never entirely sure how much he actually noticed.

She had thought Justin was different. That he saw her a person of worth. That *he* was such a person. Deep in her heart, she still knew he was, but she was too churned up and hurt to admit it to herself.

She spent the morning as usual in the garden with George. Since it rained most of the time, this was a little miserable, but George didn't seem to mind. He wore an oiled coat and trousers. Hera did not own such garments, so she watched him mostly from the French doors, with occasional forays to offer minimal help.

Lady Astley came to join them for luncheon in George's sitting room. Hera had already met her in the breakfast parlor and found her manner quite unchanged. She chattered away about a concert in Lincoln and a dinner she and Sir Hugh had attended. The only tense point for Hera was when she had asked about George's illness.

"I sent for Dr. Rivers," Hera had said, knowing perfectly well that Lady Astley already knew. "I realize you prefer to protect George from new people, but I was afraid for his life. In fact, we thought he was dead!"

"Of course you did the right thing in the circumstances," Lady Astley had told her. "And naturally, as a physician he is bound by confidentiality. He will not gossip. In any case, he is leaving tomorrow."

"Tomorrow?" Hera had exclaimed before she could stop herself. She felt suddenly bereft and panicked. Was that why he had been so eager for her to leave Denholm Hall? Because, as he saw it, he could no longer protect her? But then, who would have protected George?

"So Hugh tells me," Lady Astley had replied. "As for Nurse, this is really the last straw. I believe *you* must be in charge of any future medication, if you agree?"

"Of course," Hera had replied. She had every intention of throwing it away.

At luncheon, the subject was not mentioned again. Nurse was not present.

Lady Astley beamed at George. "How good to see you again! Hugh is going to come up this afternoon, while Miss Severne and I go into the village."

Hera almost suggested that George accompany them, but that would be too much too quickly. First, she would need to gain him access to the rest of the gardens, then work gradually from there toward a more normal and interesting life for him. If he wished it.

After Lady Astley had bustled off again, Hera cleared up the crockery from luncheon. "Do you ever wish to go beyond your own garden?" she asked casually.

"Yes," George said without hesitation, though he did not elaborate, merely pulled a book off the shelf and began to read, while Hera's heart swelled with pity and anger and determination.

⟫⟪

SINCE THE RAIN had gone off, gray skies giving way to blue with unthreatening white cloud, Lady Astley decided they should walk to the village. It would have been pleasant, too, with the happy singing of birds in the sunshine, and the fresh, after-rain scents from the fields and woods. But a pall of misery hung over Hera, interspersed with occasional bouts of anger against Justin, and determination to do her best for George.

It brought an air of distraction and unreality to Lady Astley's amiable conversation, and her trivial business in the village, which could easily had been undertaken by the cook or housekeeper. But Hera's heart beat hard as they passed the church and the vicarage, winking between the trees and shafts of sunlight.

Fortunately—so she told herself—there was no sign of Justin, or anyone else that she knew. Lady Astley seemed disappointed, as though she wished to tell her friends all about her delightful couple of days in Lincoln.

Eventually, with her household business accomplished, she suggested tea at the local inn, and here, at last, the gods favored Hera with the sight of Mr. and Mrs. Philip Rivers, clearly with the same idea.

Greetings were exchanged, and they entered the cozy coffee room together. The innkeeper's wife was delighted to welcome them and promised a "slap-up" tea. In no time, the table was covered in warm bread and scones, fresh butter, preserves, cold meats, fruit, and cakes.

By then, Lady Astley and Mrs. Rivers were ensconced on one side of the broad table, Hera and Justin's brother on the other. Pouring the tea into the inn's best cups, Lady Astley was confiding the pleasures of her time away from St. Bride, the beautiful fashions—and the frightful frumps—she had seen there.

"You did not accompany Lady Astley?" Mr. Rivers said to Hera with a faint smile.

"No. I think they wished to enjoy each other's company," Hera said.

"I gather my brother was pleased about that, at any rate. He enjoys *your* company."

Hera, wishing it were true and trying not to care, felt stricken into silence.

"To be honest," Mr. Rivers said, lowering his voice further, "I had thought your presence here might convince him to stay."

"On the contrary—I have no influence whatsoever over Dr. Rivers." She even managed to sound amused, and, rather to her surprise, an answering—if rueful—smile dawned in his eyes.

"In that matter, no one has. It is as if the whole army is his patient."

"Does he not trust any of the other surgeons?"

"A few, I suspect, but not many."

Something in his voice made her search his face more thoroughly. "He told me you didn't want him to go because you were needlessly worried about your father," she said. "I told him you didn't want him to die. Is there something we are both missing?"

"Perhaps willfully on his part." Philip hesitated. "Has he ever spoken to you of his experiences on the peninsula? And France?"

"Only amusing stories."

"I cannot imagine what it is like," Philip said in a rush, "dealing with so many dreadful wounds, so much disease and death. He will not distress us or you by speaking of it. But I know he is haunted by the patients he has lost. He has nightmares that he will rarely admit to, but I heard him when he first came home and on one occasion since. He is an excellent physician, and a finer surgeon than they are used to. I know that from many sources. But it is never enough for Justin. You may not ever think it from his outward manner, but I believe he invests his whole being in every patient, and so feels every loss, every death is his fault. Over the years, they have built up to a large number of dead men who haunt his dreams. His cries are…heartrending, and he does not even know."

Hera closed her mouth as a slow, deep ache began in her heart. Why had she never thought of that? He must feel the same about her father's death. That was why he could not leave the duel alone. More than the fate of his friend Butler troubled him. The death of another patient who should have recovered was added to his horrors.

"And that is the real reason you do not want him to go back to the war," she said slowly. "You are afraid he cannot bear it. And yet if he does not go, he cannot live with that either." He wanted to save her, too. And yet he would leave George alone? That made no sense.

"I have given up understanding him," Philip said with a quick, sympathetic smile.

"But not loving him," she said.

"No," he agreed. "Not that."

A lump seemed to have formed in her throat. She wished she had not mentioned love.

"Will you write to him?" Philip asked so hesitantly that she understood how difficult it was for him. "I believe it will mean much to him, that it will help."

She nodded, and finally asked with difficulty, "Is he really going tomorrow?" Her voice sounded small and bereft, everything she did not want to be.

"Yes, I believe so. I thought he would have told you."

Perhaps he had meant to, but their quarrel had got in the way. She swallowed. "If you tell me where to write, I shall do so."

As THEY WALKED back up to Denholm Hall, Lady Astley said lightly, "You seemed to be having a very intense conversation with Mr. Rivers."

Hera was still thinking about that conversation, which made so much more sense of Justin's obsessions and behavior, even of their quarrel. Not that she thought she was wrong. She was not. In fact, she had the odd feeling, despite his high-handed determination, that if she had allowed herself to give in to his demands, he would actually have thought less of her in the end.

With an effort, she dragged herself back to Lady Astley's words, which were not quite a question.

"He is worried for his brother," she said at last. "The family do not wish Dr. Rivers to go back to the army."

Lady Astley held her gaze. "Then you were not talking about George?"

"Of course not!" Hera said with such indignation that Lady Astley smiled and took her arm.

"There! I always knew you were an excellent find. Exactly the person we need."

Hera smiled distractedly, for the words beating constantly in her mind with both sadness and panic were: *Tomorrow. He's leaving tomorrow.*

JUSTIN HAD SPENT a largely frustrating day with lawyers in Lincoln and ended by writing to a solicitor in London called Ludovic Dunne, who investigated all sorts of knotty legal problems. Between them, he thought he had set enough in motion to begin the necessary changes.

It meant he had barely seen his family that day, which was not fair when he meant to leave on the morrow. On the other hand, he *could* stay another day—what difference would that make to Wellington? Or Bonaparte. The armies were merely mustering and endlessly drilling, not yet marching on France.

He could use that day to speak to Hera, also, to make things right between them and explain what he had done.

And yet, as he rode his tired, hired horse into the village late in the afternoon, he knew that would not do. His need to see her was an ache, a loss he would find hard enough to live with, even were there no quarrel between them. As it was...

After giving the beast over to the ostler at the inn, he strode straight past the vicarage, taking the back lanes and tracks up to the hall for speed. And he arrived, he thought, at a good time, about halfway between tea and the dinner hour, when Hera was most likely to be free.

Although he was afraid for her, he could not help but admire her loyalty to George. He would not try again to persuade her to leave, but he would tell her of the safety processes he had put in place, and the investigation he had begun. And part, he hoped, as friends.

And maybe, when he came home again…

When he came home again, she would still be a duke's wealthy daughter, and he a penniless physician. But perhaps, just perhaps, that need not matter?

Climbing the front steps, he rapped the knocker and stood back.

Simmonds himself opened the door, although a footman stood to attention beside him.

"Good afternoon," Justin said. "I'd like a few words with Miss Severne, if she is available to receive me."

"I'm sorry, sir. Miss Severne is not at home."

Disappointment and unease struck him with equal force. He eyed the imposing, if elderly, butler. "Do you mean she is not in the house, or that I am denied permission to speak to her?"

"Miss Severne is not at home," the butler repeated woodenly.

"Sir Hugh or Lady Astley, then?"

"I regret they are not at home, sir."

A second footman lurked behind the butler. Justin would never get past them without a fight, for it was clear the servants had been instructed to forbid him entry.

He changed tack. "How sad. Perhaps, then, you would allow me to leave a short note for Miss Severne?"

"I regret that will not be possible, sir. Miss Severne is not expected to return."

His stomach twisted. "She has left the hall?"

"That is my understanding, sir."

It was not Justin's. Yesterday, she had refused to leave George, even for her own safety. And today, he was meant to believe she had either gone home or left for some other position?

"I'm sure she left her direction."

"Not with me, sir."

"Then with Lady Astley."

"I'm sure I could not say."

Justin narrowed his eyes. "Then run along and ask her," he said.

The butler fell back as though involuntarily. But the footmen stepped forward into his place.

"Good afternoon, sir," Simmonds said, and one of the footmen closed the door in Justin's face.

They had seen him coming, he realized as he strode off toward the main gate. They had been ready for him, well instructed to inform him without explanation that Miss Severne had gone. Justin didn't believe a word of it.

But in a house full of devoted servants, to say nothing of the Astleys, he had no chance of getting near Hera in the hours of daylight.

Nighttime would be different.

⇒⇒⇐⇐

SOMEHOW, HERA GOT through the rest of the day—a short conversation with George, changing into evening dress, dinner with Sir Hugh and Lady Astley.

Sir Hugh was surprisingly gracious about her care of George during their absence, dwelling not on his "illness" that had required the doctor, but on his current contentment.

"He seems much better around you," he said warmly.

"He likes to talk about his discoveries and ideas," she said, then added, "He enjoyed conversing with Dr. Rivers, too. You might consider other occasional companions for him."

She felt rather daring and expected to be reprimanded for such an opinion, or at least ignored, but Sir Hugh actually nodded thoughtfully. "Perhaps."

Was now the time to press the issue of locking him in? A custom that Nurse had resumed with an air of triumph. Before she could decide, Lady Astley changed the subject, and the moment was lost.

Tomorrow. He's leaving tomorrow.

Since Lady Astley clearly did not need her in the evening, Hera excused herself after tea in the drawing room and went to see George. Lost in a new book on agriculture, which apparently Hugh had brought him from Lincoln, he barely looked up, although he smiled for the barest instant when she sat down opposite him.

Tomorrow. He's leaving tomorrow.

Restlessly, she rose and said good night to both George and Nurse, and went to her own chamber, where she paced between the walls like the caged animals she had seen at the Exchange in London. The room felt empty, more impersonal even than usual, which added to her sense of loss.

Tomorrow. He's leaving tomorrow.

Were they really to part like this, with harsh words and no peace between them? She would write, as Philip had asked, and explain… Explain what? That she loved him and would wait for him? Presumptuous! He probably had a lover on the Continent, and that was why he was so eager to return. She had the impression their friendship had taken him by surprise, as it had her. He had probably never intended to kiss her…

Butterflies soared at the memory. No one had ever kissed her before. But he had known how to make her melt. Men kissed easily, of course, as a way to more intimate favors. Aunt Hadleigh had warned her of that. Had he just been amusing himself, passing the time with a little flirtation? And she had flirted back because it was fun and different, and she had had no idea that she would fall in love, not with so complicated and contradictory a man.

Tomorrow. He's leaving…

With a gasp, she whirled around and seized her cloak that hung on the back of the door. He might be waiting for her in the maze.

And if he wasn't, she would simply walk down to the village and knock on the vicarage door. She should have done it earlier, before it was dark. She picked up the nearest candle and opened the door.

To her surprise, there was still light in the passage from the nearest wall sconce. And seated on a hard chair opposite her door was Nurse Figg, sewing. The sheer unexpectedness brought Hera to a sudden halt.

"Evening, miss," Nurse said, beaming. "Going somewhere?"

"Just for a walk. Why are you sitting there and not in your own room or the servants' hall?"

Nurse put her sewing away in her basket, picked it up, and heaved herself to her feet. "I was hoping to run into you. Mr. George was asking for you, and I said I'd see if you were still awake."

"Then why didn't you knock on the door?" Hera demanded, changing direction and heading toward George's sitting room instead of the main staircase.

"Didn't like to," Nurse said, trotting beside her. "He's not in the sitting room. He's in bed."

Hera frowned. "Is he well, Nurse?"

"Just wants to talk, and I won't do." Figg sniffed with clear affront.

Hera reached the attic door and tugged. To her satisfaction, it opened. She couldn't help glancing at Nurse, who smiled as if waiting for praise. Hera allowed her a nod and walked in and up the stairs toward the light at the top.

Behind her, the door closed. The lock turned as she did. With a jolt of anger as much as fear, she ran back down the few steps she had just climbed and wrenched at the door. It didn't budge.

"Nurse!" she cried, with a loud knock that bruised her fingers. "Figg, unlock this door at once!"

"It's no good," George said sadly from the top of the stairs. He stood in his bedchamber doorway, a lamp in one hand. "She won't come, and no one ever hears."

Her heart contracted with pity for all the times he must have tried. "They *must* hear!"

"Only Nurse. And perhaps Hugh and Caroline, but they want us here. The servants sleep three floors below, behind the baize door."

She stared at him. "Did you ask for me, George?"

He shook his head. "But they've put your things in the other room."

"What things?"

Without a word, he moved away from his chamber and along a narrow passage she had never even noticed. She ran upstairs and followed him into a tiny bedchamber with a sloping ceiling. Her night rail was laid on the bed, her toothbrush and powder beside the bowl on a washstand. A lamp and some oil sat on a chest of drawers. When she wrenched open the top drawer, she saw her own linen neatly folded.

Slowly, she closed the drawer again. "They mean to keep me here."

"They don't trust you. They think you brought Justin here."

"I did! So that you wouldn't die."

"But they're afraid you'll bring him again."

"I can't. He'll be gone at first light tomorrow." A wave of desolation swept over her.

"Then perhaps they thought you would bring others or let me out of the garden. Figg told them everything you and Justin suggested. I'm sorry. I don't want you shut up here, either."

"Well, if they imagine I will stay quiet, they will soon learn otherwise!"

"I thought that too. Once."

She regarded him. "How long have you been kept apart from everyone else?" she asked.

"Since I was thirteen years old," he said matter-of-factly.

"Are you Arthur? Sir Cuthbert's elder son?"

"Arthur George Astley," he said with a peculiar relish.

"*Sir* Arthur George Astley," she corrected him fiercely.

He blinked.

"George, they've stolen your birthright from you!" she exclaimed.

"They've stolen your estate and your wealth and your freedom!"

"I'm looking after Hugh. And Hugh is looking after me."

Hugh is looking after Hugh, and possibly Caroline, but most certainly not you! She bit back the words that could only hurt him. Instead, she said, "He only thinks he is. He can't know that you want to go out, beyond the garden."

"I want to go to Africa," he said. "And South America. They have such a variety of plants that won't grow here, apart from in hothouses, sometimes. I'd like to see them. And people with different customs and shelters and a history apart from Europe." He stopped, searching her eyes, which was rare. "You want to see these places, too."

"I would certainly like the opportunity," she said tartly.

"You should have gone with Justin yesterday."

Her mind was so full that she almost missed it. Then she sank down on the narrow bed, staring at him. "How do you know about that?"

"Figg followed him to your room and listened. She told Hugh. They thought I wasn't paying attention."

She couldn't help her distracted smile. "I suspect they think that quite a lot." Something else popped into her mind too, widening her eyes. "And they don't know you can pick the lock and get out of here whenever you like."

"Not whenever I like," he corrected her. "Has to be when Figg is snoring. Otherwise, she hears and I have to lock the door again and hide in bed."

"George, when you get out and sit in the library and drink a glass of port, why do you never go farther?"

"Hugh says people won't like or understand me. That they'll be afraid and hurt me or put me somewhere horrid full of other mad people and give me ice baths and bad food and no books or even a garden. They might even kill me."

"You're not mad, George," she said firmly. "In fact, you are the most rational, logical person I know."

His eyes slid away. "What am I, then?" he asked, with the first shade of bitterness she had ever heard in him.

"Different," she replied. "Eccentric, perhaps. Charming. And clever."

His sweet smile dawned. "Charming? Really?"

She smiled back. "Really."

He sighed. "I'll miss you. But when Nurse starts to snore, I'll pick the lock and let you out. Will you manage from here? Go to Justin, to the vicar."

Another idea was forcing itself on her, making her heart beat too hard while she considered it. But there was nothing truly to consider. What was being done to George—Sir Arthur—was monstrous.

"George…would you like to come, too?"

"To the vicarage?" he said in surprise.

"And beyond, if you wish."

He turned his back, and she wondered if he were afraid or excited or both. At last, he said, "I don't think I could manage on my own, just at first. I've forgotten how to go on. In the world."

He had only been thirteen years old.

"You wouldn't be on your own. Either Justin or I would be with you."

When he glanced back, his eyes were oddly cunning. "Or both of you?"

"Perhaps," she said quickly. She could not even think about that. It was bad enough wondering what he would think of her more or less abducting George. "But the first thing is to get out of this attic, and then out of the house."

CHAPTER FIFTEEN

I N THE PALE moonlight, Justin thought he had found Hera's bedchamber window. But there was no light in the window, or any of the windows round about, so he could not be sure. But the lack of light bothered him. Had she retired early? Or was she still with Lady Astley, or George?

Or was he wrong after all, and she had gone back to Cuttyngs? She could have been sent away, dismissed…

He could not get through the garden door to George's garden to see if his sitting room was illuminated. Someone had locked the door again, with bolts and key. But that was the unused side of the building. He had more chance of getting in from there unseen.

After considerable walking up and down the length of the wall, he found an old tree stump that gave him a little bit of a boost. From there, he was able to reach the top of the garden wall and haul himself up and over. It had been a long time, he reflected, but some skills never left one. And, of course, there had been the odd disreputable effort avoiding irate husbands in Spain, but that was something he refused to recall in the same breath as he thought about Hera.

He lowered himself down the other side, dangling as far as he could before dropping into one of George's flowerbeds. George would not be pleased. Nor was Justin, for he landed somewhat more heavily than he intended and grunted with the effort. Picking himself up, he dusted off his hands and pantaloons from habit and ran along the crazy, curving paths to the house.

Naturally, the French doors to the salon were locked, and he dared not be heard breaking the glass. There were no lights on this side of the house, so George was not in his sitting room. On impulse, he loped further along, trying all the windows, and eventually found one that lifted, although with difficulty. Perhaps it wasn't so surprising. George's garden was so secure that they had little reason to worry about people breaking in, and George himself was watched every minute of his day.

Before he could get angry about that again, Justin eased the sash open as far as he could and climbed through. He landed on the floor with something of a bump, but at least no crash of falling crockery. Unfortunately, the room seemed to be in total blackness. He could see nothing at all and wished he had brought a lantern after all. It had seemed foolish in such bright moonlight.

Then it came to him that he was surrounded by curtains that had fallen back into place as he tumbled into the room. Rising carefully, he drew them back to allow moonlight into the room. Now he could at least make out enough not to fall over the furniture as he moved.

He appeared to be in a long, once-ornate room that joined on to the salon he knew already. Part of a suite of rooms left unused by Hugh and Caroline, in order to control George more easily. There were dust sheets over everything. Clearly, the servants never came in here, would never see George in his garden.

Old Sir Cuthbert, George's own father, must have planned this concealment more than two decades ago. And Hugh had continued it, discovering his brother's talents and making use of them. Justin had never been so glad of his own annoying, interfering, caring brother.

Advancing across the room, he searched in vain for a candle or flint. Surely there would be some at the foot of the stairs, if nowhere else? Providing he could get there without bringing the whole household down around his ears.

Emerging into the main hall, grateful that the door was not locked, he moved toward the main staircase. A pale glimmer of moonlight was visible in the glass above the front door, providing him some sense of direction.

He almost fell over the half-hidden table at the foot of the staircase, and at least one candle fell over with a dull and fortunately light bump. Feeling carefully around, he found an upright candle in its holder, and the flint with which to light it. The striking flint sounded inordinately loud in his ears, but the candle ignited, and he heard nothing stir.

With the light, he could move much faster, running quickly upstairs to the first landing and rounding the corner toward the next flight that led to the bedrooms. But quite suddenly, he was aware of sounds above him, a swishing of fabric, soft footsteps on the stairs, and the glow of a candle.

Immediately, he blew his out and stepped back into the gloom beside the banister. Two people were creeping down the stairs. It came to Justin that he really did not want to be caught sneaking around the house of his father's neighbor. It would do nobody's reputation any good, and as for damaged careers…

He tried to breathe silently—difficult when his heart was racing—and hold perfectly still.

At last, a tallish man emerged, his head turned away from Justin, toward his companion and the next flight of stairs. He was fully dressed in rough clothing. Without warning, the man spun around, holding the candle high.

George's amiable, startled face lit up in the glow. And beside him, wide-eyed, was Hera.

She emitted a little gasp, whether of recognition or horror, he couldn't tell.

"Justin," George whispered. "What are you doing here?"

"Looking for you," Justin whispered back. "Where are you going?"

George smiled. "We're running away."

Justin's gaze flew to Hera's. She stared back at him, her mouth firm with determination. Several thoughts flew through his head. Triumph that George was breaking free, anxiety as to how he would cope, and how Hugh would react. In Justin's opinion, George was not mad, but he was certainly different, which meant Hugh could probably make some kind of case of abduction of his ward. Only, Justin knew no courts had been involved in his assumption of guardianship. Legally, George did not exist.

But George deserved to more than exist. He deserved to *live*.

Without a word, Justin stepped forward, lit his candle from George's, and took Hera's bag from her fingers. At first, they showed a tendency to resist, then hastily withdrew, as if his touch was too abhorrent.

She had accused him of abandoning George and sent him away for unforgivable presumption.

No one spoke as they hurried down the stairs and across the hall to a side door. They paused only long enough to light a lantern from one of the candles, and then blew out both candles and closed the door behind them. In silence, Justin led them the back way to the village, avoiding the drive and the gates.

"I remember this way," George said excitedly at last. "I used to run down here as a boy."

"Well, I wouldn't run now in the dark," Justin advised. "Why are you running away?"

"They locked Miss Severne in the attic, too. That isn't right."

Justin's breath caught. "No," he said, glancing from George to Hera. "It isn't. Why did they lock you in the attic?"

"They thought I would try to change things, tell people about George," she replied.

"What…" He cleared his throat and turned back to George. "What are your plans? Where do you want to go?"

"Africa," George said. "South America."

"He means more immediately," Hera told him.

"Oh, well, immediately, we were going to the vicarage," George said.

It has hard to tell in the lantern light, but Justin thought Hera might be blushing. But then, so might he. She had been coming to him, in spite of everything. She trusted him with George.

Even though this complicated everything, he smiled because she was safe and there was still hope, though of what, he had no idea. And, damn it, he was glad for George.

Hera's chin tilted in a way he recognized. "Why were you in the house?" she asked. "And how did you get in?"

"I came to find you because the servants told me you'd left the hall, and I didn't believe them. And I climbed in a window from George's garden. How did you get out of the attic?"

"George picked the lock," Hera said proudly. "He's very good at it."

"The secret is to wait until Figg snores," George said seriously. "Otherwise, she hears. No one else hears anything."

The gross cruelty and injustice took Justin's breath away all over again. "Well, let's stick to your plan in the first instance. We'll go to the vicarage and have tea, or hot chocolate, and make plans."

He led them in by the back door to the kitchen. George gazed about with interest as Justin lit the lamps and invited them to sit, while he stirred up the stove and put the kettle on. Part of him recognized George's nervous excitement—after all, it had been more than twenty years since he had left Denholm Hall. But mostly, Justin was aware of Hera's watching him as he went about the mundane tasks of heating water and milk.

When he glanced at her, she hurried into speech. "George knows he is really Sir Arthur. But he believes Hugh was protecting him, and he has been glad to help Hugh in return."

Justin's lip curled involuntarily. *Protecting him from what?* But, catching sight of the warning in her eyes and the agitation in George's, he bit the words back. "And now?" he asked mildly.

George shook his head. "Can't do the same to Miss Severne. It isn't right."

"It isn't really right for you either, George," Justin said gently. "You are allowed to choose how you want to live. And I don't think you want to be locked in the attic and forbidden every other place except one sitting room and your garden."

"I'll miss the garden," George said.

Justin brought over pots of tea and chocolate and set them on the table along with cups, saucers, and plates. Then he brought some milk and honey, bread and cake, and sat down.

"You don't have to miss it," Justin said, "not in the long term. You are Sir Arthur, Sir Cuthbert's heir. All the Denholm estate belongs to you."

"If I can prove who I am," George said unexpectedly.

Justin held his gaze. "And can you?"

A smile flickered and vanished. "Yes. If I want to. May I have hot chocolate, please?"

Hera set down the teapot and poured him a cup of milky chocolate.

"I've stirred up a hornet's nest of solicitors on your behalf," Justin said. "One of whom is excellent at difficult investigations. But they will do nothing you do not wish."

Hera's gaze lifted to his face. Although he refused to look at her directly, from the corner of his eye, he saw her whole face seemed to glow. He felt like basking in the warmth of her approval. She had thought he was abandoning George. And up to a point, she was right. He couldn't save everyone. But he could do something.

George said, "I don't want to fight Hugh. I want to look after him, still."

"Well, maybe you should think how best to do that," Justin murmured. "I'm sure my father will be happy to let you stay here, but Hugh has large servants. They could simply take you back by force. Or you could stay somewhere he's unlikely to find you, while you do your thinking."

George looked at him anxiously. "Where will you be?"

"Brussels."

George nodded. "Fighting Bonaparte."

"Yes. Well, patching up the wounded who will be fighting Bonaparte." Justin swung his gaze to Hera, who was now chewing her lower lip like a schoolgirl. Catching the direction of his gaze, she stopped immediately, and he found it hard to look anywhere but at her mouth. He cleared his throat. "Perhaps your stepmother would invite George to stay at Cuttyngs."

"I don't think she's there," Hera replied, coloring under the intensity of his gaze. "But Victor would. Actually, George, you and Victor would probably like each other!"

"Who is Victor?" George asked.

"My brother." She drew in a breath. "Actually, he's the Duke of Cuttyngham. And I'm afraid I'm not really Miss Severne. I'm Lady Hera Severne."

George looked only faintly surprised. "Like I am really Sir Arthur Astley?"

"Something like that."

George glanced at Justin. "I suppose you are really the prince regent?"

Justin laughed. "No, I'm plain old Justin Rivers. Do you really remember me from our childhood?"

"I never forget anything or anyone. Though you *are* different now."

"I should hope so! So would you like to stay at Cuttyngs with Lady

Hera and her brother?"

George considered. "Actually, I'd rather go to Brussels."

Justin blinked. "Why?"

"My old governess is there. Mademoiselle Villière. She is part of my proof."

Hera closed her mouth. Justin knew how she felt. At last, she said faintly, "Then you will fight Hugh?"

"If I need to. Can't lock ladies in the attic."

"Quite right," Justin said hastily. "My only concern about the Brussels scheme is that I will have duties, possibly far away from you."

"And I won't know how to go on, just at first," George said, almost as though repeating a catechism. "Perhaps Lady Hera could come, too."

"Lady Hera," Justin said, "cannot travel unchaperoned with two gentlemen."

"But she may pick up a maid anywhere on the journey," Hera pointed out. "No one need know I did not start out with one. But I think the quicker we leave St. Bride, the better for George."

"Hera…" Honor compelled him to dissuade her from doing anything that might hurt her reputation, and yet his heart was singing because she wanted to come. Whether it was for George or him, he didn't mind at that moment. He just wanted her with him.

And she could not be.

"Yes?" she said haughtily. But it was too late. He had read the light of adventure in her eye, and it spoke quite recklessly to his own.

He laughed. "Let us take George to Brussels!"

At that point, the kitchen door opened, and Philip appeared in his dressing gown. "Justin?" he said. He then stopped abruptly, a half-finished yawn vanishing into his hand. "I thought I heard voices… Miss Severne!"

He blushed to be greeting her en déshabillé, which caused Justin to emit a crack of laughter. At which Philip, with a glance of brotherly dislike, pulled himself together.

"Is something wrong?" he asked. "Shall I wake my wife?"

"No, no, please don't," Hera said at once. "Dr. Rivers is looking after us very well."

"Miss Severne finds herself in the position of having to leave Denholm Hall in a hurry," Justin said smoothly, but even then, he knew it would not be enough explanation.

"And this…gentleman?" Philip inquired, gazing at George, who had sprung to his feet in the manner of a schoolboy before an adult.

Justin sighed. "I *would* introduce you and tell you where he is going, but then you would have to lie."

Philip met his gaze until his scowl dissolved into a sardonic twist of the lips. "Is this lie in a good cause?"

"Yes."

"Then you had better tell me."

So Justin did.

By the time they left the vicarage, Philip had dressed. He walked with them to the inn, where he helped persuade, cajole, and threaten the ostler into preparing the horses and an ancient coach, which Justin drove himself.

Leaning down from the box, he took his brother's outstretched hand. "You'll give Father my farewells, and apologies? I *will* write."

"Of course. It's an iniquitous crime, but I hope you're doing the right thing."

"So do I."

Philip's face lightened. "I'm glad she is with you."

Justin's brows flew up. "Now that was where I was sure you would object."

"You see? You don't know everything, little brother."

Justin smiled. "I don't. Thanks, Pip." He straightened, and when Philip stood back, he set the horses in motion, driving them out of the yard and onto the road to the port of Boston.

✦✦✦✦✦✦

NURSE FIGG DID not trust the Severne girl, so, having left the breakfast in George's sitting room, she listened at the attic door for sounds of anyone lurking right behind it. Hearing nothing, she slid her key into the lock—and only then realized the door was unlocked.

Her heart seemed to fall all the way into her shoes. Her throat dried up with fear. Opening the door very slowly, she began to climb the stairs.

"Mr. George?" she warbled. "Miss Severne?"

No one answered. And she knew in her heart, before she even looked, that both bedchambers and dressing areas were empty.

With a cry halfway between a sob and a wail, she hurried back down the stairs, closed the door, and fled down the back staircase before waddling and puffing her way to the breakfast parlor.

If she still hoped for anything, it was that she could tell Lady Astley first, and not have to break the news herself to Sir Hugh. But by ill luck, they were breakfasting together, her ladyship reading letters over her coffee, Sir Hugh with a newspaper folded beside his plate.

Involuntarily, Figg let out another sob of distress as she whisked herself into the room and closed the door.

Leaning heavily against it, she uttered, "They've gone."

Sir Hugh ignored her.

Lady Astley sighed. "What has gone where, Nurse?"

"Mr. George and the girl! They've vanished."

That got even Sir Hugh's attention. For an instant, they both stared at her. Then, almost as one, they stood and bolted from the room, brushing past a maid with an empty tray who had to flatten herself against the wall to let them pass.

"Clothes," Sir Hugh said between rigid lips. "Are their clothes gone?"

Nurse looked. "He's taken fresh linen and a change of outer

clothes. Soap. Tooth powder. Brushes." She made her way past Lady Astley into the smaller room and looked in the drawers. They were all but empty.

Sir Hugh swung on his wife. "Go to the vicarage. Take Figg and—we shall have to risk it—two of the footmen. If George is there, bring him back."

"Why would he be at the vicarage?" asked Lady Astley, bewildered.

"Because Justin bloody Rivers is at the bottom of this! And in case we're too late, I shall go to the inn and discover where the devil they've gone."

"And follow them?" Lady Astley asked. "Seriously?"

"Seriously. *She* doesn't matter. She's a hysterical nobody with no family, whom no one will believe. But it is absolutely imperative that we get George back as soon as humanly possible."

Lady Astley said what they were all thinking. "Dr. Rivers was going to Brussels."

"Surely he would not hamper himself with George as well as the girl? But if we have to," he added grimly, "we will go to Brussels, too."

CHAPTER SIXTEEN

Hera's first impression of the continent of Europe was that it was full of British people. And soldiers of many nationalities, although the ones she spoke to were largely from British regiments. Justin was known to several of them, who greeted him with cheerful irreverence but never, she noticed, disrespect, even among more senior officers.

They finally arrived in Brussels late in the afternoon and found rooms in a cramped hotel, where George, exhausted, went straight to sleep.

"Do you want to rest also?" Justin asked her at the door of her own chamber. "If so, I can ask them to wake you in time for dinner."

They had lived in such cramped quarters, thrown so much in each other's company, that she suspected he must need time to himself. "Oh, I'll find something to do."

"And I. I feel if I don't stretch my legs now, I'll never walk again! Do you want to come?"

It was a casual but quite genuine invitation, and she could not help smiling. "Oh, I do! Give me five minutes to change my dress and I'll meet you in the foyer."

Feeling somewhat refreshed and excited, she left the hotel on Justin's arm, and they strolled around the nearby streets to get their bearings.

"Will you go in search of your old regiment tonight?" she asked.

"Tomorrow is time enough. I know where they are now, and I can start gathering supplies. There is no sign of an imminent march. But it could come suddenly, so we need to find somewhere for both you and George to be comfortable. The maid you rescued in Boston is useful, but I think you really need a companion or a housekeeper…"

The "maid," a skinny, rather grubby girl called Ruby whom they had found hiding on the docks from some unspecified threat, had been more than happy to go anywhere with Hera for a sandwich. Since they had no time to find someone more suitable, Ruby had been recruited, washed, re-dressed, and lectured if not into submission, then at least into not stealing. So far. Hera rather liked her.

Hera said, "If we have a housekeeper, then we'll need a house. I don't know what our chances are with the town bursting at the seams! Ghent might have been better."

"I'll make inquiries."

"So will I. You have enough to do, and I imagine you are not planning to stay with us!"

"No, I'll make camp with the men. As long as you are comfortable with George?"

Actually, George had been something of a revelation on the journey. Sometimes his whole body had shaken, sometimes with nerves or downright fear, but usually with so much excitement mixed in that Hera had no doubts they were doing the right things for him. He had slept as soon as Justin bribed them passage on a cargo ship about to sail, and that seemed to help his adjustment to the unfamiliar surroundings and noises and the strange rolling of the vessel.

There was no passenger accommodation as such, though the captain had let them make up little cubicles from the crates and boxes in the hold. And he'd provided lots of bedding, more than they needed, so Hera had used blankets to make doors for their "rooms." They had even set up a table at which they took their rations, getting George used to the idea of eating with people.

Interestingly, Ruby treated him with the same suspicious respect she accorded Justin.

The seamen had taken to George with casual friendliness, letting him play cards with them on deck. He beat them quite often and was boyishly pleased, although he was never ill-mannered enough to gloat. In all, the voyage had been a successful introduction to other people, although the land journey afterward had stressed him more. Hera wasn't surprised. Transport was difficult, even now that most of the gathering soldiers were in their proper camps, for the various armies had taken most of the horses and vehicles available.

"I think George will be fine," Hera said cautiously. "My problem is to find a reason for him living in my house! The town is full of British people who will know he is not my brother. Victor does not mix in society, but the world knows he is lame."

"An unjust way to be recognized," Justin replied. They walked into a large green park, scattered with paths and well-to-do people strolling in the sunshine. It reminded Hera of Hyde Park at the fashionable hour. "Perhaps lodgings with another family would be best. Or we could even stay on at the hotel. It's comfortable enough."

"It would save moving George again," she said. "I'm just not sure he will take to the constant noise and movement as people come and go."

"At the moment, he is interested enough not to mind."

"He goes to sleep when he is anxious," Hera pointed out. "And he is asleep."

"We'll see how he is in the morning. I shan't abandon you, you know." He smiled down at her as he spoke, and her heart gave one of those little somersaults that she never quite got used to, no matter how often they struck.

He had barely touched her on the journey, although they had developed a quiet, companionable closeness that included George, and brought its own gladness. At times like this, though, it wasn't enough. She wanted his strong arm around her, holding her close. She wanted those smiling lips on hers.

"Rivers!" someone shouted, and they both looked up, startled.

Another couple, also arm in arm, were approaching along the path in front of them—a young officer and a lady in dark blue who began to look weirdly familiar.

"Butler!" Justin sped up, throwing out his free hand, which the officer seized with enthusiasm.

Mr. Butler's companion and Hera stared at each other in shock.

"*Your Grace?*" Hera said, for some reason unable to believe her eyes. Perhaps because her stepmother looked so beautiful, glowing with vitality and a happiness Hera had never seen in her before.

The duchess tried to smile, drawing in a deep breath. "Not *Your Grace* anymore," she said firmly. "I have just married Major Butler. Giles, my stepdaughter, Lady Hera Severne."

Major Butler. Abruptly, the name hit her like a club.

The infectious smile on the officer's handsome face faded as he turned from Justin to her and bowed with strange care. "Lady Hera."

"Major Butler," she whispered, whipping her gaze back to Justin. "Major Butler who—"

"Yes," Justin said gently. "Major Butler fought the duel with His Grace, your father."

"Oh…" Shocked and fascinated, she gazed from the lean, good-looking officer to her stepmother. "I know we meant to forgive him, but you *married* him?"

Her Grace—how long before she would stop thinking of her as Her Grace?—glanced nervously around her. "Don't make a scene, Hera, for all our sakes."

"Oh, I'm not going to," Hera assured her. "I'm just…flabbergasted. How? Does everyone know?"

"It's a long story. I wrote to Victor and to you, though you've clearly crossed with my letter. But yes, society here is aware of our marriage and has not yet crucified me. We have the Duke of Wellington and the Duchess of Richmond to thank for that, largely."

"And your own dignity," Major Butler added. "And the war. Can't revile the soldiery until Bonaparte's defeated. For what it's worth, Lady Hera, I deeply regret the death of your father. God knows I would undo it if I could."

Hera blurted, "Justin doesn't think you killed him at all. He thinks His Grace was poisoned before the duel."

"Poisoned!"

"We can't discuss this here," Justin said hastily. "Where are you staying?"

"With a Mrs. Edwards," said Her Grace. "We're pretending she's my cousin, though she isn't really. Come for dinner. She won't mind."

"Um, we have someone with us whom we can't leave alone for too long," Hera said.

"Bring them, too," Her Grace said. "Who are they?"

"Sir Arthur Astley," Justin said with some relish. "And you'll understand all when you meet him. Perhaps you should show me where you live, and then I'll walk back and fetch him, or at least tell him I'll be late back to the hotel."

Still dazed, Hera found herself walking beside her stepmother. "Your Grace," she began in a rush.

"Perhaps you should just call me Rosamund. I don't mind if you find Mrs. Butler too difficult."

"It isn't that," Hera assured her, surprised by the hurt Her Grace—Rosamund—could not hide. "For some reason, Mrs. Butler seems much more formal than *Your Grace!*"

"I expect you have a thousand questions," Rosamund murmured ruefully.

"All intrusive and personal."

"Talking of which, why are you in the company of Dr. Rivers

without the remotest shadow of a chaperone?"

"*You* are my chaperone, Stepmama."

Rosamund let out a little crow of laughter. "So I am! At last. I wonder if Mrs. Edwards would let you stay? She is terribly good-natured, as I have cause to know."

"She'd have to let George stay, too."

Rosamund frowned. "Who is George?"

Hera began to laugh.

⤛⤜

THE FIRST PART of the story was told on the walk to the Edwardses' house—how Hera had applied for the position of companion on the day the duke died, and how she had been offered and accepted it with Victor's good will. By the time they reached the house on a quiet residential street, still close to the center of town, Hera was telling them about her duties and George's excessive supervision.

Rosamund was clearly eager to hear more, and all but dragged Hera to her sitting room. The men followed, and Major Butler issued everyone a glass of sherry, before gazing expectantly at Hera for more. By the time she got to herself being shut in the attic, both he and Rosamund were outraged and all but cheered her escape with George and Justin.

"Good Lord," Rosamund said faintly. "I feel my own adventures are quite tame by comparison! What do you mean to do now?"

"In the short term," Justin said, setting down his glass, "I had better go back to the hotel and George."

Rosamund jumped up. "Let me speak to Mrs. Edwards and the cook. One moment, only…"

In the end, Mrs. Edwards came herself to welcome them. A much younger woman than Hera had expected, she did indeed seem to be thoroughly good-natured, and on excellent terms with both

Rosamund and her very odd choice of new husband. Justin was dispatched to invite Sir Arthur and bring him back if desired.

Mrs. Edwards bustled off to give her husband and niece the good news, taking Major Butler with her, no doubt in the belief that the stepmother and daughter would appreciate privacy. Hera wasn't sure she did.

"I have just realized I am not dressed for dinner," she said, hoping it didn't sound like nervous small talk.

"I won't change my dress either, then," Rosamund said. "The Edwards and Izzy may, just because they are always at parties in the evenings. Do you hate me for marrying him, Hera?"

Hera could no longer avoid thinking about it. "Of course I don't hate you!" In fact, the very idea distressed her.

Rosamund said, "It happened too quickly, and absolutely at the wrong time, though I doubt there is ever a correct time to marry the man who shot your husband."

"Except in tales of old where he carries you off over his saddle bow," Hera said.

"He didn't quite," Rosamund said with a fleeting smile, "although we did rescue each other a few times. But I do love him, Hera. I never loved anyone before."

Hera nodded, a lump forming in her throat because she understood. And because, despite how little she deserved it, her stepmother was trusting her. Hera understood so much now. "He adores you."

Rosamund blushed. "I hope so."

"You deserve it," Hera muttered. "And to be clear, I could never hate you. I know how His Grace treated you, how helpless he tried to make you... And us, Victor and me. But you should know that you made a difference to us. Somehow, our life was better just because you were in the house. An ally we could not admit to."

Rosamund waved her hand in a quick, nervous gesture, as though dismissing the distressing past. "I was little more than a child myself when I married him. I didn't understand at first the damage he did to you and Victor. When I did, my intervention only made it worse."

"No. He stopped maligning Victor in public after you told him how bad it made him look."

"Did he?" Rosamund looked surprised.

"Yes. And...and I should have asked for you to present me in London, but I was too selfish. I knew His Grace would have to come too. With the Hadleighs I was in a different house, and he could abdicate responsibility to them. But you were still stuck in Cuttyngs."

"It is past," Rosamund said with finality. "And you and I can both look forward."

"Not quite," Hera said lightly. "I want to know how you came to meet Major Butler in the first place!"

Hera was laughing with delight at the story by the time they went to join the rest of the family in the drawing room. She was introduced to Mr. Edwards and to Mrs. Edwards's lively and pretty niece, Miss Izzy Merton.

And shortly after that, Dr. Rivers and Sir Arthur Astley were announced. Although George, now wearing Justin's spare coat that was too big for him, looked quite tense and agitated, he bowed and said the right things to his hosts. Justin stayed beside him, and Hera led the conversation away from him to give him time to settle and feel comfortable. A glass of sherry seemed to help, although the contents vanished with rather alarming speed.

Fortunately, they did not go into dinner formally, so Hera was able to walk in beside George and sit beside him. He ate with rather studied concentration, as though the familiarity of food was a lifeline.

Hera, wondering if they had pushed him too far, too soon, murmured, "Are you comfortable, George? Shall we make an excuse and leave?"

"Oh, no," George said, and reached for his wine glass. He wasn't yet used to facing the unfamiliar, but in his own way, he seemed to be enjoying the challenge. He lowered his glass, looking surprised.

"You don't like the wine, sir?" Mr. Edwards said genially. "I'll have them bring you something else, if you'd prefer."

"On the contrary, I like it very well," George said. "Never really cared for wine before, but this, I like."

Mr. Edwards beamed. He was not what Hera's family would have called a gentleman, being something of a self-made man in trade who had married into gentry. She suspected he was more used to polite disdain than praise from people of rank.

Across the table, her eyes met Justin's, and she knew they were both proud of George.

"Where is it you are staying, Lady Hera?" Mr. Edwards asked her.

"The first hotel that had rooms! We plan to look around tomorrow, though."

"Oh, you could stay with us!" Izzy Merton beamed. "Couldn't she, Aunt?"

"The rooms are rather small," Mrs. Edwards said hesitantly, "but I suppose it would be pleasant to be with your stepmama. In fact, if we alter..."

"It would be good for Mrs. Butler too," Izzy interrupted blithely. "When the world sees how friendly the duke's daughter is..." She broke off under her aunt's glare and blushed. "Sorry," she muttered. "I was thinking aloud."

"Sensibly, I must allow," Hera said. "Though I fear it would make you too cramped, Mrs. Edwards!"

"Not at all!" Mrs. Edwards insisted. In fact, her eyes sparkled at the prospect of having another titled person under her roof. "Please consider our house as yours."

"Only if you agree not to turn anyone out of their rooms for my benefit," Hera said. "And I should tell you I also have a maid who is not yet quite trained."

Justin grinned at this description, but she avoided his eyes.

Mrs. Edwards thought rapidly, while the servants removed the first course and brought in the fish. "We can make use of the ground-floor study as a bedchamber. If you should not object to being so close to the kitchen, Dr. Rivers?"

"You needn't include me at all, ma'am," Justin said. "I will have my own arrangements with the army. But if you have room for Lady Hera and Sir Arthur, I own my mind would be considerably the lighter."

Mr. Edwards smiled. "Then that is settled. You'll accept the invitation to stay, sir?"

George looked from Hera to Justin and back. Hera, reading no dislike in his eyes, nodded very slightly. "Thank you, you're very kind," he said formally.

"What do you think of *this* wine, sir?" Mr. Edwards asked him, pouring from a different bottle that had been opened for the new course.

Obediently, George tried it. Again, his eyes widened. "Delicious. You know I think Hugh must have bought inferior wines. Do you think so, Hera?"

"Actually, yes," she said, "though perhaps you shouldn't give him away."

Justin snorted.

Rosamund said, "What did you mean about His Grace being poisoned, doctor?"

It seemed their hosts, even young Izzy, were deep in the Butlers' confidence.

"It was merely a possibility that struck me," Justin said at last. "I have no proof either way, and little chance of ever obtaining any. But I keep thinking back to the morning of the duel." He swung around to Major Butler. "Did it not seem to you that the duke held himself very stiffly?"

Butler thought. "Well, yes, but it was the nature of the man. And he was about to fight a duel. I was pretty tense myself."

"You think he might have been in pain and hiding it?" Rosamund asked.

"It crossed my mind," Justin admitted. "But I might simply be trying to fit the facts to my suspicions. I've written to Frostbrook and Anthony Severne for their thoughts, and I intend to speak to your seconds, too, Butler. I don't suppose they've mentioned any such thing?"

"Well, no, but they're liable to jump at any chance of—er…getting me off," Butler said, "so I'm not sure how much use they would be. Anthony Severne is here in Brussels, though."

"He came to stop my marrying Giles," Rosamund put in, "but is now resigned to the marriage."

"Good. I'll speak to him again." Justin nodded, then turned back to Butler. "One more thing, though. There was a woman watching the duel from not very far away. Do you have any idea who she is?"

"No, but I saw her too," Butler said. "I think she was young, though I couldn't make out her face. Was she staying at the inn?"

"I never saw her there. But it struck me…" He trailed off with a quick, apologetic glance at Mrs. Edwards and Izzy. "Forgive me—this is hardly a fit conversation for your dinner table. I have grown too used to speaking my mind. Where are you off to this evening, Miss Merton?"

Only after their hosts had gone out for the evening, and Major Butler accompanied Justin and George to the hotel in order to bring back Hera's baggage, did the conversation about the mysterious lady resume.

"If she was His Grace's mistress," Hera said bluntly, "she might well have had reason to poison him."

"A lover's tiff?" Rosamund said.

Hera's mind boggled to imagine her father in such a situation. "Did he *have* a mistress?"

Rosamund shrugged. "Anthony would know. Have you any idea how bizarre it is for you and I to even be having this conversation? Apart from anything else, you are not supposed to be aware of such things. We shall leave the questioning of Anthony to your Dr. Rivers."

Hera flushed. "He is not *my* Dr. Rivers!"

"Isn't he?"

Hera opened her mouth, then closed it again. "He would be the first to tell you it was impossible."

"Nothing is impossible," Rosamund said. "Look at me!"

CHAPTER SEVENTEEN

IN THE MORNING, Butler appeared at the hotel again, this time to help transport George and his things to the Edwardses' house. After which, Justin intended to accompany Butler to the camp beyond the town.

Justin was delighted to be in Butler's company again and looking forward to his reunion with many other old friends. On top of that, he was glad to have ensconced Hera with her stepmother, and he thought the relaxed Edwards house would be excellent for George, as long as he had his own space. The duchess—Mrs. Butler—had said something about a kitchen garden where she was growing herbs. Hardly on the scale of George's garden at Denholm Hall, but no doubt he could make some improvements.

Everything, in fact, was working out better than Justin could have hoped when he first found Hera and George escaping their attic prison in the middle of the night. So why, as he accompanied the luggage in the Edwards's borrowed coach, did he feel a large knot of anxiety in his stomach, an inexplicable sadness in his heart?

Because he had left home again? Because he didn't know how vindictive Hugh Astley would be toward his father?

Or because he was about to leave the woman who had been constantly in his company and his thoughts?

All of those. But the one that twisted so painfully was leaving Hera. He had always known this mad dash to Europe in her company was reckless, even foolish, but the encounter with her stepmother had brought the truth home to him with all the force of a punch to his gut. A lady's reputation was not a game, however much he might deride "propriety" as pointless hypocrisy. And the duchess's shock had told him so without words. He might not have touched Hera on the journey, but nevertheless, he had behaved like a scoundrel.

There was feeling between them. Too much. He should never have allowed that to develop, never flirted with her, never kissed her. But her company, the teasing possibilities of a future, had been too beguiling. And plain wrong.

By a stroke of good fortune, she was now safe with her stepmother. He owed her an apology and the decency to step back from her life before he made matters even worse.

The short journey was soon accomplished, and everyone spilled out at the Edwards's house. Justin kept his own bags separate, while servants carried in George's and the rest of Hera's.

Mrs. Edwards herself showed George to his bedchamber, which was quite small but bright, and looked over the gardens, before bustling off about her other household duties. In the Edwards's garden below, Justin glimpsed Hera and Rosamund Butler, apparently deep in conversation about plants. Fresh pain flooded him.

He turned away before either saw him. "You'll be comfortable here, George?"

"You're going?" George said with a first hint of anxiety since arriving.

"Yes, but not forever. I'll call whenever I can. And, of course, Hera will be here."

George nodded. "If I am the baronet, I should have money to pay my way."

"Indeed you should. We need the solicitors to sort that out, though. It may take some time. Hera and I will see you right until then."

"I need new clothes, don't I?" George said ruefully.

"If you want to cut a dash."

George laughed and clapped him on the shoulder. And Justin, his heart growing heavier by the step, went to say farewell to Hera.

As he stepped out into the little garden, he all but bumped into Butler coming in, hand in hand with his wife. Neither of them looked remotely embarrassed to be caught in such a display of affection.

In fact, Butler grinned. "I'll wait for you in the hall. Ten minutes?"

Justin nodded curtly and kept walking. He found Hera crouched beside an herb garden, pulling up weeds with her bare hands, much as she had done in George's garden at Denholm Hall. She looked up and smiled at him, and his heart turned over.

"Rosamund is making use of the herb garden," she said. "She makes potions and pastes for the sick and injured. She always has, but now she wants to use them to help Major Butler and his men. You should speak to her, Justin. Perhaps she can help you, too."

"I expect she can," he said, "providing she tells me what's in them all." He reached down to help her rise, and she took his hand with a faint flush.

"My hands are earthy," she apologized. "Are you going with Major Butler?"

"Yes. There will be a lot to arrange. I'm not sure when I'll be back. Will you manage George?"

"I don't think he needs managing. Just a friend or two."

He couldn't help smiling. "I'll miss you, Hera Severne."

Her expression slipped. "That sounds like more than *au revoir*."

Her brave attempt at humor almost destroyed his purpose, but he held on grimly. "You know it has to be. I shan't abandon you. I'll always help you when needed, but you know as well as I do that anything more is not possible."

She met his gaze. "Anything more?" she repeated. "Such as...?"

"Don't make me say it, Hera."

But she was relentless. "If you have the courage to do it, then the least you can do is say the words."

"Very well," he said, stung. "Your rank and mine are incompatible. No matter what I wish, that will always come between us. I cannot ever ask a duke's daughter to marry me."

"Why not? In case she says yes?"

His lips twisted. "Exactly. I'm sorry. I behaved badly. I should never have touched you. Or kissed you."

Fresh color flared along her delicate cheekbones and spread outward. "Then you are sorry you did?" she challenged. She really thought he couldn't say that either.

"Yes," he said, while his heart ached. "I am very sorry I did."

Her hand flew out so quickly to strike that he almost missed it. As it was, he caught the full force hard against his palm and closed his fingers around hers. But at least she had made things easy now. "Goodbye, Hera."

Only, it wasn't easy at all, for tears brimmed in her eyes, and her whole beautiful face spoke of such misery that *he* might have slapped *her*. The anguish was intolerable. For an instant longer, he let himself gaze at her before he needed to stride away.

And yet he didn't stride. He groaned beneath his breath and yanked her into his arms before bringing his mouth down hard on hers. She gasped into his mouth, and her taste, her smell, her softness against his body, reduced him to raw emotion. To a terrible longing for what could never be. For a moment, startlement held her completely still, and then her lips moved beneath his and her response was absolute.

Passion surged between them, hot and powerful and undeniable, even through the taste of her tears and his own unforgiveable triumph.

"Don't lie to me, Justin," she whispered against his lips. "You can't."

And then she had torn herself free and walked away into the house with her head held high, leaving him alone to control his own desire and shame and utter misery.

FORTUNATELY, THE NEXT few days were so busy that he had little time to dwell on Hera or unrequited love. He was greeted with relief and pleasure by commanding officers and men, some of whom even raised a ragged cheer for him. He had sewn many of them up in the past, although the numbers of raw recruits and untried militias disturbed him. He set about amassing supplies and the means to transport them and worked from dawn until dusk.

In those first few days, he made one brief expedition to the pleasant town of Ghent, and one to Brussels, returning with his cart piled high with bedding, cloth for bandages, and a large supply of buckets and bowls and mops.

At the last minute, Butler joined him on the Brussels trip, leaping onto the cart just as he urged the horse forward.

"Off duty for a few hours," Butler said cheerfully. "Drop me at the Edwards's house, my good man."

Despite his own pain, Justin was glad to see Butler so happy with life. It was a bizarre marriage he had made to the woman he had, at least in the eyes of the world, widowed, but she clearly made him happy. More than that, he seemed content on some deeper level, even with the uncertainty of the charges he faced at home over the duel.

Obediently, Justin pulled up the horse at the Edwards's front door.

"Not coming in?" Butler asked. "One of the servants can hold the horse."

"Perhaps later. Am I collecting you again?"

Butler pulled a face. "Sadly, yes."

They arranged the time, and Justin drove on without once glancing up at the windows where he longed just to see Hera's face.

His first call was at a tall, narrow house where he knew Anthony Severne, heir to the Duke of Cuttyngham, had rooms.

After leaving an urchin in charge of the placid horse and empty cart, he knocked on the front door. He more than half expected to have to push his way into Severne's lodgings, but the landlady, after leaving him standing in the hall for a mere minute, came puffing back down the stairs to beckon him up.

Severne was fully dressed and suave as ever.

"Doctor," he greeted Justin, graciously offering his hand. "I suppose it is unsurprising to see you here, though I admit I had not expected your call."

"Indeed, how could you?" Justin said. "It was Mrs. Butler who told me of your presence in Brussels."

The faintest of spasms crossed Severne's face. Unsurprisingly, the duchess's indecently quick marriage to Butler bothered him. "And what might I do for you, doctor?"

Severne waved him to one of the two uncomfortable chairs in the tiny sitting room and took the other.

"As you know," Justin began, "I have been concerned about the precise manner of His late Grace's death. Yet I have discovered nothing to indicate he was not in perfect health when he challenged Major Butler."

"I did tell you," Severne said mildly.

"All the same, did it not appear to you that his manner on the morning of the duel was markedly different from that of the evening before?"

Severne blinked. "Well, yes. It would be, would it not?"

"I would expect him to be more serious, yes," Justin admitted. "A little grim, even, perhaps covering a very understandable fear with insouciant remarks. I don't recall such remarks, do you?"

"It wasn't his nature," Severne said. "I don't recall any from Butler, either."

"What did His Grace have for breakfast?" Justin asked, clearly taking Severne by surprise.

"Breakfast? Nothing. I doubt that surprises you, either! He wouldn't even drink coffee with Frostbrook and me."

"Why not? Did he have an upset stomach? A pain in his gut?"

Severne stared at him, his gaze no longer supercilious, but still impossible to read. "I very much doubt it, but he did not say one way or the other."

"But he ate or drank nothing that morning?" Justin asked. "Not even a cup of water? A slug of brandy for courage?"

"He didn't need courage," Severne said impatiently. "To be quite frank, doctor, I don't believe he had the imagination to fear his own demise, only to keep his own dignity. He ate nothing, drank nothing that I saw."

"Then he did not seem to you unnaturally stiff, as though in pain?"

"No! He was always a stiff old martinet. What are you trying to prove now? That bad water rather than Butler's bullet killed him? My advice to you, doctor, is to abandon Butler to his fate. He shot His Grace, and His Grace died. No sane person would fail to connect the two, least of all a man of medicine."

Justin smiled. From sheer dislike, he made it rather wolfish. "And how much medicine, exactly, do you know, Mr. Severne?"

Severne sprang to his feet. "Exactly what are you implying, doctor?"

Justin raised his eyebrows. "Why, that your knowledge of medicine is inferior to mine. It was more of a statement than an implication." He rose and bowed slightly. "I thank you for your time. Good morning, sir."

HERA WAS WITH her stepmother and George in the garden when Major Butler strolled out of the back door. With a little gasp, Rosamund dropped her basket and ran to him, only to be wrapped in his arms and swung around in an exuberant circle.

"Why so happy?" she asked. "Is Boney beaten?"

"Because I'm with you, of course. And no, not to my knowledge."

Hera barely absorbed their banter. Her attention was glued to the door, but no tall, sardonic doctor followed Butler into the garden.

"Rivers might call in before he has to collect me," Major Butler said, so casually that Hera knew it must be aimed at her. She appeared to be an object of pity to a man wanted in England for murder. "He's hunting down medical supplies."

George looked up from his gardening only long enough to say good morning. While the Butlers wandered into the house arm in arm, Hera sat on the stone bench and picked up her book. George's silent, unjudging presence was curiously soothing, but still, she was too churned up to concentrate.

They all joined the Edwards for luncheon, and there was talk of a military review the following day.

"We could go, if you like," Rosamund said to Hera. "I'm sure it's patriotic enough for mourning not to interfere, and we might as well show that we approve of each other." She frowned. "Although, actually, I'm not sure that my approval would help you!"

"She doesn't need approval," Mrs. Edwards said. "She has done nothing wrong."

Except travel more or less alone in the company of two men unrelated to her. But hopefully, no one who mattered had witnessed that. Although, now Hera came to think of it, Justin might consider marrying her if she was ruined. Then he might convince himself he was doing his wretched duty.

Rosamund, perhaps seeing the speculation in Hera's face, scowled at her.

Mrs. Edwards said, "And I'm sure it would be quite appropriate for both of you to appear at our party, providing you did not dance. Since you are our guests, it might look odder if you did *not* appear. As if you were quarreling or had something to hide."

When they were alone, briefly, after luncheon, Hera asked her stepmother if she thought Mrs. Edwards was right.

"Probably," Rosamund replied distractedly. "Though she also wants you there as the duke's daughter to improve Izzy's chances in the Marriage Mart."

"Is that likely?" Hera asked.

Rosamund smiled. "Actually, no. But not because of you. Izzy is devoted to a young man in England, and I doubt anyone can turn her from him."

After luncheon, George went to the tailor with Mr. Edwards. It was not the sort of expedition into which Hera could insert herself, and she could not help worrying. She had to content herself with saying hastily to Mr. Edwards, "If he gets agitated or...or strange, just bring him back."

Mr. Edwards looked faintly surprised by the advice, but merely smiled in response.

Hera spent an hour with Izzy, hearing all about her betrothed in England, and rather more interesting adventures explaining how they had first met Rosamund and Giles Butler. In fact, this finally distracted Hera to the extent that she was actually surprised when the drawing door opened and Justin walked in.

He was frowning and brisk, no warmth in his expression, no softness in his naturally hard eyes. Hope died quickly with the remnants of her smile. Anger did not.

"Dr. Rivers," she said coolly, and to the maid who had shown him in, "Tell Major Butler that Dr. Rivers has come to collect him."

If he was surprised by such a cold greeting, he gave no sign of it, merely bowed. It was Izzy who seemed startled and invited him to sit.

"Sir Arthur has gone out with my uncle," Izzy informed him.

Justin's eyebrows flew up, and he glanced at Hera.

She looked out of the window. "They might be back in time for tea," she said.

"What have you been doing today, doctor?" Izzy asked a little desperately as the silence stretched.

"Just buying supplies," he answered.

Hera yawned.

"Oh, you will come to our party, will you not?" Izzy seized on the topic with clear relief. "On Thursday?"

"You are kind to ask me, but I'm afraid I cannot commit my—"

"Ah, that is Rosamund's voice," Hera interrupted, as though quite unaware of her rudeness.

An instant later, Rosamund and Major Butler came in, she laughing at something he had said. In marked contrast to Hera, Rosamund offered Justin her hand in greeting and smiled as she said, "Have you come to take my husband away, doctor?"

"And to tell you I spoke to Mr. Anthony Severne, who claims His Grace neither ate nor drank at all the morning of the duel."

Hera could not help looking at Justin this time, though fortunately his gaze was on Rosamund.

"Could it have been from the night before?" Rosamund asked.

Justin shook his head. "I can think of no poison that would take so long to act."

Butler clapped him on the back. "Then we're back to the original premise. Thanks for trying, my friend."

"Oh, I haven't given up yet. I doubt Severne was with him every moment. I've still to hear from Frostbrook."

It was one of the many things Hera admired about him, that he never gave up. Except on her, apparently. Pain seemed to rise up from her toes, freezing the blood in her veins. She needed him to go quickly. She couldn't bear him to leave again, not like this, and yet if she did not have her pride, what was left? A pathetic, lovesick puddle of a female, and that she refused to be.

"Are you ready to go, Butler?" Justin asked. "Or shall I leave you to follow later?"

Butler sighed. "No, I need to be back this afternoon. Farewell, my lady, Izzy. I expect I'll see you at the review tomorrow."

"Goodbye, major," Hera said with a quick smile, and then turned away toward the window, adding over her shoulder, "Doctor."

Izzy jumped up to accompany the men to the front door.

As the door closed behind them, Hera felt her stepmother's gaze on the back of her neck.

"Have you quarreled with the doctor?" Rosamund asked.

Hera shook her head. "A quarrel would imply some involvement. Some feeling."

"Oh, he has feeling," Rosamund said. "One only has to look at him."

"I suppose contempt is a feeling."

"That is not contempt in his eyes when I catch him looking at you, Hera." Rosamund came up beside her and touched her hand.

"Then what is it?" Hera whispered. "That I am not good enough for him? That he does not wish for a wife? That he lacks the courage to defy the convention that declares us of different rank?"

"Not the courage, never that. The man goes on the battlefield to tend the wounded!"

Her throat ached from unshed tears. "Then it is me. Something lacking in me that allows him to draw a line which he will not cross."

"Honor," Rosamund said with a sigh. "Giles was the same. They think it dishonorable to ask us to marry beneath our own rank."

At last Hera turned her head to meet her stepmother's gaze. "Does he imagine he is saving me for someone like Lord Nimmot, or the Marquis of Tarrleton's son?"

"Possibly, though I doubt he has got as far as individuals."

Hera gave a rather wan smile. "Then I should flirt with men of birth and fortune to make him jealous?"

"Could you?"

Hera thought about it. "No. I only ever flirted with him."

"Oh, my dear," Rosamund said with enough understanding to force the tears into Hera's eyes. "Then perhaps you should not stop. There are times when you cannot leave such matters solely in the hands of honorable men."

AT THE SAME time, as the cart rattled its way through the suburbs of Brussels, Justin was staring grimly at the road and seeing only Hera's cold, dismissive face. He couldn't deny that her manner hurt, nor that he had brought her contempt on himself. He knew that she perceived his standing back from her as an insult, which hurt him as much as it did her, though to explain that would only make the parting harder for her. Let her hate him if it helped her.

Only it doesn't help her, does it? In her manner this afternoon, he saw again the Lady Hera of his very first acquaintance at Cuttyngs. Beautiful, distant, as rude as she needed to be to get her own way. She had intrigued him even then, yet the return of that Hera was unbearable after the delightful, passionate companion he had come to know.

"Made a mess of things with Lady Hera?" Butler asked.

"Yes."

"You're the physician. There must be a remedy."

Justin's lips twisted. "It's one I cannot use."

"Why not?"

"Because I'm an army surgeon. If all goes well, I have the prospect of becoming a country doctor. She is the daughter and sister of dukes."

"If you want approval for the mess you've made, you're talking to the wrong man. I married the duchess, remember?"

"You've still got the mess," Justin retorted.

"Yes, but I've also got a happy wife, not a face like a smacked arse."

Justin gave a short bark of laughter. "True."

They trundled along into open country until Butler broke the silence once more. "I married Rosamund because I discovered that my honor was about more than myself. I could live with my own unhappiness. I could not live with hers."

Justin closed his eyes, feeling his jaw clench. "Stop," he said between his teeth. "Just stop."

CHAPTER EIGHTEEN

H ERA ATTENDED THE troop review mostly because it was George's first public outing. A food hamper accompanied them so that they could enjoy an al fresco luncheon while watching the soldiers be inspected. But she was amazed by the crowds of fashionable British who had turned out to do likewise. It was like attending a Venetian breakfast at the height of the London Season.

No one cut Rosamund. No one looked overtly disapproving of Hera, either. In fact, she was greeted by acquaintances with surprised pleasure, for the most part. Perhaps because she at least wore dark colors, if not black, and was sitting quietly beside her stepmother in a small party that included only the Edwards and George. George himself caused a little interest, which he carried off with unexpected aplomb. Judging by their expressions on being introduced, none of these people had heard of the Astleys of Denholm Hall.

As luncheon was set out, the soldiers commenced their display of marching and riding in orderly lines. The Duke of Wellington himself watched, apparently relaxed in the company of his staff officers and several beautiful women. Rosamund amused herself by spotting her husband and his friends among the officers.

"Is Justin there, too?" George asked.

"No, Justin is here," said a familiar voice right behind them. By force of will, Hera did not twist around to see him. She did not want

CAPTURED

him to see her flush of pleasure and anticipation.

But she saw George gazing up at him. "Don't you march?"

"Not a soldier," Justin replied.

"Won't you join us, doctor?" Mrs. Edwards invited him. "Have a sandwich. And those little pastries are very good."

"Thank you," Justin said, dropping down on the blanket beside George. "You're looking very fine, Sir Arthur," he said with a quick smile. "New coat?"

George grinned. "Cutting a dash."

Hera picked up the two plates nearest her and offered them to Justin. His surprised gaze flew to hers for a pregnant moment before he took a sandwich with a murmur of thanks. Mr. Edwards passed him a glass of wine.

Hera's stomach was twisted so tightly, she could not eat anything further. Her heart beat hard with excitement, and with her own doubts, because before she had only ever been able to flirt when he began it. She had to remind herself how he had looked at her, how he had kissed her, in order to believe in her own attraction. If he had tired of her, she had nothing to lose but her pride. But if there was a hint of love for her, then she had everything to gain.

She could command him haughtily to walk with her. Or she could aim for lightness? She allowed him time to eat, to talk to George a little, and then, before the conversation could become more general, she rose to her feet.

"I feel the need to walk," she announced. "Your escort, Dr. Rivers?"

If he was surprised, he hid it. He and George had already begun to rise since she had. He replied, "Of course. You'll join us, Sir Arthur?"

Drat the man!

But unexpectedly, George saved the day. "Don't believe I will just yet." And he sat back down again.

Hera, her lips twitching, appropriated Justin's arm and strolled away. There was plenty of space to walk between other parties and onward toward the trees and the road.

"Do you feel the need of protection?" she murmured with undisguised mockery.

"Yes," he said.

"Afraid I shall hit you?" she taunted him.

"It's not you I fear. Do you have something urgent to say to me?"

His words gave her a surge of hope. Rosamund was right—he was being honorable. "Oh, I have many, many things to say to you. My trouble is knowing where to begin. Do I tell you off for stupidity or cruelty? Praise your selflessness? Demand the truth? Because it seems to me there was always honesty between us before, and we owe it to each other still."

"Don't, Hera."

She stared at him. "You are afraid of the truth? *You?*"

The words broke from him, almost inaudible and yet so intense, a shudder seemed to pass through him. "I am afraid of the *hurt*, for both of us."

"Then why are you doing this?" She halted and turned to face him. "If I were to kiss you now, in front of everyone, would you feel obliged to marry me?"

His breath caught. His gaze lingered on her lips, then lifted slowly, deliberately, to her eyes. "I'd be more inclined to take you into the trees and ravish you. Is that what you want?"

She almost laughed because he actually thought his words would scare her away. Instead, they aroused her. "Yes."

Surprised laughter sprang into his eyes, and something else much warmer and more desperate. He drew her on. "You have just escaped the life you saw as a prison," he said. "Don't even think of trapping yourself in marriage to a man like me. You of all people must be aware of the power a husband has over his wife."

"I would not feel trapped. Not with you."

"Maybe not at first. But in six months? Six years? In *my* world, not your own."

"Oh, stop it," she said impatiently. "Do we not breathe the same air? And if you are so concerned for my lost freedoms as a wife, why will you not even listen to me now? What right do you have to make such a decision for both of us?"

They were almost at the line of trees that separated the meadow from the road. He stopped again, as though he suddenly realized she had deliberately led him in this deserted direction. There was an air of harassment about him as he whirled them about to face back toward everyone else.

"What right?" he repeated. "None. Except that you are nineteen years old, and I am almost a decade older and wiser."

Older and sillier! She looked up at him and met his gaze. "Then you don't love me. Say it and I will walk away."

For an instant, pain stared out of his face, turned down the corners of his expressive mouth, breaking her heart. And then it was gone. "It is because I love you that *I* am walking away."

Happiness seemed to explode within her, along with massive frustration. Her fingers tightened on his arm. "Justin…"

But his gaze had shifted, and she didn't know whether to laugh or cry that even at this moment she could not keep his attention. But from instinct, she followed his gaze and saw Rosamund sitting alone on the blanket they had all previously shared. And standing before her, confronting her, were two people, rigid with anger.

"Oh, no," Hera breathed. "That's my aunt and uncle, and they've found Rosamund!"

As one, she and Justin quickened their pace.

"They'll ruin everything for her!" Hera said. "What are they even doing here?"

"Well, half the *ton* is in Brussels already. And I expect they got wind of the marriage."

"Anthony," Hera said with fury. "He was always a wretched snitch! Where is everyone else? Before Aunt Hadleigh destroys what Rosamund has won…"

"Closer to the soldiers. And Butler's with his men."

"That, at least, is probably a good thing."

"If you walk any faster, it is you who will be drawing all the attention."

"Why? I am merely in a hurry to greet my aunt."

Of course, she had already drawn attention. Most who had come to admire the troops were now gleefully watching her rapid approach to her stepmother, or the confrontation they suspected was already taking place between Rosamund and the Hadleighs. A few more blatant gossips were strolling deliberately closer, so Hera opted for distraction.

Raising her hand, she waved like a hoyden and all but dragged Justin with her into a run. "Aunt! Uncle! What a delightful surprise! Why did you not warn us you were coming to Brussels?"

As she had hoped, her behavior halted Aunt Hadleigh in mid rant. She stared at Hera—now holding on to her bonnet with one hand and Justin with the other—and a small spasm crossed her face.

"Hera," she said coldly.

Hera released Justin's arm and all but skipped up to her aunt, kissing first her cheek and then her uncle's. "How wonderful! You will join us, will you not?"

"Allow me to fetch more suitable seats," Justin murmured, veering off toward a couple of abandoned folding chairs close by. He used the opportunity to glare at the approaching nosy couple so hard that they veered away in alarm.

"When did you arrive in Brussels?" Hera asked her aunt with forced amiability.

Lady Hadleigh sniffed.

Her husband said, "Last night."

"We did not even know you were here," Lady Hadleigh said furiously. "Is this—" She flapped one contemptuous hand toward Hera's gray and lavender dress. "Is this your idea of mourning?"

"Half mourning," Hera said pleasantly. She lowered her voice. "Let us be honest. He was really only half a father. Do sit."

"Yes, do," Rosamund invited them as Aunt and Uncle both goggled, speechlessly, at Hera's disrespect. They collapsed rather than sat down on the chairs Justin placed for them with a strange choking sound that may have begun as a snort of laughter.

Rosamund's smile was amiable, though her eyes were not. "It is up to you, of course, but I hope you will consider Hera and Victor before you cause any more scenes guaranteed to bring the family into scandal."

Hera felt a burst of pride in her stepmother.

Aunt Hadleigh almost exploded. "You, *you* dare say that to me?"

"Yes, I do. I hope you remember Dr. Rivers, who called on us at Cuttyngs?"

The Hadleighs barely spared him a nod.

Hera dropped onto the blanket beside Rosamund, declaring her allegiance without words.

Rosamund said, "There is no need to refer to my remarriage. I can guess your views, but they are in a minority here, and if aired will merely provide food for the gossips. Giles and I have the support of the Duke of Wellington, who gave me away, and the Duchess of Richmond. I would rather your outrage did not damage Hera."

"*You* damage Hera," Lady Hadleigh uttered intensely. "Your indecent marriage, your encouraging her to gallivant about the countryside with another nobody, and live in the house of her father's murderer!"

"Mr. Edwards never met my father," Hera said tartly. "As for Giles, I doubt he was even responsible for His Grace's death."

"But speaking of the Edwards," Rosamund said, "here they are.

Allow me to present Mr. and Mrs. Edwards, their niece, Miss Merton, and Sir Arthur Astley. This is Lord and Lady Hadleigh. Lady Hadleigh is the sister of my late husband."

There was nothing the Hadleighs could do or say. They had been essentially roped into the group that had been lent respectability in their eyes by Sir Arthur's name. And now they could not leave it without causing the kind of scene Lady Hadleigh abhorred. Almost spitting mad, she could only nod graciously at the introductions, her mouth thin and rigid.

In the end, she could not even turn her back on Major Butler, who appeared unexpectedly and slightly breathless. Hera greeted him with the air of an old friend and offered him a sandwich.

Justin poured everyone a glass of wine.

JUSTIN HAD CAUSE, over the next few days, to be glad of the Hadleighs' unexpected arrival. Hera's nervous yet impassioned arguments had almost begun to make too much sense to him. Especially when Butler's earlier words were still ringing in his ears: *"I could live with my own unhappiness. I could not live with hers."*

Of course, Butler's situation and Justin's were vastly different. Admittedly, Butler had shot Rosamund's husband in a duel, but Rosamund herself was a widow, and more than nineteen years old. Hera…

Damn it, there was no excuse for what he had done to Hera. But if he walked away now, she would recover and, in time, move on to a better man.

Oddly enough, even that bleak argument stopped making sense to him.

He lost himself in work, building and administering medical supplies, treating the minor illnesses that occurred, and insisting on conditions for the men that would not breed more serious disease. If Hera was never far from his thoughts, at least he did not speak of her, and neither did Justin. In time, the ache of loss would lessen.

He was with Butler and two other officers, MacDonald and Elton, late one afternoon, preparing for a convivial evening with their colonel, when an ensign appeared to distribute post. Mac and Elton seized theirs with joy and departed. Butler tore his open on the spot, so Justin sat down on his truckle bed and broke the seal on the first of his own.

He already knew it was from his father, but he was unprepared, when he unfolded it, for another sheet of paper to fall out. Absently, he bent to pick it up without looking. *My dear Justin*, the letter began…

Butler's hand brushed Justin's off the fallen paper, and he picked it up. "Do you know what this is?"

"Not yet," Justin said impatiently, holding out his hand.

"It's a special license."

"*What?*" Justin's gaze flew to his, then to the document in question. He snatched it.

"It's a marriage license," Butler said amiably. "Made out in your name."

And Hera's. Blood flooded into Justin's face. "Of all the interfering old…"

In case your honor requires it, his father had written. *I have every trust that the lady's does not.*

"Damned honor," Butler said. Rot him, he was laughing at Justin. "Requiring you to walk away, and now demanding that you marry her. What to do?"

"I'm sure you have an answer," Justin said bitterly.

Butler clapped him on the shoulder and sauntered toward the door. "Follow your heart, old boy. It won't let you down."

And for no reason that made any sense, Justin began to laugh.

⟫⟫⟫✦⟪⟪⟪

AN HOUR LATER, Justin turned into the residential Brussels street where resided all his hopes. He was driving the familiar old horse and cart that had been the most easily available mode of transport when he left camp. For the first time, it struck him that this was hardly the equipage of a gentleman, let alone one aspiring to the hand of a duke's daughter—which was amusing when he considered that their disparity in birth and wealth were what had held him back from her. Nor was he dressed for a formal evening, for he had not even changed. Once the way forward had become so clear to him, like the shining light on the road to Damascus, he had simply sent his apologies to the colonel and left camp.

Only now, with the Edwards's house in sight, and his heart, his entire being, in knots of nervousness, did lesser, unimportant anxieties add themselves to the only important one. Would she accept him? Would she punish him first? Or come to her senses and recognize that he was unworthy? Though he deserved the last, he didn't know how he would endure it. Was this how she had felt since their conversation in the garden? He had surely been cruel and blind.

Someone crossing the road in front forced him to slow the horse and pay attention to the present. A carriage was waiting on the left, only a little beyond the Edwards's front gate. Were they going out for dinner? Was Hera going with them, or had he hopes of seeing her alone?

With a jolt of surprise, he saw that George stood at the side of the road, talking to whoever was inside the carriage. The door was open, but George was shaking his head as though declining to enter.

A twinge of unease pierced Justin's personal concerns. George stepped back, almost into the garden wall, just as a large stranger jumped down from the carriage and seized him.

Justin shouted, lashing the reins to make his horse shift. A female whirlwind—Hera?—flew out of the Edwards's gate, but it was too late. Both George and the stranger were inside the carriage, and the horses took off at the gallop.

The cart horse roused itself to a fast trot. Hera—oh yes, it was Hera—spun wildly around, looking for help.

"Tell Edwards!" he shouted to her, and had no time to swerve as she hurled herself at the cart. To his horror, she clung to the side of the vehicle. If the horse stopped suddenly, she would probably be shaken off. Already, it was snorting and shaking its head, annoyed by the weight imbalance pulling at it.

Abandoning the horse to its own devices, Justin threw himself toward Hera, catching her hands and tugging so that he could grasp her under the arms and haul her onto the cart. By then, he had to grab at the reins, since they approached the end of the street, and he hadn't even seen which way the carriage went.

"Left!" Hera yelled, climbing onto the seat beside him.

Justin hauled on the reins, and the horse trundled to the left, so late that they almost collided with a carriage going in the opposite direction. The coachman yelled at Justin. Justin ignored him, for he had had already seen the fugitive carriage some distance in front.

"What is going on?" he demanded. "Who forced George into that carriage? Did you see?"

"Yes." She looked at him, her eyes wide and frightened and yet so brilliant that they caught at his breath. "It was Sir Hugh Astley. I saw him in the carriage. He was talking to George, but George wouldn't get in, and then that other man appeared from nowhere…"

Justin swore beneath his breath. At least, he hoped it was beneath his breath. "What brought you outside in the first place?" he asked, keeping his gaze fixed on the carriage ahead, which turned right.

She shivered. "George and I were going for a walk before dinner. Ruby told me he was waiting outside. The carriage could have been waiting there all day. I never noticed it."

"Hugh must have followed us. Not difficult, since he knew where I was bound. Though I admit I didn't think he'd have the nerve to follow."

"He has everything to lose," Hera said bleakly. "It was George who made the estate profitable, George who told him where to invest. Without George, it all begins to fall apart, and Caroline Astley has no new gowns or jewels to play the grand lady over her friends and neighbors."

"Worse—they probably know George is accepted here as Sir Arthur. They're on notice of charges against them of fraud and false imprisonment and God knows what else. They have nothing left to lose. George alive and free is the worst possible outcome for them."

Her breath caught as his reasoning added to her instinctive alarm. "Faster!"

"This is as fast as the poor old horse goes." Justin veered right and saw no further sign of the carriage except the end of a wheel turning right again. In the absence of any other vehicle, he urged the horse after that one.

This street was teeming with traffic, not least because it ran parallel with one of the wider canals running through the town.

Damnation…

Choosing a direction at random, he turned left. A barge was being pulled along the canal by horses, but no carriage was driving at speed. Justin asked a few pedestrians and the driver of a brewer's dray, making himself understood more by mime than by language, but no one seemed to have seen the speeding carriage. Justin turned into the next street and came around again, pointing the horse in the other direction.

This time Hera asked the question, with appropriate hand gestures, and a woman pointed to a carriage stopped at the side of the road. Its door was open, and the carriage was empty. No coachman sat on the box. The horses, unmoving, seemed glad of the rest.

"They couldn't drag him through the street!" Hera exclaimed. "Unless they hurt him, knocked him unconscious…"

Justin turned his head slowly toward her. "Or bundled him onto a canal boat. They must be taking him back to England. They have no other choice."

"The boat we saw back that way!" Hera cried. "Isn't it sailing toward Ghent and Ostend? Oh, quick, Justin, turn!"

He turned via the back streets once more and set off along the canal.

CHAPTER NINETEEN

THEY WERE SEVERAL miles outside the town before they caught up with the canal boat. By then, it was dark, and since they had no lantern, traveling had become dangerous. On the directions of a farmer who claimed to have seen the boat they sought, they had turned away from the main waterway, along a quieter stretch of water.

"I should take you back to Brussels," Justin said, as though just noticing the dark, and therefore the time. "There's a light shining from what seems to be a farmhouse over there. We could try to beg a lantern off them for the journey."

"We can't just go back and risk them taking George on to England," Hera argued. "Besides, I doubt your poor old horse would last the journey back to Brussels without a rest and a meal… We could let her rest here while we borrow the lantern. She can crop the verge and then be more able to go on."

"Rosamund and the Edwards will be worrying."

"Ruby saw me throw myself at the cart," Hera said ruefully. "They will know I've gone with you. They probably think we're eloping… Justin, are those lights ahead? On the canal?"

She leaned forward peering, as did Justin.

"Yes…and they're not moving," he said with a hint of excitement. "They've stopped for the night, never imagining that we're following still."

"Then we should go on!" she insisted, almost snatching the reins from him.

He let her have them but didn't release the brake on the cart. "Wait here and let the poor old mare rest and eat. We're going to need a light whether we catch up with George or not, so I'll run up to the house."

Although she couldn't bear to be sitting still, she knew he would move faster than her. Still, she felt his loss as he jumped down and vanished into the darkness. After a while, she got down herself and went to the horse's tired head to give her a grateful pat. Her ear flicked, though she didn't stop munching.

The wait seemed interminable, while Hera kept her gaze on the unmoving lights ahead. By the time Justin loomed out of the dark once more, she could only see one light.

"To stop another boat colliding with it, probably," Justin said, one side of the lantern flaring light over his saturnine face. He had covered the other side with some cloth. "Either they've left the boat, or they're sleeping on board."

Together, they moved along the track. Now she could make out the hoof marks of earlier horses, probably those that had pulled Astley's barge. *If* it truly was Astley's barge ahead. They had no proof of that.

Justin took her hand in his free one, and in spite of her anxiety for George, she felt both soothed and warmed. She hadn't even asked him why he had been outside the Edwards's house at just the right time. She was only glad he was.

It took longer than she had thought, but at last they could make out the unmistakable shape of a long, narrow barge. Justin drew her back from the track, where trees supplied some cover. Hera wondered if Hugh Astley had chosen that spot in the hope that the trees would also mask the boat's presence.

"They probably hide it from the main Brussels road, which is just over there," Justin murmured. "According to the farmer I spoke to."

They crept through the trees until they were level with the boat, which sat quiet and unmoving. It was impossible to tell if anyone occupied the space below.

"I'll step on board and poke around," Justin said. "You hold on to the lantern, but keep it shaded. I've memorized my way."

She took the lantern but grasped his wrist with her other hand. "Justin."

"What is it?" He didn't sound impatient, just concerned, and without warning, she wanted to weep, which was foolish as well as unhelpful.

"Be careful," she whispered.

A smile flickered across his face, and he drew her hand to his cheek before releasing her and turning away.

There is hope, she thought in wonder. *There really is. Once George is safe.*

She stared toward the boat, and it seemed to her that something moved on the deck. A shout of warning rose and was quashed. She could not shout in case it warned Hugh on the boat. Instead, she set down the lantern and walked cautiously after Justin, who stopped so suddenly that she bumped into his back.

He seemed to know her at once, for he made no move to defend himself.

"Someone's on the deck," she whispered.

She felt rather than saw his nod. "I know. Wait until the light strikes him."

A sudden, mad idea caught at her breath. *It cannot be...*

The light at the back of the boat briefly touched the man's face as he crept cautiously to the side. It was George.

A breath of laughter shook Justin. "We'll need the lantern," he murmured, and while she went back for it, he moved forward.

By the time she caught up with him again, Justin stood in front of a tree, while George seemed to be searching for something on the deck.

"What the devil is he doing?" Justin muttered.

"Looking for a lantern," Hera said, and risked turning her own.

George paused at once.

"George!" Justin whispered.

George's head jerked and then froze. Hera raised the lantern higher. George grinned and, without a word, stepped off the boat. He loped immediately to Justin, and they gripped each other's shoulders before George's gaze fell on her and his smile widened.

Hastily, she raised her finger to her lips, then led the way back through the trees toward the horse and cart.

"Where is Hugh?" Justin asked him, low-voiced, once they were sure of not being heard.

"On the boat," George said.

"And the big brute?" Hera asked.

"On the boat too. I punched him on the nose."

"Oh, well done," Hera said, then frowned. "That is, as long as he didn't hit you back?"

"No, but it taught him to be more careful around me," George said. "He wanted to put me in the cargo hold, but Hugh made him lock me in a cabin instead."

Justin smiled at him. "Did you pick the lock?"

George grinned back. "I thought he would be too wise to it after we escaped from the attic at Denholm Hall, but they seemed to blame that on Figg not locking the door in the first place." His smile faded. "I lied. I said I would be good, provided they didn't give me the medicine."

"Escaping *is* good," Hera said.

"Exactly," Justin agreed.

A snort in the darkness and the stomp of one hoof warned Hera to raise the lantern. They were almost upon the horse and cart.

"I wondered how you'd got here," George said. "Did you follow us?"

"Lost you in Brussels at the canal, but guessed you would come this way," Justin said, patting the horse's drooping neck. "This poor beast isn't really up to the journey back to Brussels tonight. She needs a proper rest and proper feed. According to the farmer, there's an inn on the main road. We could change her there."

Justin handed Hera up to the seat and climbed up to join her. George hauled himself onto the main part of the cart and lay down.

"George?" Hera said over her shoulder. "Are you…well?"

He appeared to think about it. "I will be after a sleep. Like the horse."

❯❯❯❮❮❮

THE INN WAS easy enough to find, but it had already closed for the night, and neither the innkeeper nor the ostler were best pleased. They insisted they did not "change" cart horses and clearly thought their British visitors were either mad or criminal.

"It will be the middle of the night before we get back to Brussels in any case," Hera said. "Why don't we just stay here for the night?"

"Because you are with us," Justin said. "And even Ruby is not."

"Coming home in the dark will look worse," she said. "Besides, Rosamund will cover for me. And I really think George needs to sleep. In a bed, not a jolting cart."

"You cannot stay here," the innkeeper's wife said, catching the gist of the conversation. "The young lady is not married to either of you!"

The contemptuous way she spoke the word "lady" showed her meaning plainly enough. Hera adopted her haughtiest daughter-of-the-duke look, while George's expression grew grave and Justin snapped, "My good woman, the status of your betters is not your concern. You will provide three bedchambers and hot chocolate. And we shall

214

breakfast at six. Now show us the way."

The innkeeper's wife swallowed, the light of battle wobbling but not quite fading.

"Besides," George said, "the lady is betrothed to me."

Hera turned her head to stare at him, but no one paid her any attention.

The innkeeper's wife threw up both hands but, interestingly, seemed too cowed by Justin's continued glare to object further. Perhaps she feared the long-term damage a refusal could do to her business.

"We only have two bedchambers, milord, but—"

"Two will be sufficient," Justin barked.

While the ostler took care of the cart horse, the humans of the party were shown to two bedchambers and given every comfort they required, including hot chocolate. They drank it together in Hera's room, since it was the largest, with the door quite properly open while the innkeeper, his wife, and the maid all retired to bed, and George told his tale.

"I was waiting for Hera in the street and noticed a carriage waiting there. I assumed it was to do with the house next door, but the coachman called to me, asking me something in French. I went closer, and I saw that the man inside was Hugh."

"Were you glad or frightened to see him?" Hera asked.

George considered. "I was glad to see him. I thought he might have come to apologize to you, and he was kind, at first. Said he and Caroline had missed me."

That was the pity of it, Hera thought, swallowing the lump in her throat. Hugh and Caroline didn't believe George had feelings because they weren't obvious or demonstrative. Yet everything George had labored over and endured at their hands had been done for Hugh. And Hugh just thought he was manipulating the embarrassing family idiot. She could see the anger in Justin's face, too, quickly hidden from

George.

"But then," George continued, "he said I had to go with him in the carriage. I explained that I didn't and wouldn't. Then another man I hadn't even seen seized me and threw me into the carriage. I tried to push my way out again—I saw you in the cart, Justin, and Hera running after me. So, I punched that man in the nose, but Hugh made me sit down and tied my hands together. They bundled me onto the boat so quickly, I didn't know where I was for a bit."

He fell silent. Then, rubbing his forehead, he said, "The movement of the boat was quite pleasant, like the ship when we crossed the sea, only this boat was pulled along the canal by horses. I wished you were there. For one thing, you wouldn't have locked me in a cabin so that I couldn't go on deck."

"That's true," Justin said gravely. "Did you wonder where they were taking you?"

"Home," George answered with a sigh. "Hugh told me from the beginning, said he had to look after me, but I don't believe that's true, do you?" He looked from Justin to Hera and back.

"No," Hera said hoarsely. "He might believe it, but he's thinking of himself, not of you."

George nodded. He didn't appear to be hurt, though it was hard to tell.

"Were you anxious?" Justin asked. "When darkness fell?"

George shook his head. "I knew I could get out when I wanted to. When they moored the boat and took the horses away, and everything went quiet, I knew it would be just like escaping Figg. So, I picked the lock and left. I couldn't find a lantern, though, and had no idea where to go, except back the way we'd come." He smiled with sudden brilliance at Justin. "Then I saw you. You were looking for me. You and Hera."

"Yes, we were."

George finished the last of his hot chocolate with relish. "Do you think they'll give up and go home without me?"

Justin hesitated. "I don't know. I suspect that was merely their opening volley. They may try to force us to give you up to them."

"We won't," Hera assured him. "In fact, we can't. The choice is yours."

"And don't let him frighten you with the law," Justin added.

"I won't. I know the law. I found Mademoiselle Villière, my old governess," George added. "I was going to take you to meet her, Hera, when I ran into Hugh. We can go tomorrow instead. Or perhaps she can come to Mrs. Edwards's house." He stood up. "I'm going to sleep now. Good night."

"Good night," Hera said, smiling at his suddenness.

Justin rose too. "Leave the lamp turned low, if you will," he said to Justin. "I just want a quick word with Hera."

"Of course." George went out and closed the door.

"He is resourceful and courageous," Hera said. "I wonder if Hugh has any grasp of that?"

"More than he had this morning, I imagine." Justin still stood beside one of the two armchairs, gazing at her so intently that she sprang up and walked toward the shuttered window. "You are tired. I shall leave you to sleep. Before I do, I just wanted to say...what I was looking for you earlier to say."

"You were looking for me?" she said quickly, swinging back to face him. With amazement, she saw that he was actually nervous, unsure.

"Yes," he said. "To apologize. To ask forgiveness for my blindness, my condescension, my cruelty to you."

Unreasonably disappointed, she dropped her eyes to hide the fact. "There is no need," she said.

"There is," he insisted. "It was as if a part of my brain was isolated, blocked off from all understanding. I was desperate to do the right thing by you, without seeing what that was."

"And what is it?"

"To ask you to marry me."

Her heart thudded once, then an odd little smile sprang to her lips. "Because George showed you the way by claiming to be my betrothed? Because you think, finally, that marriage to me is now compatible with your honor?"

"No!" He took an involuntary step forward and forced himself to stop again. Surely that was desperation in his eyes? Almost...fear? "Because I love you."

She couldn't bear it. She spun away from him again. "I don't believe you," she whispered. It was true, and she didn't know why. She should tell him to go, but her tongue seemed too dry to speak. She heard him move behind her, inhaled the warm, distinctive scent of him, and when his hands landed lightly on her shoulders, her knees threatened to buckle.

"Forgive me," he said again, low, and somehow emotion seemed to vibrate from his fingers through her whole body. It might have been his, or hers, or some volatile combination. "That you don't believe me is my fault, too. When I first met you, I sensed the kind, warm, passionate person trying to get out. You are all of that, and so much more. Like the other half of me, the better half I didn't even know existed. I tried because I thought it was right, but I cannot bear to walk away from you, not if you feel even a tiny fraction of what I feel for you."

Warmth seeped into her. Dear God, were those his lips on her nape? Soft and beguiling, they teased her skin, sweet and arousing. Her head twisted with a pleasure she could not hide.

"You...love me?" she whispered. Somehow, she seemed to be leaning back against him. His cheek rested against her hair.

"I adore you. I always have. And you have always known."

"I hoped. And then I doubted."

"I'm sorry," he whispered, turning her to face him, his gaze on her lips. "I don't know why you even look at me, but..." As though he couldn't help it, he bent his head and covered her mouth with his.

Long and tender, his kiss ravished her. She clung to him, one hand caressing his nape, the other cupping his rough cheek while she kissed him back with delight and wonder and growing sensuality.

He swept his hand down her back, pressing her closer until her hips fitted against his and she felt the hardness of his arousal. Heat surged within her, exciting, overwhelming. The kiss turned into another, and then another, each more devastating than the last. He shifted her within his arm and slid his hand around to settle over her breast.

She moaned softly with pleasure as he caressed and kissed, and she slid her own hands beneath his coat in search of greater closeness, in search of *everything*. His fingers found the fastening of her gown, and she gasped with new, urgent gladness, because she knew somewhat hazily where this was leading, and she welcomed it with all her heart and all her desire.

He groaned into her mouth, stilling his fingers with apparent difficulty. And slowly, gradually, he disentangled their lips.

"I seem to be seeking much forgiveness today," he said unsteadily. "Please just say you will marry me. Soon. Very, very soon. And then I'll have the strength to leave you. I can sleep and dream of you and hope you dream of me."

"You know I will marry you," she managed. "Whenever you wish."

A smile, warm and delighted, gleamed in his eyes and played about his sensual lips. "Thank God. Then I'll bid you good night. It's not so long until morning."

"No," she agreed, as, with flattering reluctance, his arms fell away. She swallowed. "Good night."

Her heart beat hard as he backed away and finally, resolutely, reached for the door handle.

She couldn't bear it. "Justin."

He paused and glanced back over his shoulder.

Slowly, she held out her hand. "Don't go," she whispered. "Stay with me."

His breath sounded labored, ragged. "Do you know what you're offering?"

"More or less. I know I want you to stay. I want to be close to you. And I know we're going to be married."

The smile flickered once more. He turned back to face her. "So we are," he said, and prowled back toward her like a large, predatory cat.

Her knees gave just as he caught her and swung her up in his arms. "Then tonight is for you," he said, laying her on the bed. "A taste of love and delight. My promise to you."

He threw his coat on the floor, his cravat following to reveal the strong column of his throat. She reached up to help tug the shirt up over his head, and then, at last, she could touch his skin, hot and velvet smooth, save for the dusting of coarse hair across his chest and a thin line pointing downward from his belly into his pantaloons. In moments, they were gone, too, and she could not take her eyes off him. From head to toe, this man was beautiful. Strangely, arousingly beautiful.

He let her get used to his maleness while he slowly unlaced her and drew off her own clothing. There was the wonder of his naked skin on hers, of his murmurs of delight in her beauty, the sheer pleasure of his knowing hands and mouth. He taught her the ecstasy of her own body, and then, with the intimate intrusion of his, the ultimate joy of finding bliss together.

And only then, awed and dazed with love, did she fall asleep in a tangle of limbs and sheets and a warmth that spread from the inside out.

CHAPTER TWENTY

J USTIN WOKE AT dawn, as he always did. But this morning it was with blinding pleasure in his heart and Hera Severne in his arms.

He had not meant to fall asleep in her bed. But then, he had not meant to take her there in the first place. He had intended to wait for their wedding night, knowing as he did that young girls were taught never to grant premarital favors, for the protection of their reputations, their families, and their entire lives. But when she asked him to stay, he had known this was yet another piece of conventional wisdom that she was throwing off. That, in fact, physically loving her would be the best proof he could give her of his feelings.

And since this coincided so perfectly with his personal desires, his answer had never been in doubt.

So much for good intentions. He smiled down at her soft, contented face, still awed that the sight could be one he enjoyed every morning of his life. Now that she had agreed to be his wife. He loved the curve of her lashes against her cheek, the tangle of hair about her face, the tender shape of her slightly parted lips.

Desire, always stirring in the mornings, grew more urgent.

No, he shouldn't have fallen asleep. He should have returned long before this to the room he was meant to share with George. But watching her expressions change from the wonder of physical pleasure to the perfect trust of sleep, he had been reluctant to move. Her passion had been a revelation to him, her beauty a constant delight. And when he had allowed his own joy to consume him—something else he had foolishly intended to eschew—she had wept tears of sheer emotion.

This was the love he had avoided for so long. And yet with her, he was its willing slave.

But they still had to get out of the inn early, breakfasted and without being chased by the innkeeper's wife wielding a large saucepan in the name of morality. Very gently, he began to disentangle himself.

Her eyes flew open, and it was yet another joy to watch her memory and her happiness return, along with a long, rosy blush of mingled embarrassment and, he hoped, desire.

"Good morning," he murmured, softly kissing her lips.

She kissed him back, moving against him as though she could not help it.

He drew back with reluctance. "I have to go back to my room before I'm caught."

"Didn't you say that last night too?" she asked innocently.

"Minx," he said, before grinning and kissing her again.

For one more instant, he hesitated as lust took hold. But concern for her won. She was new to physical love, and he would not hurt her for the world.

"As soon as we get back to Brussels," he growled, "I'll dig up a chaplain from the army or some ordained younger son from the fashionable throngs. And then…"

"Yes?" she asked breathlessly, and he laughed, sliding out of bed.

"Definitely, yes. Breakfast at six, remember?"

He hauled on his shirt and buttoned his pantaloons while she watched, then grabbed his coat, blew her a kiss, and marched determinedly to the door. After checking the passage was free first, he departed with a last smile and walked rather dazedly into the room he shared with George.

George was up, perfectly dressed and pacing. In the growing day-light, Justin could see his grazed knuckles where he had punched Hugh's henchman. George stopped pacing and peered at him.

"Sorry, George, you weren't worried, were you?"

Slowly, George began to smile. "Not now."

Did he mean because Justin had returned? Or because he could read his friend's happiness? For the first time Justin wondered what George would think of his marrying Hera. It was George, after all, who had claimed to be her betrothed last night. Perhaps he was in love with her, something Justin had never considered.

"Is it breakfast time?" George asked.

"Almost. Let me just wash and tidy up a little…"

An hour later, duly breakfasted, they set off back to Brussels, with Justin driving, Hera beside him wrapped from head to toe in a voluminous and disguising cloak, and George sitting with his legs dangling over the side of the cart. Even the mare seemed happy enough to trot back to town.

"I hope Rosamund and the others haven't sent out search parties," Hera said. It was the first trace of unease she had shown. To Justin's delight, a glow of happiness seemed to surround her. She had never been more beautiful, never shone so brightly, even half-hidden in the shrouding cloak.

"They might not notice," George said.

"Rosamund always notices," Hera said. "Though she doesn't al-ways say so."

"It's Mrs. Edwards's party this evening," George pointed out. "They are bound to be busy. At least, Hugh and Caroline always were before a party."

"So it is!" Hera exclaimed, turning to Justin. "Are you coming, Justin?"

And Justin, who had once assured Butler that wild horses would not drag him there, smiled and said with determination, "I hope so."

⫸⫷

WHEN HERA ENTERED the breakfast parlor with a cheerful "Good morning!" everyone was there.

Rosamund sprang to her feet. "Hera!"

"I'm fine, honestly," Hera assured her, walking to the table and helping herself to a cup of coffee, "though we had a bit of an adventure."

"The servants told some tale of you hurling yourself at a cart driven by Dr. Rivers," Mr. Edwards said. "If it wasn't for Mrs. Butler here, and your girl, Ruby, we would have had the army out looking for you. But Ruby seemed to think all would be well if the doctor was with you, and Mrs. Butler said any fuss would merely damage your reputation! And then Sir Arthur vanished at about the same time in a strange carriage!"

"He is back, too. He's just changing his clothes." Hera sat down beside Rosamund. "I'm sorry to have worried you, but in truth, our flight was not for nothing. And if we are careful, it should not amount to any more than servants' gossip."

Rosamund said, "*Any* gossip is particularly bad for you, because of my marriage to Giles. We both need to be faultless. What were you thinking of, Hera?"

"Saving Sir Arthur," Hera said. She looked around the faces of the Edwards, Izzy Merton, and Rosamund. "I had better tell you all about him and about our adventure…"

⫸⫷

INEVITABLY, THE EDWARDS'S party did not go according to Hera's overoptimistic plan.

Lack of space prevented the event being on the scale of a ball, but Mrs. Edwards made best use of what public rooms she had. The gracious drawing room, with much of its furniture removed and the rest pushed back against the walls, became the ballroom, with a fiddler in the corner to supply the music. The dining room was used for both buffet and dowagers, according to Izzy, who declared the older ladies needed somewhere to gossip where they could hear each other above the music and mirth. The breakfast parlor had become a small card room.

After much discussion, Rosamund and Hera ensconced themselves in the drawing room, the former to act as permanent chaperone for the young people dancing.

"Don't you want to dance with Major Butler?" Hera asked her stepmother as they took up residence in the corner.

"Yes," Rosamund admitted with a fleeting smile. "We danced at our wedding. But I am still a recent widow, despite being a bride, and I shan't upset convention any more than I have already. It wouldn't be fair to Giles's career, or to you and Victor."

"I can't really see Victor being out much in Society," Hera said, "let alone pandering to it. Can you?"

Rosamund didn't answer at once. Then she said, "Your father's death has changed us all. I look forward to seeing Victor grow into his dukedom."

George came up to them, looking slightly self-conscious in his new black evening coat, and just a little nervous. "The first guests are arriving."

"We're not hosts," Rosamund said kindly, "so nothing is required of us except amiability."

"And we appreciate the male escort," Hera added to make him feel useful.

"Then I'll just stand with you. Let me fetch you a glass of something."

If Hera kept one eye on George to make sure the noise and press of people did not overwhelm him, it seemed George also meant to look after her and Rosamund. He was introduced to everyone and bore his part manfully in polite conversation. In fact, being both good-natured and unexpectedly humorous in a quiet way, he appeared to be well liked.

"Ask someone to dance if you wish to," Hera murmured to him.

"The mothers are more my age than the daughters," he observed. "Besides, I can't actually dance."

Hera blinked in consternation. "Why did I not think of that before?"

"Why didn't I?" George responded.

Hera would have responded further, but Lady Hartley, who had become something of a fashionable hostess in Brussels, came to pay her respects to Rosamund. She duly greeted Hera and Sir Arthur, to whom she had been introduced at the troop review some days ago. Then, unexpectedly, she sat down on Hera's other side.

"I am so glad to see you here and looking so well, Lady Hera."

"Thank you," Hera said in surprise. "I am always well."

Lady Hartley smiled. "I am relieved to hear it. It was just that I saw you being driven at high speed through the city in an unlikely vehicle, with that doctor fellow at the reins."

"Dr. Rivers," Hera said dangerously, before she noticed the warning pressure of Rosamund's elbow in her arm. She had fallen into Lady Hartley's trap.

Lady Harley smiled. "That's the fellow. Naturally, I was concerned for your health, but when I met Mrs. Edwards later in the evening, she seemed to know nothing about it. So I called here at the house. Her Grace—that is, Mrs. Butler—was not at home, and no one could tell me anything about you. Except that you were not home either." She pursed her lips in a solicitous manner. "I was afraid you had been taken very ill and were in some hospital or other run by the army!"

Hera willed herself not to blush and bit her lips to prevent an equal response to the woman's insolence.

Rosamund said, "There are no circumstances in which Lady Hera would not be treated by the best doctors in her own home, which, for the duration of her visit, is here with me."

"Then she was on an expedition of pleasure?" Lady Harley's eyes gleamed. "With the good doctor? For so long?"

Rosamund raised a haughty eyebrow. Hera realized it was the best way to deal with such blatant prying, but the effort to keep silent caused her hands to clench in her lap.

Perhaps George saw her distress, for he hurried into speech. "I was on the same expedition, most enjoyable. And quite proper, for Lady Hera and I are betrothed."

There was short, stunned silence, not least because George's voice had pierced further than he had intended, and several other people heard his declaration, too.

"Indeed?" Lady Hartley purred. It was not the gossip she had come for, but she clearly had no doubt that she had forced an announcement the couple in question were not entirely prepared for. "Then let me the first to congratulate you, Sir Arthur. Charming match. Quite charming."

Behind her smiling lips, Hera's teeth ground so tightly together that it hurt. She could not deny the betrothal without making George look foolish at best and herself... Well, she had no idea, but the gossips were going to have a field day when she married Justin Rivers.

Fortunately, Lady Hartley bustled off soon after that, no doubt to enjoy spreading what she had just learned.

"Why did you say that?" Hera groaned quietly when they could not be overheard.

George flopped down in the chair beside her. "I thought it would help. It worked on the innkeeper's wife. I shouldn't have said anything, should I?"

"Never mind," Hera said with an effort. "At least it has given her something to talk about other than my wretched health. As for being driven at high speed through the town, I defy anyone to make that cart horse travel at anything quicker than an undignified trot!"

A little later, while George went to fetch them more lemonade— "Brandy would be more useful," Rosamund muttered—Izzy Merton dropped into his vacated chair.

Still breathless from dancing, she said, "Why are they saying you are engaged to Sir Arthur, Lady Hera?" She lowered her voice. "Is it to make Dr. Rivers jealous?"

"No, it is not," Hera replied between her teeth.

"Well, I think it might. He's not going to be pleased when he hears."

Where is he? Her need of him felt like an ache, and not just because of George's betrothal nonsense.

"Speak of the devil," Izzy murmured, and sprang up again, darting into a crowd of young people while Hera, her heart racing, gazed toward the door. She glimpsed Justin through a throng of other guests. His expression was familiarly sardonic. Worse, while Major Butler managed to enter the drawing room and skirt the dancers to reach his wife's side, Justin appeared to be in no hurry.

Unable to be still any longer, Hera rose. She wanted to pace rapidly to relieve her tension, but had to settle for strolling, while she kept a faint, amiable smile on her lips. Past experience during the London Season at least helped with that.

And then, without warning, Justin stood right in front of her. "What a jilt you are," he murmured. "Betrothed to George already?"

"Oh, Justin, he just blurted it out and I couldn't stop him!"

The mocking gleam in his eyes changed to one of concern. "Don't look like that. I was only joking."

"I was afraid you were angry," she said in relief.

"What kind of monster do you take me for?" He took her hand, threading it through the crook of his arm, and began to walk. "If I am angry, it's on George's behalf. Do you suppose he really does want to marry you?"

She stared at him. "No. He thinks I'm young enough to be his daughter."

"You are," George said, appearing as from nowhere and thrusting a glass of lemonade at her. She had to release Justin's arm to take it. "Think I said the wrong thing, Justin. Are you angry?"

"Not at all," Justin replied. "We'll sort it all out."

Abruptly, Hera's tension eased. Too soon, as it turned out.

"Oh, no," George said anxiously.

The waltz had just come to an end, and through the milling couples on the dance floor, Hera followed George's gaze to the pair at the door. Haughty, proud, and beautifully dressed stood Hugh and Caroline Astley.

"How dare they?" Hera gasped.

"Last stand," George said. "Last roll of the dice. I need to go and see somebody."

"Good idea," Hera said. "Go round behind them and up to your room. Take one of the footmen in case they brought that ruffian whose nose you punched…"

But it seemed to be too late for any of that. The Astleys had seen them and made a determined start toward them. Somehow, a passage opened up in the crowd, making clear space between the Astleys and Hera, Justin, and George. Worse, curiosity killed much of the conversation.

Beside Hera, George was rigid. In quick comfort, Hera touched his arm.

Hugh's hand flew up as though he would point, then he dropped it to his side and uttered in a strong yet shaking voice, "Madam! Stand away from my ward!"

Justin stepped in front of both of them, though Hera immediately moved to peer around him. So did George at his other side.

Hugh and Caroline came closer.

"Sir," Hugh began disdainfully, "I do not know—" He halted and broke off, blinking rapidly in recognition. "Doctor? What lies has this loathsome creature told you? For I should hate to believe you could be part of this fraud, this deceitful abduction!"

If Hugh had wanted the attention of the entire room, he had succeeded. The fiddle was silent. No one spoke except, very quietly, people excusing themselves to squeeze into the room.

Justin said sarcastically, "Well, I am glad of your good opinion, at any rate. Certainly, I have never committed any such crime as you seem inclined to accuse somebody. But who, pray, is the *loathsome creature* to whom you refer? I take leave to doubt that Mrs. Edwards would invite any such into her home."

"No doubt Mrs. Edwards has been as duped as we," Caroline said stoutly. "That woman inveigled her way into *my* home in the guise of a companion and stole away our ward with the intention of lying to the world that he is my husband's poor dead brother, in order to gain wealth for herself through marriage to our helpless George!"

By this time, Hera had moved to Justin's side. George stood at the other.

Justin laughed. "You mean *this* helpless George? Sir Arthur Astley? I'm surprised you still find him helpless after he escaped imprisonment by you twice."

Hugh's face grew mottled with anger. Caroline's lips curled in contemptuous outrage. But Justin had not finished.

"However, to return to your *loathsome creature*, Mr. Astley. I really hope you did not mean this lady?"

"She is a deceitful criminal," Caroline said, her voice throbbing with a passion Hera had never heard in her, "and I want her taken up with the law. Please, someone arrest Miss Harriet Severne!"

Many people exchanged glances, but nobody moved. Izzy stood nearby, her eyes shining with excitement.

"Mrs. Astley, you are entirely mistaken," Justin said with silken, entirely false pity. "This is Lady Hera Severne, only daughter of the late Duke of Cuttyngham, and sister of the current duke. Why should Lady Hera seek employment in your home? Let alone abduct Sir Arthur here in the hope, as you imply, of marrying an elusive fortune—which, at best, must be a fraction of her own. I apologize for the vulgarity, my lady."

"L-Lady Hera?" Caroline repeated, swaying slightly. She looked suddenly very white.

But Hugh seemed made of sterner stuff. Through the faint, shocked titters scattered about the room, he said, "Then she has fooled you, too! Why would Lady Hera seek to ally herself with a penniless idiot like our poor George?"

"How dare you?" Hera cried, finally too outraged to be silent. "Your brother is a good and gentle and highly intelligent man who has been keeping you and your wife in the lap of luxury for years! Through the goodness of his own heart and the quick brain you now choose to deride!"

"Hera," George said uneasily.

"Deny, then, that you are betrothed to him," Hugh said with triumph.

"I am not," Hera said. "But if I were, I would count it an honor and a happiness. In fact, were I not already betrothed to Dr. Rivers, I would *love* to marry George!"

"Would you?" George asked, such a mixture of delight and unease in his face that Hera suddenly wanted to laugh.

Justin did laugh, a short, breathless bark that made George grin at him.

"Yes, I would," Hera said. "And since everyone else has heard the rumors now, I might as well tell you all that George—Sir Arthur— pretended to be engaged to me in order to save my reputation from gossip."

"A step that became necessary," Justin added, suddenly not laughing at all, "when Lady Hera and I were forced to rescue Sir Arthur from the clutches of this man who bundled him into a coach, then onto a barge where he was locked in a cabin."

"Ooh!" The breathy sound seemed to echo around the room as everyone looked expectantly at Hugh and Caroline.

Caroline laughed a little wildly. "If that is true, then how, pray, did he get out?"

Hera and Justin both turned to George, who looked alarmed and then both shy and modest.

"I picked the lock," he said apologetically. "Just like I did in the attic. I used to do it so I could sit in the library for a change. I liked the library and there was always decent port there. Though I don't care for your wine, Hugh. Only then you locked Hera in the attic, too, and I couldn't have that, so I picked the lock again and took her to the vicar."

It sounded like some wild tale by Mrs. Radcliffe. Certainly, the faces around the room betrayed both shock and bewilderment.

"Nonsense," Hugh declared. "I will take my ward back with me and the lawyers will establish—"

"The lawyers will indeed establish that this is Sir Arthur George Astley, your older brother," Justin interrupted. "The matter has already been set in motion."

"No one believes these trumped-up lies," Hugh stated.

In fact, belief wasn't really the issue. The sheer, avid excitement in the room was.

"I do," said an unexpected female voice clearly.

The passage that had closed behind Hugh and Caroline opened again to let Rosamund come through with an unknown lady of late middle years.

"Mademoiselle Villière," George said, beaming and going at once to take her hand.

"I was waiting quietly for you," Mademoiselle Villière said in faintly accented English. "But Mrs. Butler came and said she thought you might need me now."

"Who the devil is this?" Hugh blustered, betrayed into less-than-perfect language.

"This is your old governess and mine," George said amiably. "Mademoiselle Villière. I found her in Brussels."

"I don't know her," Hugh said. "She could be anyone."

"But I know you, Monsieur Hugh," the governess said tartly. "And more to the point, I know your brother. He has a birthmark shaped like a comma in the middle of his back."

"*He* told you that!" Hugh said furiously.

"She knows, you fool," Justin said with contempt. "Dr. Watling, who delivered you both, told me of the same mark, and the lawyers know all about it. Since you were not even invited here, I suggest you return forthwith to England and remove whatever actually belongs to you from Denholm Hall, because Sir Arthur is coming home."

"And I don't want you in the attic," George added.

This time, Hera couldn't help herself. She laughed and squeezed George's hand and felt Justin's arm slip around her waist.

All was right with the world as Hugh and Caroline spun on their heels. They tried to storm off, but people were less eager to get out of their way now. They looked down their noses at Hugh and Caroline, who were obliged to utter, "Excuse me," more than once in order to get out of the room, where a large footman awaited them.

CHAPTER TWENTY-ONE

"D O YOU THINK they will try again to abduct him?" Hera asked Justin anxiously as the conversation started up again and the fiddler resumed.

"No. We have men watching them now, all the way to the coast. One wrong move and they will be arrested."

"Is that why you and Giles are late?"

"One reason. Have we ever danced together, Hera?"

"You know we have not. I am in mourning."

He smiled so warmly that she almost felt she was in his arms. "No, you are not."

"No. But I think we have probably shocked the polite world enough for one day."

"I hope this polite world of yours will not punish George for what was revealed this evening."

Hera's worried gaze found George in a group of people who included Mademoiselle Villière, clearly the center of attention, and looking a little surprised but not distressed. "No, I think they're intrigued, and too much on his side to be cruel. They like him. And he... I think he has discovered he quite likes being with people. At least after a glass or two."

She saw her stepmother approaching and turned toward her. "How did you conjure up Mademoiselle Villière so quickly?"

"Giles and Dr. Rivers brought her to the house with them," Rosamund said, apparently surprised Hera did not know. "But she would not come in to the party unless it was necessary. It seemed to me it *was* necessary. To more personal matters, why did you not tell me you were betrothed? Or is this another ruse, like Sir Arthur's?"

Hera blushed, though with a tilt of her chin, she took Justin's arm. "It is quite true. I meant to tell you, but I didn't want you to think it was only because of the impropriety—"

"Hush," Rosamund said in mock outrage. "Never speak that word in public. Will you wait for Victor's approval?"

"Not unless I have to," Hera replied with a quizzical glance at Justin.

"We have a special license," Justin said.

Hera stared at him. "We do?"

"My father obtained it," he confessed, "and sent it to be helpful. Or commanding. One is never sure which with him."

Laughter bubbled up. "Well, at least he approves!"

"I found a harassed chaplain who can marry us next week," Justin began.

"If you're interested," Rosamund interrupted, "Izzy has been flirting with the ordained son of a marquis. I think you might find he is available sooner. Would you care to be introduced?"

⟫⟫⟩⟨⟨⟪

THE REST OF the evening passed in a blur. The marquis's son, Lord Rupert, turned out to be an amiable young man with a rakish gleam in his eye. He didn't appear to take himself or anyone else too seriously, but he was perfectly happy to marry Justin and Hera after the party.

"If you would like more time to be sure, that is probably better," he added with an attempt at earnestness, his eyes straying to Hera, who, in sudden panic, glanced at Justin.

Justin gave a fleeting, rueful smile, and abruptly all her anxieties dissolved.

"Tonight would be best," she said firmly, and won her reward in the exciting glow of Justin's eyes.

And so, as the guests departed, only Lord Rupert stayed behind. And Giles Butler to give Hera away. And the fiddler for some reason.

With Izzy attending Hera, and George as groomsman, the simple ceremony was quickly and joyously performed before the eyes of the entire household and the grinning Ruby. The hint of mischief about Lord Rupert was oddly beguiling, and Hera's being filled with happiness, even before she and Justin were pronounced man and wife.

Giles proposed a toast in champagne to Dr. and Mrs. Rivers, and after a few minutes of congratulations, Rosamund shooed everyone from the room, leaving Justin and Hera alone with the fiddler.

Hera glanced at the musician in some consternation. If he wanted paid, why had he not spoken to Mr. Edwards? But beside her, Justin nodded, and the man raised his violin and began to play a waltz.

Justin bowed and held out his hand. And Hera, with a gasp that was half laughter and half tears, laid her fingers in his and walked into his arms.

Half an hour later, still gently swaying in the sweetness of her husband's embrace, Hera realized the music had stopped and the fiddler departed. Smiling, she raised her head from Justin's shoulder.

"Thank you," she whispered, as his mouth found hers.

With sweet, heavy pleasure, passion grew, and overcame them before they even left the room. Hera found that exhilarating, almost as exhilarating as she found the rest of the night with him in the safer privacy of her bedchamber. It was the beginning of something new and wonderful, and she embraced it with all her heart.

EPILOGUE

THE MONTH OF June in the following year of 1816 was cold and wet. On the first anniversary of their wedding, Hera and Justin trudged home through the village of St. Bride toward their cottage. The rain had gone off, temporarily, leaving a good deal of mud and a blink of cool, watery sunshine.

"Thank you for the assistance," Justin said, squeezing her fingers. "You kept her calm and brave, and that was half the battle."

The blacksmith's wife had had a difficult labor but, with Justin's help, had finally given birth to twin boys. Mother and children were exhausted but healthy.

"I like to help," Hera said. It was true. Since returning to England last autumn, Justin had set up his practice on the edge of St. Bride, close to his father, and to George up in Denholm Hall, now the perfect—if eccentric—lord of the manor.

Hera had worked hard to make their home comfortable, welcoming, and even gracious. Victor had visited a few times. The Hadleighs never spoke to them, since Hera had, in their opinion, married so far beneath her. Which merely proved how little they knew or understood.

Naturally, their home had a separate consulting room for Justin to see patients. Hera organized his appointments, made sure he remembered to eat, and welcomed him to her bed every night, whether he was amorous or exhausted or both. But this was the first time she had helped physically with a patient, and it had certainly been something of a trial by fire.

At least she knew now what was ahead of her.

"You are a natural," he said proudly, and for an instant, she let her head rest against his shoulder. "You have no regrets?" he murmured.

"None." She didn't even need to think about it. "Do you?"

He had given up roaming the world with the army after Waterloo. The carnage of the battle and its aftermath had brought back his nightmares with a vengeance. She had held him through many, wept with him over losses, including old friends and comrades, and celebrated all those he had saved. Some would never be whole, but many had life and hope because of him.

Life in St. Bride was quieter, but no less busy. Gradually, he had lost the nightmares in this new work, while involving himself in new ideas and experiments for the future. She loved being part of all of it. As she loved the sheer fun of their leisure moments, and simply being with him, whether in banter, serious conversation, or companionable silence. She knew a deep sense of belonging, to him and to the life they created together, and she was sure he felt it too.

They were happy. And there would be no better time to tell him.

"I learned much today," she said. "Much that will be useful."

"You intend to take up midwifery?" he teased.

"Only in a personal way."

He glanced at her, a quizzical smile playing on his lips. "Is this your way of telling me you are with child?"

"You know!" she gasped, tearing her hand free.

"I'm a physician," he said dryly. "I know the signs. And you must admit, we are frequently intimate!"

"Why did you not say?" she demanded crossly.

"Why did *you* not?"

"I wanted to be sure," she admitted. "And I wanted to surprise you. And make you happy. I hope."

At that, careless of the Miss Pinktons approaching from the church, he flung his arm around her shoulders. "Happy? Oh, my dear, I could not be happier." He pressed his lips hard to her temple and smiled, his delight open in his eyes. "Two shall become three."

"Or four," she said, thinking of the blacksmith's wife.

"Or four," he agreed. "Or even five, although it is rare." He searched her face and then glanced upward at the lowering sky. A few spots of rain had begun again. "Do you ever feel *lucky*, Hera?"

"All the time," she said, kissing his shoulder.

"So do I," he said happily. "So do I."

About Mary Lancaster

Mary Lancaster lives in Scotland with her husband, three mostly grown-up kids and a small, crazy dog.

Her first literary love was historical fiction, a genre which she relishes mixing up with romance and adventure in her own writing. Her most recent books are light, fun Regency romances written for Dragonblade Publishing: *The Imperial Season* series set at the Congress of Vienna; and the popular *Blackhaven Brides* series, which is set in a fashionable English spa town frequented by the great and the bad of Regency society.

Connect with Mary on-line – she loves to hear from readers:

Email Mary:
Mary@MaryLancaster.com

Website:
www.MaryLancaster.com

Newsletter sign-up:
http://eepurl.com/b4Xoif

Facebook:
facebook.com/mary.lancaster.1656

Facebook Author Page:
facebook.com/MaryLancasterNovelist

Twitter:
@MaryLancNovels

Amazon Author Page:
amazon.com/Mary-Lancaster/e/B00DJ5IACI

Bookbub:
bookbub.com/profile/mary-lancaster

Made in the USA
Monee, IL
01 June 2023

35077244R00138